HANDS OFF

Bennett Security Book 1

HANNAH SHIELD

Cover design by Damonza

Editing services by The Wicked Pen

Published by Diana Road Books

Edgewater, Colorado

HANDS OFF

Chapter One

*A*urora Bennett stood on the balcony, staring down at the partygoers below. The champagne was flowing, the music was loud, and people danced with abandon in their sparkling evening wear.

The "Angels and Demons" theme had turned out just the way she'd imagined, complete with devil horns and feathery angel wings for the guests to put on.

A quick spot-check proved that the appetizers were circulating right on cue. The photographer looked busy, snapping candid shots. And most important? Her clients, Brandon and Nadia Wolfson, were dancing right in the middle of the room, basking in the adoration of their guests.

Wow, she thought. *Did I actually pull this off?*

Brandon looked up, as if feeling Aurora's gaze. He smiled and nodded at her, then grabbed another glass of fizzy wine from a passing tray before dashing off. Probably to greet more of his business associates.

The Wolfsons owned this venue, The Lighthouse Club. It was the couple's wedding anniversary, yet their party was more about deal-making for the Wolfsons than it was a simple

celebration. For Aurora, it was one of the biggest events she'd
planned on her own, not as an assistant or intern.

"He's definitely happy," said a bubbly voice beside her.
"That's not easy to do."

Jennifer Scoville, Brandon's assistant, stood at her elbow,
wearing a blue silk cocktail dress. Her long, straight hair
trailed down her back.

"You think so? Your boss can be hard to read."

"You kidding? He and Nadia both love you." Jennifer
nudged Aurora's arm playfully. "Look at you, all dolled up.
You should be down there, enjoying yourself."

Aurora glanced down at her dress. Floor-length black
sequins, cut-outs at the waist, showing the sides of her ribcage.
A rental. Hardly anyone had seen her in it tonight, but Aurora
didn't care. She dressed for herself, and feeling sexy gave her
confidence. Even though she'd ended up sweating through the
fabric, she was so nervous.

"I just wanted to make sure everything was perfect."

Jennifer winked. "And it was. So, relax."

Aurora breathed out a sigh, one part relief and one part
disappointment that she'd completed her role in tonight's
festivities. Months of planning, stress, and spreadsheets, and it
all came down to a few hours of showtime. She should've
been thrilled. After all, this was her first major party-planning
gig since moving back to her hometown. If socialites like the
Wolfsons recommended her to their friends, she'd have no
shortage of work coming down the pipeline.

She didn't have a ton of experience with swanky events,
but this one felt a bit anticlimactic now that it was almost over.
As if it all should've meant something more than just a short
release, no matter how intense. Kind of like sex with a guy
you'd met at a bar. Fun, memorable, yet you knew you'd never
see him again.

Of course, after her eight-month dry spell, a short release

with a sexy partner sounded pretty darn appealing. Any day now, her vibrator was going to give out from overuse. It was huge and green—nicknamed the Incredible Hulk—and it was the only penis in her life these days. Sad, but true.

"As long as the Wolfsons are happy with their anniversary, I'm happy."

"It's been great working with you," Jennifer said. "Brandon will have another soiree for you to plan before you know it. And hopefully your brother can make it to the next one?"

Aurora's smile turned sour. Her brother.

Max Bennett was part of the reason she'd moved home to West Oaks after a disastrous break-up with her ex. Aurora's entire support system was here in California, small though it was.

Then Max had been quick to offer his help, and without questioning his motives, she'd accepted it. The Wolfsons had been Max's clients first. He'd recommended Aurora to them.

But after spending four years away from home for college, Aurora felt like she hardly recognized her brother. He'd gone from a clean-cut soldier, fresh from an honorable discharge after serving his country, to an entrepreneur who owned a multi-million-dollar security company.

Thank goodness he'd been busy tonight and had to decline the Wolfsons' invite. Otherwise, he'd probably be on this balcony right now, checking up on his little sister instead of enjoying the free booze.

Jennifer had dropped more than one hint about getting together with him on a more "personal" level. But sadly—for Jennifer and all the other single ladies of West Oaks, anyway —Max was a chronic bachelor, workaholic, and all-around control freak. Yes, Aurora had accepted his help. But she hadn't thought he'd still be so *nosy*. She wasn't a teenager anymore.

Jennifer held out a sealed envelope. "The remainder of your fee, plus a little extra to show Brandon's appreciation. Text me, okay? We'll drive into L.A. for a shopping and spa day?"

Aurora felt herself glowing at Jennifer's offer. The woman seemed so sophisticated. Exactly the kind of image Aurora hoped to project. "You know how to sweet talk a girl. I'm totally in."

They hugged goodbye.

Aurora popped open the envelope and glanced inside, then did a double take. This check couldn't be right.

"Jennifer, wait—" But the assistant was already gone.

A little extra? Brandon had doubled her fee.

But she didn't feel appreciated. Instead, she felt sick inside. This wasn't right.

Max, she thought. *My overprotective, bossy brother is behind this.* She wasn't sure how, but she just knew.

She couldn't accept this money. It wasn't professional. How was she supposed to make it on her own if people treated her like a charity case? Or even worse, used her to suck up to her brother.

Aurora marched toward Brandon's office, heels clacking against the stone flooring. Down below, the music continued to throb.

In her purse, her phone buzzed. It was a text from her best friend. Her biggest reason for moving back to West Oaks.

Lana Marchetti had written, *Pick up any hot men at the party tonight?*

Aurora groaned aloud. She texted back, *I wish. Max's spies are probably here. Not to mention his cameras. Just wait until you hear what he's done now.*

Was she being overly dramatic? Yes. But who could you vent to, if not your best friend? She thought about calling Lana, but the yelling would have to wait until she was safely away from the party.

Aurora tucked her phone away as she reached the outer door to the Wolfsons' suite of offices.

It was cracked open. Odd. But just as well. She could put the check on Jennifer's desk with a note, politely but firmly refusing the extra pay.

She pushed the door open. A light was on.

"Hello?"

Nobody answered. A half-empty glass of champagne sat on a bookcase, left here sometime tonight. Maybe the person was going to come back. If it was Brandon, she wanted to talk to him. She could graciously turn down his gift and assure him that no special treatment was necessary, regardless of whatever her brother might've suggested. She didn't want to offend the man and ruin her chances of further business.

But after standing around for almost five minutes, nobody had returned. She slid the envelope under the door to Brandon's private office.

Then she heard footsteps. Voices came from just beyond the outer door to the office suite.

"I told you, this isn't a good time," Brandon was saying.

Aurora took an instinctive step back. She'd never heard him so anxious. Usually, her client exuded an effortless confidence. He came from a rich Pasadena family, nothing but private schools and yacht clubs and weekend jaunts to Vegas via helicopter. "If somebody at the party sees you here, there will be questions—"

A new voice spoke, low and dangerous.

"It's time when I say it is. I have concerns about our arrangement, and I don't wait."

Something about that harsh voice turned Aurora's skin cold. A sense that the man, whoever he was, didn't have a single ounce of mercy in his soul.

She ducked into the nearest open door—the office that belonged to Nadia, Brandon's wife. The room was a dark expanse of modern furniture and expensive art. At the same moment, Brandon and the other man entered the main door from the hall. Aurora backed up into the shadows, crouching down, but she could still see the men through the doorway.

The new man was tall, early thirties, with handsome features and wavy dark hair. He carried himself with an almost-royal bearing, looking down his nose at Brandon.

"Dominic, I don't know what people have been telling you, but—"

Dominic lunged. Grabbing Brandon by the throat, he shoved him up against the wall. The half-glass of champagne tottered from the bookcase and smashed onto the floor.

Aurora thrust a hand over her mouth, covering her gasp.

Two more men stood on either side of Dominic. One was as big as a linebacker, with his long gray hair back in a pony-tail. The other was slighter, with a pointy nose and cunning eyes.

Their faces were impassive as they watched Brandon struggle to breathe.

Below, she could still hear music and laughter coming from the party. But it might as well have been another world. Aurora looked around Mrs. Wolfson's office, as if she'd find some way to help her client. If these men were as serious as they looked, Brandon was in trouble.

She felt her phone in her pocket, but her hands were shaking too hard to take it out.

"James told me everything," Dominic hissed. "How he fixed the records when he brought you my money, so the two of you could skim your extras off the top? As if I wouldn't find out?"

Brandon clawed at Dominic's hands around his neck. The man released his hold, and Brandon tumbled onto the floor, coughing and wheezing. His face had turned bright red.

"He's lying." Brandon got onto his hands and knees. "Please, Dominic." His voice was hoarse. "You know me. I'm a friend of your father's. I wouldn't… If anything's missing, I'll pay it back…"

Dominic was nodding along. "Oh, I have no doubt of that. But you didn't just steal from me. You took my money and started a little business on the side."

Aurora could hardly breathe, but a voice in her mind broke through. *Phone*, she told herself. *Snap out of it and do something.*

She managed to pull the device from her pocket, though her fingers felt numb. She checked that it was on silent. But what now? Should she contact the police? Her brother? Max got on her nerves, but he or his employees could actually handle a situation like this.

She glanced back up at the scene in the main office. A look of horror had crossed Brandon's face. He clutched at the other man's pant legs.

"Wait, listen, it wasn't my idea."

Dominic kicked him away. "You disgust me. I'm finished with you."

"No, please, I'll do anything."

"You betrayed me. Do you have any idea how much that hurt? Eric, why don't you show him exactly how it feels?"

He nodded at the one with the ponytail, then stormed out of the office, the door swinging shut behind him.

The two goons stared down at Brandon. Ponytail—Eric—dug a hand into his pocket and came out holding a pistol. A silencer fit onto the end of the muzzle.

"Shit," Aurora whispered.

They were going to kill Wolfson.

SOS, she typed into her phone, and sent the message to her brother. *Gun. Brandon's office.*

Again, her gaze darted over the darkened room. She needed a weapon. Or something, anything, to distract Dominic's men. But what could she do? She couldn't go up against two guys with guns.

These men were criminals. Mobsters or gangsters. What would they do if they found her here?

Her eyes lit upon a white panel on the wall. It bore a familiar logo. A stylized "B." Bennett Security. She crept over. Out in the main part of the office, Brandon was blubbering and trying to scream. It sounded like the goons had shoved a gag into his mouth. Bile rose in Aurora's throat.

She reached the panel and touched it with her finger. It flashed to life, showing a digital screen. Aurora hit the icon for the silent alarm. A red light began to flash on the panel.

Right now, a notification would be ringing out at her older brother's company headquarters.

But he hadn't written back to her text. Where was he? What if nobody got here in time?

I have to do something, Aurora thought, just as the pistol fired. Blood sprayed across the carpet. She cried out. Her hand flew to her mouth, but too late to cover the sound.

Brandon had collapsed in a heap.

Eric looked up at his pointy-nosed friend. "Did you hear that? Just now?"

Aurora's body flooded with panic, every nerve tingling painfully. Yet she couldn't move.

"I didn't hear anything," the friend said.

"Could've sworn I did. Came from over there."

No. No, no, no, this can't be happening. Nadia Wolfson's desk hid her from view. But if they came fully into the room—if they turned on the lights—they'd find her in an instant.

Their footsteps came closer.

Her blood rushed in her ears. Her lungs burned from holding her breath.

"Oh fuck, you see that red light? That panel? Wolfson must've tripped a silent alarm before you did him. We need to get the hell out of here."

She heard the outer door open. Footsteps, running.

Then silence.

Even when they were gone, Aurora stayed crouched in the dark in her evening gown, shaking so badly that her vision blurred. Brandon was out there. If she went past him, she was sure she'd see the accusation in his face.

You hid and saved yourself. You coward.

Chapter Two

*D*evon Whitestone circled his opponent, waiting for the moment to strike. A fist drove toward his face. He leaned to the side, narrowly avoiding the blow. Jeez, his reflexes were slow today. He felt like he was moving through sand.

A jab. A hook. Bob and weave.

Focus, he told himself.

But he was sloppy throwing his next punch. Left himself wide open. He didn't even see the fist coming, only felt knuckles driving into his chin, even through the padding.

Devon went sprawling onto the rubber flooring.

"Oh, shit." Chase, Devon's friend and sparring partner, threw off his headgear and pulled the gloves from his hands. "Are you okay?"

Devon let the bite guard drop from his mouth. The room was spinning, but only a little. "Yeah. No worries. I'm slower than usual today."

"What happened? Late night?"

"Yeah. Got called in."

"Again? What time did you get home?" Chase held out a hand, helping Devon up.

"Uh, three maybe?"

Chase whistled. "Jesus, Devon. I mean, you're making me look good on the mat by comparison. But you should be home asleep." He led Devon over to a bench and made him sit down. "You need a day off."

Devon managed a weak laugh. "This *is* my day off."

"I don't know how you keep going like this, man," Chase said. "I really don't."

Because I don't have much choice, Devon thought.

Chase handed Devon a water bottle. He took a long swig.

"Tell me the truth," his friend said. "How have you really been?"

Fucking tired, he responded silently. *I'm coming apart at the seams. But I'm going to keep acting like everything's fine, and eventually, it will be. I hope.*

"Hanging in there," Devon said.

He didn't like talking about his problems. Devon wasn't a fan of showing weakness, not so much because he looked down on vulnerability. He wasn't a hyper-macho, men-don't-cry sort of asshole. He had feelings, even if he couldn't afford to show them. Getting caught up in his own wants and needs would be selfish. His family needed him to be strong.

It had been a year and a half since his world turned upside down. Since his twin brother, Kellen, had died in the line of duty.

Devon and Kellen came from a family of Los Angeles cops. Uncles, aunts, cousins, all proud to be blue. The twin brothers had wanted nothing more than to join the club. Then their father had been shot and killed while on patrol when they were ten. It had been a terrible time. Yet the family bonded together even closer and got through it.

After they'd graduated high school, Kellen wanted to uphold their dad's legacy. He'd applied to a criminal justice program with the intention of entering the police academy after he got his degree. But Devon, on the advice of his school counselor, went through the difficult process to apply to West Point. His grades were stellar. He'd always welcomed a challenge. And he still had a lingering ambivalence about a life patrolling the streets of L.A.

And then—to his surprise, most of all—he'd actually gotten accepted with a full-ride scholarship. Four years later, he graduated and began his career as a lieutenant in the army. Then he'd completed the Ranger Assessment and Selection Program and joined the Army Rangers.

There were things he couldn't stand about being a soldier, like losing people he'd grown to love and admire. He'd lost too many people in his life. But overall, Devon was happy with his career. He had a purpose, serving his country with pride, and that meant everything to him.

Then came the phone call last year, when he'd learned that Kellen had been shot trying to stop a gunman at a shopping mall. By the time Devon heard about it, Kellen was already gone.

Devon's mother and sister had begged him to come home. They couldn't take the risk of losing another member of their family. It took nearly a year to get his honorable discharge. Finally, Devon made it back to Los Angeles, just in time to find out that his mom's mortgage was underwater. And his sister Ruby gave birth a week later, her deadbeat ex nowhere to be found.

So taking care of his family became Devon's new purpose.

The job offer from Bennett Security came at just the right moment. Devon moved his mom, sister, and baby niece out of Los Angeles and into the beautiful beachside community of West Oaks. It wasn't easy to afford the rent, but this was the kind of life that he wanted to provide for them, away from the crowds and the smog and the bad memories.

Since they'd moved to West Oaks, his family was actually smiling again.

"You could always get laid," Chase said. "That might take some pressure off."

He snorted. "When would I have time for that?"

Devon wasn't in the service anymore, but he still lived by a schedule. Wake up at five, run two miles to the gym, train. Clean up, eat, and head to work by eight. In the evenings, he picked up extra shifts or spent time with his Mom or Ruby. Bed by nine, unless he was working. On Friday nights, whenever possible, he babysat his niece so his sister and mom could take a little time for themselves.

Devon had to be their rock, both financially and emotionally. They had the support of their extended family and the police community, too. But nobody else was going to take responsibility for them the way that Devon would.

His schedule kept everything moving smoothly, no unexpected surprises. His mom and sister needed certainty in their lives, and so did he. Dating had a tendency to throw mud into the gears.

If he had to take extra shifts to make ends meet, and if he had to just keep pushing relentlessly to keep himself from sinking—well, that was how it had to be. Once he'd saved enough money to get Mom and Ruby and the baby into a real house, no more noisy apartments or unreliable landlords, then maybe he'd back off a bit. Take a nap.

If he broke under the stress? His family would come crashing down along with him.

"You can't spare one night for a hook-up?" Chase asked. "You're practically a monk."

Devon grunted dismissively. He got up, and they headed for the showers. "What about you? What's new at the station?"

Chase was an officer with the West Oaks Police Department. This gym, in fact, was a popular place for cops to work out and train. Even though Devon was ex-military, the officers here accepted him as an honorary fellow cop because of his family legacy. His friendships with police often came in handy working for a private security company.

Chase stripped off the rest of his gear, throwing it into his locker. "You haven't heard? That murder over at The Lighthouse Club is what everyone's been talking about. I figured the sirens woke the whole town last night."

"Oh, I heard. Actually, that was the reason I got called in to work. We did the security system at the club, and Bennett himself responded to the silent alarm. He'd even gotten a tip-off beforehand, apparently, though I'm not sure how. I had to cover the office while Bennett and his team were gone."

Devon usually sold security systems these days or worked behind a desk. His mom couldn't handle the stress of him being in danger.

Chase whistled. "Then you must know a lot more about it than I do, man. People are saying that Wolfson, the guy who got killed, had ties to a Los Angeles crime ring. They've been moving into West Oaks, trying to expand their territory. And the rumor is, there was a witness to the murder. Some woman."

From a nearby locker, another guy looked over. He wore a towel around his waist, and he'd laid out his West Oaks P.D. uniform on the bench. "I heard that, too. I wouldn't want to be her right now. These mobster guys are no joke. Remember that eyewitness last summer who got gunned down on the L.A. County courthouse steps, right before testifying?"

"That was brutal," Chase said. "They couldn't tie the hit to anybody, either. Unsolved. Sickening that that kind of shit is coming to West Oaks, now."

Devon didn't like the sound of that. West Oaks was supposed to be a safer, quieter place for his family to settle and heal. It was like L.A.'s problems had followed him here.

His phone buzzed, and he checked the message. Damn. "That's my boss. I gotta head out."

"But what about your day off?"

"Duty calls."

"And Devon Whitestone always answers," Chase joked. Devon heard his friends' rueful laughter following him out the door.

DEVON SWIPED HIS KEY CARD, entered his code on the pad, and walked into Bennett Security's main office. The place was full of large windows and chrome, with fancy flat-panel TVs lining the walls along one side. A couple of his colleagues looked up and nodded hello from behind their computers.

He had worked for Bennett Security for three months now. He was still the new guy, so he didn't have his pick of assignments. But Max Bennett knew that Devon wanted as many shifts as possible and seemed to be pleased with the work Devon had done so far.

He jogged up the open-riser staircase to his boss's closed door. The room was lined with glass walls, and Devon could see his boss on the phone, pacing back and forth across the luxuriously appointed space.

Bennett noticed him through the glass and waved for him to come inside.

Still listening to his phone, Bennett pointed at the leather couch across from his desk. Devon sank into the cushions.

Max Bennett had been running Bennett Security for just a few years. Bennett had grown up here, so it probably had been easy to get started. Maybe he had a built-in client base from his former classmates, no doubt some fancy private school.

The company installed custom security systems and provided personal protection to the wealthy around West Oaks. Their clientele was elite and filthy rich, so Bennett must've been making a mint off the fees. As his swanky head-quarters showed.

If Devon hadn't known, he wouldn't have guessed his boss had been Army Special Forces.

"Yes," Bennett said into the phone, "make sure she has a detail twenty-four-seven. If West Oaks P.D. can't provide it, I want to know. If anyone from the Syndicate so much as farts in her direction, I want to know." A pause. "Of course, I'm being demanding. Who do you think I am?"

Bennett said goodbye and ended his phone call. Then he came around to the front of his desk and leaned against it.

Devon sat up straighter. "What can I do for you, sir?"

Bennett regarded him for a moment. "I like you, White-stone. You seem like the sort of man I can trust with some-thing sensitive. Do you think that's fair?"

"Yes, sir. Of course."

Bennett nodded. "You remind me of myself when I was younger. You want to prove yourself. And you want to take care of the people close to you."

Bennett knew a little about his personal history and his family situation. Though Devon doubted that Bennett could truly understand the financial pressure he was under.

"I hope so."

He'd been lucky to get this job in the first place. The commanding officer of Devon's unit of Army Rangers had also been an old friend of Bennett's. When Devon got his discharge, his commander passed on a strong reference.

A lot of former military worked for this office, which was a sensible move on Bennett's part. With those who had their level of training, Bennett would know what to expect, and he'd know that the job would get done.

"You also have a sister, correct?" Bennett asked.

"Yes, Ruby is my younger sister. And I have a niece as well. Haley." She was six months old.

"Of course, I remember. I called you in today to ask a

favor. For *me*, personally. My own younger sister is in trouble, and I'd do anything to ensure her safety. I need someone close by, someone I can count on. I think that person is you."

Devon opened his mouth, but Bennett held up his hand. "Before you accept this assignment, I need to make a few things…explicit. You heard about the murder at The Lighthouse Club last night? A young woman witnessed it."

"That was *your sister?* A witness to some mob hit?" Devon blurted without thinking. He clamped his jaw shut. Damn, he really was tired. He wasn't in top form today.

But Bennett didn't seem to hold the outburst against him. "That's right. My sister Aurora was the witness. She'd tried to text me, and I missed it at first. Thank god she triggered the silent alarm. I don't want to think about what could've happened otherwise."

He rubbed the skin between his eyes. "Turns out, the people she saw take out Brandon Wolfson came in from L.A. The Silverlake Syndicate. They're organized crime, and they don't fool around. I need to know that Aurora is protected at all times. I was just on the phone with the Assistant District Attorney about a police detail for her. They've promised that her identity will remain sealed for as long as possible. But it's entirely feasible this will get out. And if that happens, I don't want those thugs anywhere near her."

So, this would be a bodyguard assignment. Not Devon's usual role. In fact, it was a promotion. He felt pride that Bennett would choose him. Excitement made his nerves sing.

But Devon's mother wouldn't like it. She'd freak if she found out. Maybe Ruby would, too.

He wanted this assignment, though. For the first time in weeks, he felt completely awake.

"Would your family be okay with that?" Bennett probably saw the uncertainty on Devon's face.

"I could make it work. May I ask for more details?"

"Of course. You shouldn't take this decision lightly. You

would be staying close to my sister until the DA is able to make an arrest and get my sister's testimony on the record. I don't know how long exactly that would take. It could be a week or two. It could be a month. Perhaps even longer if we think the Syndicate plans to retaliate. I'll have a remote team here at the office watching the cameras twenty-four-seven, and you would have time off whenever I can arrange suitable backup for you. But I'm talking about extended hours."

Which would mean extra pay. Devon was already thinking about his savings account balance and how much this could add to the nest egg he was building up for his mom's new house.

"But that's not all," Bennett went on. "My sister is... How can I put this? Spirited. She's much younger than me, not far out of college. She doesn't like me getting involved in her business, even though she clearly needs my help. So, until I can convince her otherwise, she can't know that you're working for me. She can't know that you're there to protect her at all. You'll have a cover story. She's never met you before, so that helps."

"But how close are we talking? To be frank, I'm not the best liar. That's what the other guys tell me, at least." His Ranger buddies had loved to give him hell about how uptight he was.

His boss laughed. "And that's what I like about you. You're a straight shooter. Just what I need. But don't worry. You would be staying in the apartment next door to hers. Close enough to keep an eye on her, but there would be no need for a lot of conversation."

"But why me? If you don't mind me asking, sir. I've been warming a desk lately." Devon didn't want to lose this opportunity, but he didn't feel that he was the best fit, from what his boss had explained so far.

Send him into a war zone to help seize an enemy airfield?

He'd know what to do. This was an undercover operation among civilians. He was no spy.

"You're up on your training, though? You've put in your time at the range?"

"Yes."

Bennett crossed his legs at the ankles, gazing into the distance for a moment. "Like I said, you remind me of myself. You keep a cool head under pressure. You care about your family more than anything else."

"Yes, sir," Devon responded softly.

"And you're not a womanizer. Yes, I've noticed. I pay attention to my employees. In fact, that leads into my last requirement—that you keep a certain distance. I need to know, with absolute certainty, that you can keep things completely professional around Aurora."

"Professional? I'm not sure what you mean."

Actually, Devon was pretty sure he did know what Bennett meant. But he was a little shocked that Bennett was even suggesting it.

The man's keen eyes said that he sensed Devon's thoughts and didn't give a shit about causing offense. "Let me be clear, Whitestone. Unless you're actively shielding her from an assailant, you'd better keep your hands off my sister. That goes for every other part of you, too. Unless you want to lose them." The man's eyes bored into his. "I assume that won't be a problem?"

"No, sir. No problem whatsoever."

Devon thought the secrecy was a little weird, and that his boss didn't need to worry about his professionalism. But in Bennet's shoes, he might've been asking for the same thing where Ruby was concerned. Especially after that piece of shit ex had left Ruby pregnant and in the lurch.

"Excellent. I expected no less. If you handle this job well, you'll have a very bright future with Bennett Security. Fuck it up?"

The rest went unsaid. His ass would be toast.

But Devon was, through and through, a man who believed in duty. He would sooner cut off his own balls than mess around with his commanding officer's sister.

Bennett extended his hand, and they shook.

Chapter Three

*A*urora burst into her apartment, kicking off her shoes and throwing down her purse. The night from hell had followed her into day, and now it was one chaotic blur. She didn't even know what time it was right now.

She couldn't stop thinking of the look on the ponytail man's—Eric's—face when he pulled the trigger. The high-pitched yet shockingly small sound that the gun's silencer made. The dull thud as Brandon's body hit the carpet.

Aurora flinched at each memory.

Lana Marchetti walked in behind her and shut the door. "Should I run a warm bath for you first? Or maybe a glass of wine?"

"Don't baby me, L. I get enough of that from Max."

Poor Brandon Wolfson. And his family. Aurora had liked him, though she hadn't known him well. But nobody, kind or not, deserved to meet such an end. Bile rose in her throat. No, she couldn't think about it. She'd already cried and vomited enough. No more of that.

Last night, after those horrible men had run from Wolfson's office at the sight of the blinking alarm, Aurora stayed hidden until her brother had arrived. She had mixed feelings about Max, but she'd been so thankful to see him in that moment. He'd wrapped her in his arms like she was still a little kid.

The police had shown up at The Lighthouse Club on Max's heels, followed by the district attorney. They'd questioned Aurora all night and well into today at the police station, long after Max had returned to work. She'd told the detectives everything she could about the murder.

At the station, Aurora had changed out of her black evening gown. But the clothes the police gave her didn't fit. They belonged to someone else. She scratched at her skin.

"I don't want a bath or wine." Aurora opened a cabinet in her chef-ready kitchen and pulled out a bottle of vodka. "A shot is more like it."

Lana slid onto a stool at the countertop. "Maybe one. But getting drunk isn't going to help, believe me. I've seen this before, and I know how it goes. You need to relax. Rest. Your stress hormones are off the charts right now."

Aurora's best friend was a district attorney, the second in command of their small county. Lana prosecuted hardened criminals on a daily basis. She was the most poised, intelligent, fearless woman Aurora had ever known.

Lana's family had taken Aurora in as a kid, back when Max was overseas and the rest of their family imploded. Lana was years older, but they'd been dear friends ever since.

I should be as brave as Lana. Instead, I'm a mess, and I didn't even lose anyone close to me.

What about Brandon's wife and the rest of his family and friends? Or Jennifer? What were they going through, even now?

She poured a shot of vodka into a coffee cup and tipped it back. The liquid made her shiver. Right away, she went to pour another, but Lana stayed her hand. "Uh uh, no way."

"Would you stop being so reasonable?"

"Everything's going to be all right. We have detectives

investigating Dominic Crane as we speak. We're going to make sure the case against him is airtight."

Max had already checked the Bennett Security cameras around The Lighthouse Club. Many hadn't been functioning, and Crane had avoided the rest. But Lana had said Crane could be held liable for murder, even though he didn't pull the trigger himself.

It all depended on Aurora's testimony.

"We're going to file a sealed complaint," Lana went on, "charging Crane and his accomplices. Within a day or two afterward, they'll be under arrest, and they won't have a clue about your identity until after that happens."

"And then I'll have to testify?"

Lana nodded. "But I'm planning to arrange a special deal with the defense attorneys. It's possible to have a witness testify early when there's a risk they may not be available at trial. Usually it's elderly witnesses, but there's no reason it wouldn't work here. Crane's lawyers would question you, and that way your testimony will be on the record."

"Because they'll want to kill me once they know I exist."

"Aurora…"

She threw back the second shot. "I know what you and Max were talking about. I'm not dumb. Crane will want to get rid of me before I can testify. Right?"

"Well… That's what we're afraid of. Yes. By having you testify early, I'm hoping they'll back off. Though I can't guarantee it."

"Okay." Somehow, she felt better hearing it out loud. As if having the worst in front of her made it easier to face.

You're not a victim, she told herself. *You can handle this. Be brave.*

Fake it till you make it, right? That was Aurora's motto for starting her party-planning business. It could work for this, too.

"When will I testify?"

"I don't know yet. Like I said, several things need to happen first. And we have to get the defense to agree—"

"I just want it over with."

"I know, sweetie. I know."

How was she supposed to keep her fledgling business going? Earlier last night, her prospects had seemed so bright. The party had been a success, and she was supposed to hold a birthday party for Mrs. Wolfson next week at their gorgeous estate up in the hills. She'd actually thought she could do this. Have a business, a *life*, of her own.

And now, everything was ruined. A man was dead, his wife despondent.

And I could be next.

But that thought didn't make her want to hide. She'd done enough hiding inside that office. She wanted to run.

"Can we go outside? It feels stuffy in here."

"Well…"

Don't say I'm trapped here, Aurora thought. *Please.*

"How about the rooftop terrace? If you eat something first, *and* we leave the vodka here."

Aurora smiled at her friend. "That'll work. Thank you."

AURORA SAT ON A WICKER CHAIR. A cool breeze blew from the water. The Pacific Ocean stretched out towards the horizon, sun glinting off its surface.

The commercial district along Ocean Lane bustled down below them. Waterfront seafood restaurants, trendy boutiques, and art galleries.

The Lighthouse Club was farther down the strip, in a building she could see from here. Police cars still lingered outside. Aurora suppressed a chill.

"Maybe we shouldn't have come up here," Lana said.

"No, it's fine. I'm okay. But…I feel awful about what

happened. I wish there'd been something I could do to stop them." Her voice cracked on the words.

Lana hugged her. "But thank goodness you stayed out of sight."

West Oaks didn't have much crime, usually, and hardly any murders. She'd grown up in this town, though her family hadn't lived anywhere near the beach. They'd lived a very different life back then.

Now, her brother Max owned this building. He'd offered her an apartment rent-free when she told him she was moving back. He hadn't mentioned it would be one of two pent-houses, with access to exclusive amenities like this rooftop terrace. She'd been saving up money to get a place of her very own, but apartments in West Oaks weren't cheap.

Everywhere she looked here, she saw her past. Her brother. She was incredibly grateful for his help with moving back. But she also wanted to forge her own life, like Max already had. He'd founded a successful company, paid for their parents to retire early and travel, conveniently out of their children's way.

People around here had no idea the founder of Bennett Security had been born on the wrong side of the freeway.

"Look." Lana leaned over the railing. "There's one of the squad cars. They're keeping watch over your building. That should make you feel safer. You know, Max offered to send a—"

"Uh, no. No bodyguard. I already told him."

"Rory, your brother runs a private security company. Assigning you a bodyguard is the easiest thing in the world for him. He knows what he's doing. Max is only trying to look out for you."

Aurora didn't like when her friend called her "Rory." That was what Max called her when she was a kid. But Lana had always gotten along better with her brother than Aurora did.

"Yes, Max has done a lot for me." For much of her life,

he'd been more like a parent than a brother. "But he's done enough. He treats me like I'm a child. Like I'm stupid." Like her ex, Justin, did. "He has no faith in me."

Aurora had every intention of making sure that Wolfson's killers were punished. But she wasn't going to sacrifice her freedom in the process. She'd already started over once when she'd moved back here. She couldn't do it again. Much less become a prisoner in her own home.

After her identity as the witness was revealed publicly? Then *maybe* she'd consider it. Not before.

"I think you're being too hard on Max and on yourself. Which is understandable. You've had a terrible shock, and it's easier to focus your anger on him than on what happened. I might be working on the case against Crane and his men, but I'm your friend first. You can tell me what you're feeling."

Lana put a hand on Aurora's arm, but Aurora shrugged it away. "You know, I'm tired after all. I'm ready to lie down now."

Lana sighed.

They took the stairs back to the penthouse level. But just as Aurora reached the bottom of the steps, she stopped.

"Something's wrong."

It took a moment for Aurora to pinpoint the issue. The other penthouse. Its door was open.

But nobody lived in that apartment. Max kept insisting his property manager hadn't found the right tenant with the necessary level of income. Translation—*I haven't found anyone I trust to live next to you, dear sister.*

What were the chances he'd found a tenant *today*, of all days?

As she watched, a man came out of the open doorway, closing it carefully behind him. Tall, muscular. Like Crane's men.

Then he looked over at the other penthouse door. *Her door.* He dug into his inner coat pocket.

A gun. He had a gun.

Aurora pushed Lana backwards into the stairwell. She couldn't breathe. Her heart rate had spiked, and her blood was racing.

"Go back up. Hurry."

They reached the terrace. Aurora yanked out her phone. "I'm calling the police."

"What? Why? I don't understand—"

"There was a man."

"So?"

"He had a gun."

Lana gasped. "Are you sure?"

"Excuse me," a male voice said. "Is everything all right?"

Aurora spun around, stretching out her arms to shield her friend. "Lana, get behind me!" No way was she going to lose someone else, and she cared a heck of a lot more about Lana than pretty much anyone.

The man from downstairs stood before her, his arms up. He was holding a phone. There was no gun in sight.

"Who are you? What were you doing in the other penthouse?" she demanded.

Lana peered over Aurora's shoulder.

"I was just moving in, and I heard voices up here. It sounded like someone was upset, so I wanted to come and check things out."

"See?" Lana put her hand on Aurora's back. "I don't think he means any harm, sweetie. He's just a new neighbor."

The guy nodded. He wore dark jeans, loafers, a white button down with a blazer over the top. The type of outfit any number of rich guys who lived in this building might be wearing. Yet he was a lot more built than the typical rich guy. The way he held himself conveyed strength, even danger. He was over six feet, with broad shoulders that strained the seams of his jacket. His hands were large, his fingers wrapping deftly around his phone.

He had a striking face. Lean, sharp cheekbones, a prominent nose. More like Dominic Crane, the crime boss, than like Crane's henchmen.

Aurora didn't trust him.

But her friend was already crossing the rooftop deck toward the guy. "We had a rough night. I'm Lana Marchetti. She's Aurora Bennett. Did you move into the apartment next to hers? The other penthouse?"

"Um, yeah. That's me." The guy tucked his phone back into his pocket. "If everything's okay here, I'm going to head back downstairs and unpack."

He hadn't even told them his name. His eyes kept moving across the deck, as if he was checking for something... Checking for threats. And there was a grace in the way he moved, the way he shifted his weight between his feet. Almost like a dancer. A smoothness to his movements that seemed predatory. He'd had training.

Wait a minute. Aurora knew exactly where this guy had come from.

Un-freaking-believable.

"You're military, aren't you? You're the bodyguard. My *brother* sent you."

His eyes fixed on her, and the rest of his body had gone still. Betraying nothing. Which only confirmed her suspicions.

She had met army guys through her brother. Max had shed many of the mannerisms of his military days, at least the most obvious ones. The stiff, straight back, the solemnness of his expression. Now, Max could be just as charming and easygoing as any wealthy playboy in West Oaks. When he chose to be.

But this guy? He was fresh. It was like he'd come here straight off the base.

He shook his head. "Afraid you have me mistaken for someone else." He spoke in a monotone. "I'm just renting the apartment."

"Bullshit. Max sent you."

"I don't know what you're talking about."

She took out her phone. "Then I'll ask him. What's your name?"

His eyes flipped over her quickly, and then he said, "Rick Harrison."

Aurora started texting. "You're a crappy liar, Rick Harrison. I know military when I see it. And you expect me to believe you just happen to move in today, the very day that my brother told me he wanted to send extra protection for me? Does Max really think I'm that clueless?"

The man's face changed. The blank, soldier-like expression was gone. Instead, his lips slid into a smirk. His brows arched, his eyes narrowing on her. His beautiful features sharpened into something more wicked.

"Afraid I have better things to do than chase after a spoiled little rich girl. If we're done here, I really need to get back downstairs. I have my own work to do."

"Spoiled little…" Anger flooded through her as her fists clenched. How dare he speak to her that way? As if he knew anything about her. "You have no idea what…"

But clearly, she'd been wrong. This guy wasn't working for Max. Otherwise he'd never be so rude.

She was seeing phantoms everywhere, like that gun. So, this was really her fault, not his.

My fault.

She saw danger when there wasn't any. But when those men shot Brandon? Killed him? She'd hidden and done nothing.

My fault.

Why was her vision feathering at the edges? Why couldn't she breathe?

"I'm not… I'm not feeling…"

Suddenly, the floor raced up to meet her.

"Rory!" Lana cried.

Aurora felt strong arms lifting her up. She was distantly aware that her new neighbor, the asshole Rick Harrison, was carrying her. He held her gently, his feet gliding down the steps.

The scene around her changed. They'd reached her apartment. Rick lay her down on the couch. He was saying something else to Lana, but that was when exhaustion finally overwhelmed Aurora, and her eyes couldn't stay open anymore.

Chapter Four

"*S*hit." Devon was back in the other apartment, pacing. Aurora had pegged him as security from minute one.

How was it possible that a tiny woman could be harder to manage than the men he'd used to command?

This was never going to work. She'd seen right through him. Then that condescending tone had come out of his mouth. He didn't even know where that came from. Probably some asshole he'd overheard in a bar back in L.A.

Spoiled little rich girl?

Okay, so maybe he thought that could be true of Max Bennett's younger sister. But it had been an awful thing to say, especially considering what she'd been through, and he didn't even know if it was accurate.

And then the girl had practically fainted. He figured that she was worn out from everything she'd endured in the last twenty-four hours. That was what her friend Lana had assured him. But Lana's tone had become clipped and professional with him. Which he'd deserved because he had been a complete jerk.

He had deflected Aurora's suspicion, but he hated the way he'd had to act to do it. *God, I can't manage this.*

He took out his phone and dialed Bennett's number.

"How're things going, Whitestone?"

"Sir, I'm not sure I'm the right person for this job."

He explained what had just happened: how Aurora had seen through his weak cover in about five seconds. But Bennett reassured him.

"It sounds to me like you did fine. I'm sure that she or Lana will call me any minute, and I'll back up your story. And from now on, our team in the office will keep an eye on things remotely, and you'll only step in if it's necessary. If you offended her, I promise she will get over it. She's been facing a lot worse."

That was true. His rudeness didn't even rank on the scale of Aurora's problems. "You're right. I'll get back to work."

"I know she's in good hands. Get to it."

After Bennett hung up, Devon realized that he hadn't mentioned the other thing that happened. Picking her up off the ground, carrying her down the stairs. He hadn't meant to leave that out. Technically, he had been touching her, which he wasn't supposed to do. He hadn't been protecting her from an imminent threat. But surely Bennett didn't mean emergency situations. Devon couldn't have left her lying there. Right? He might be playing the part of an arrogant business-man, but the act could only go so far.

And he was really trying not to think about how good she had felt in his arms. She'd been wearing an oversized T-shirt and sweatpants, yet the shape of her body had been clear enough underneath. Ample curves, tiny waist, long legs. And the way her hair draped over his arm, how her lips had been slightly open, and her long lashes had splayed on her cheeks…

No, he was definitely not going to think about any of that. He adjusted his jeans, telling his dick to calm down.

No wonder Bennett was so concerned about guys getting

handsy with her. No straight, single male could be around that girl for long without wanting to have her.

Devon would just have to think of her as his own sister.

But as he opened his laptop and logged in, he knew that would be impossible. The way his body was stirring without his permission revealed that he didn't remotely think of Aurora Bennett as his sister.

He would just have to ignore those impulses. He knew how to control himself. He would steer clear of her as much as possible and focus on his mission.

Devon spent the rest of the day getting acquainted with the building's security system. Bennett had installed it himself, so most of the protocols were familiar to Devon. In his three months so far with the company, he had been tasked with reviewing the security for several of their big clients, and the system here was as fancy as they came. Closed circuit, motion sensor cameras in all the common areas and the garage. Biometric access controls and landlines in every unit that connected directly to a specialist at Bennett Security.

The penthouse level boasted an additional unique feature —access to the rooftop terrace. It wasn't just a beautiful place to relax and take in the ocean views. The rooftop also connected to a secret escape route out of the building. Max Bennett had designed the upgrades himself. Apparently, he'd had visiting Middle Eastern royals and A-list celebrities in mind, but such exclusive digs weren't in high demand in West Oaks at the moment.

Briefly, Devon had been worried that Max might've included cameras throughout his sister's apartment. Like, her bedroom. That would've gone way beyond Devon's comfort level. In fact, Devon would've started second-guessing whether Max Bennett was an honorable leader at all. But the inside of Aurora's place was entirely hers.

Of course, she had cameras aimed at the front door from several angles and multiple locks. The elevator up to this floor required a key fob or fingerprint scan. Only Devon and Aurora, and her invited guests, had access. So, all he had to do was keep in touch with the team at headquarters and serve as a last line of defense.

He felt gratified that Bennett had trusted him with this assignment, and he intended to make the most of the opportunity. But in truth, he wasn't likely to see much action. This was going to be a quiet assignment, hardly all that different from manning a desk at the office.

So, he probably shouldn't worry his mom by telling her.

He made himself a quick dinner with some of the supplies he'd brought along with him. Bennett had promised a grocery delivery later. While he waited for the food to heat, he did push-ups and sit-ups on the living room carpet. One of the tough parts of this job would be remaining in this apartment, in front of a computer screen, instead of being able to take his daily run or go to the gym.

When he'd left the military, he'd just finished his second year in the Army Rangers. Devon liked to think his training hadn't worn off yet, despite six months as a civilian. He'd been working hard to keep himself in shape, and he'd been sparring at the cops' gym ever since he'd arrived in West Oaks. That was how he'd met Chase.

He knew he didn't have the breadth of training that Bennett's other bodyguards did, guys who'd spent a decade in various special forces and had even more time as elite personal security under their belts. But Devon could strip down and reassemble any weapon within a matter of seconds, had skills in marksmanship and emergency medicine, and he excelled at close combat with hands or a knife.

He itched to use his skills in the real world again. He didn't want Aurora to see any more danger, but if threats did happen to emerge, Devon was determined to be ready.

After dinner, he was back in front of the computer. Only a few residents had come in and out of the building, and nobody had ventured up to the penthouse level. Nor had Aurora or Lana come out of the other apartment. He assumed that the women had gone to sleep for the night.

Devon checked his video chat and saw that his mom was active. He pressed her name, and the call connected.

"Hi, sweetheart. Where are you?"

So she hadn't failed to notice the new background behind him. This apartment was far more ostentatious than his own. The place had come fully furnished, complete with art on the walls and expensive looking vases on the shelves.

"I'm on a special assignment. Don't worry, just manning a computer terminal. How was your day?"

His mother told him about her day at work. She'd been an ICU nurse for decades before retiring due to her arthritis. Now, she answered calls as a customer service rep. She was able to work from home, and the hours were flexible. But the pay wasn't much. Her clients, big retail companies, liked that she didn't mind working late at night. His mom had suffered from insomnia ever since they'd lost his father. It had only gotten worse after Kellen.

His mom kept her voice low since Ruby and the baby were no doubt asleep in their own room. "I hope you're taking care of yourself. I don't think you should be working these long hours."

"Look who's talking."

"We're doing fine. You put too much pressure on yourself. If you're on a special assignment, you must be busy. What can I do for you? What do you need?" She stood up, carrying her phone with her. "I know, you'll need to eat. I'll just throw some things into the slow cooker, and—"

"Mom, please. You don't have to do that. I've got plenty to eat here."

Devon knew that she would go without sleep if necessary to provide for him and his sister. And that was exactly why he had to work so hard. So that his mom would give herself a break.

"I'm sure you've got things handled for yourself, son. I just wish there was more that I could do for you. And you know your birthday is almost here. If you can think of a gift…" She trailed off, and tears filled her eyes. His birthday meant Kellen's birthday. Their second since his brother's death. Devon would turn twenty-seven, another age that Kellen would never reach.

"We'll do something special." He knew that was what his mom and sister needed. They would want to spend the day together remembering his brother, and yes, probably crying and hugging each other a lot. He would grit his teeth and get through it. He had to stay strong for them.

The hardest part was watching them fall apart, feeling all the same anguish inside of himself, yet pushing it down and away. He couldn't show how shitty he felt because they needed him to be the stoic one.

They talked a little more about plans for his birthday, and Devon managed to coax a smile out of his mom before saying good night.

After his mom was gone, Devon pulled out his phone and sent off a text to Chase, his friend and sparring partner.

On assignment. Going to be busy for a while. Would you mind checking on Ruby and my mom for me tomorrow? See if they need anything?

Chase wrote back, *Of course, man. No prob. Will do.*

He changed into his sweats and did a few more push-ups before getting ready for bed. The new surroundings kept him up and alert even though it was late, so he streamed a TV show for a while.

He was just switching off the light when a thump came from next door.

Immediately, Devon sat upright, listening. He checked his

phone, but it didn't show any warnings from the team at head-quarters. Maybe there was no reason for concern.

But then he heard another thump.

Then a shout.

In half a second, he was on his feet and charging for the door.

Chapter Five

$\mathcal{A}$urora sat up in bed, breathing hard. She'd been having strange, disturbing dreams. She looked around the room. Lana was asleep in the bed next to her. But Aurora couldn't remember exactly why her best friend was spending the night.

Then, in a flood, the events of the past day came back to her. The "Angels and Demons" party at The Lighthouse Club. Hiding in Mrs. Wolfson's office. She flinched as she recalled the gunshot. The splattering of blood.

Tears welled in her eyes, and her stomach burned with nausea.

And then that man on the rooftop in the afternoon. Rick Harrison. She had accused him of working for her brother, which made her sound like an idiot. She was paranoid. Plenty of real threats and problems were looming, and she certainly didn't need to invent new ones.

Spoiled little rich girl.

Why did she even care what that guy thought of her? So what if he was her new neighbor? He was some jerk, probably working in tech or finance, and he no doubt hadn't given her a second thought after he left.

Except for the fact that he had to *carry her* back to her apartment, she remembered now. She'd basically fainted in front of him, like some fragile debutante. God, how mortifying.

She had to get her mind off everything that had happened, especially her new neighbor next door.

Aurora strode into the bathroom, where the light was already on. She closed the door most of the way, so she wouldn't wake Lana, and washed her face.

Her closet connected to the bathroom. She went inside.

This was one of the best features of this apartment. The huge walk-in closet space. She'd only filled half of it with her clothes and shoes, and sometimes she daydreamed about what she might buy to fill the rest of it. Someday, when she had money of her own to spend.

Rick Harrison probably had a closet full of overpriced stuff he didn't even use. Multiple closets at various houses because he hadn't brought much with him here. Aurora hadn't seen any movers.

True, if you overlooked the arrogant personality, Rick was extremely attractive. Objectively speaking. But he wasn't even her type. Guys with a military bearing usually reminded her of Max. She couldn't imagine having a sexual thought about any man who resembled her brother. Gross.

But that guy. *Rick.* Who was even called Rick anymore? It was straight out of an eighties movie.

She pictured the strong, lean shape of his body. His dark tousled hair, cut short at the sides.

Nope. Not her type. She was determined to forget about him.

She dug into a drawer to find her favorite yoga clothes: a halter-top sports bra and a pair of high-waisted leggings with mesh cut-outs along the sides. She slipped them on and turned back and forth in front of her full-length mirror. Her hands ran along the smooth fabric.

It had been such an indulgence, buying clothes this expensive and this impractical for herself. She'd bought these items right after Brandon Wolfson's first payment for her party-planning services.

That indirect connection to Wolfson's death stole a little of her joy in owning the clothes, but she banished that thought. She wouldn't let those thugs destroy this small source of happiness.

She loved the way the bra lifted her breasts, and how her stomach looked flat and toned where it was exposed. She hadn't even worn these clothes out of the house yet, just enjoying them here on her own when she streamed yoga videos. Actually, she was afraid to mess up the nice fabric.

But this was exactly what she needed. A reminder that she was strong and didn't need anybody else to make her feel safe or secure. She didn't need any man's approval to feel good about herself, did she?

Justin, her college boyfriend back in St. Louis, had done a number on her self-confidence. Justin had been controlling and condescending, and she'd let him get away with it for too long. He'd subtly poked fun at her "easy" business classes, amazed that party-planning was even a career. Thank god she'd come to her senses. But when she broke up with him, she'd realized she had nothing of her own.

Aurora didn't have much of her own in West Oaks, either. She'd been trying to change that.

She was grateful that Lana had stayed overnight, and Aurora would've done the same for her best friend. But it was essential for Aurora to know that she could make it through this no matter what, regardless of who else was surrounding her.

A bodyguard, she thought dismissively. She didn't need any damned bodyguard.

But she did feel a surge of nervous, restless energy pumping through her veins. She needed to be productive. She needed something to do. A glance at her clock told her it was three in the morning, not exactly a reasonable time for starting new projects.

But suddenly she just couldn't be still. She couldn't imagine going back to bed and trying to sleep. And even if she did fall asleep, those dreams might come back.

Awful, blood-soaked dreams.

Aurora snuck out into the living room, scanning for something to keep her occupied. It was pretty clean already. Most of the time, she wasn't tidy. Her ex always complained about her messes. But this fancy apartment seemed to demand a higher standard. The place was so beautiful that she couldn't help feeling like a guest here, instead of at home.

Max had recruited a top interior designer to decorate these penthouses. It wasn't Aurora's style, with all the floral patterns, the thick fabrics, and ornate light fixtures. She would've preferred something cozier. Bright colors, a few cushy pillows, and framed prints on the walls that didn't look like they'd been sold at auction.

Spoiled little rich girl, Rick had called her. What a joke. If he only knew where she really came from. But still, his assumptions stung.

Her hands fluttered at her sides, desperate for something to keep them busy. Some way to keep her mind off her obnoxious neighbor and his even more obnoxiously handsome face.

She eyed the living room furniture. From the moment she'd walked into this place on her first day back in West Oaks, she hadn't liked the layout of the furniture in the space. It was cold and impersonal, like a hotel lobby instead of her apartment. And it was *her* apartment, even just temporarily. Who said she couldn't make it more comfortable? Make it more her own?

She grabbed a chair and tugged it out of the way. Aurora knew exactly what she wanted to do with all this nervous energy.

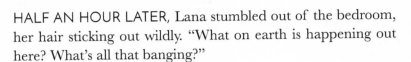

HALF AN HOUR LATER, Lana stumbled out of the bedroom, her hair sticking out wildly. "What on earth is happening out here? What's all that banging?"

"I'm redecorating."

"In the middle of the night?"

"I felt inspired." She had already moved the sofa into a new position and banished one of the striped chairs that she absolutely hated to a different room. Right now, she was in the process of switching out an ugly landscape for a canvas from the dining room, one that she actually didn't mind. It was an abstract piece, clearly based on the ocean view from the roof. Cool, calming shades of blue and green and beige.

"I just need to change the picture hanger in here. This one isn't going to work with that other canvas."

She charged over to the laundry room, where she'd stashed her toolbox. Lana's footsteps trailed behind her.

"Okay," her friend said, sighing. "How can I help?"

Aurora found the picture hanger she wanted, but now her hammer seemed to be missing.

"My hammer is gone. I swear if Justin stole it from this box before I left…"

She'd had to leave at least half of her tool collection in St. Louis because Justin had claimed they were his. But she was missing her favorite hammer, the one with a bright pink handle that Lana had gifted her back in high school.

Lana perched a hand on her hip. "The pink one? I can't imagine that Justin wanted that. It must be here somewhere. I'll look."

Lana dug through the various levels of the toolbox. But Aurora couldn't stand around watching, nor could she focus on a making an organized search. The thought of losing her special hammer, such a small yet precious thing, filled her with panic. And she didn't even know why.

She just knew she had to keep moving.

Just find something else, she told herself. She was resourceful. She could handle things on her own, no matter what came her way.

I'll fix this.

Aurora went into her bedroom, scanning for anything heavy that she could use as a hammer.

Then she had a brilliant idea. She went to her nightstand.

Ha, perfect.

Out in the living room, Aurora held a drywall anchor to the wall and started tapping it in.

"Oh my god," Lana said behind her. "Is that…"

Aurora raised the object she'd fetched from her nightstand. "The Incredible Hulk. Remember him? He's good for *all kinds* of things around the house."

Lana started to giggle.

The Hulk was another gift from Lana. The woman knew how to pick a birthday present. It was nine inches long at least, covered in rubbery material, thick and stiff in Aurora's hand. Not the typical hammer, true, but it would do the job.

"Brings new meaning to the term 'getting pounded,'" Lana said.

Unfortunately, the Hulk slipped and hammered Aurora's finger instead. She yelped.

Furious knocking interrupted them. Someone was trying to break down her front door. Lana ran over and checked the video screen.

"It's your neighbor. Rick."

Oops. "Well, might as well let him in." She figured she should apologize for waking the guy on his first night here, even if they didn't like each other.

Lana opened the door, and he barged in. Aurora's breath caught. He was wearing nothing but a pair of thin sweatpants. A light dusting of dark hair covered his broad chest and washboard stomach, leading down to his waistband.

Veins traced his biceps, his torso carved from lean, ropey muscle.

Aurora opened her mouth, a contrite apology already on her lips.

But then Rick started talking.

"What the hell is going on in here?" He looked around at the mess in the living room. "I thought someone was being attacked. Do you have any idea what time it is?" His eyes widened. "Is that a *dildo*?"

No way was she going to apologize to this arrogant douche. So what if he was hot? That was irrelevant. *He thinks you're a spoiled brat*, she reminded herself.

"We're just doing a little home improvement in here." She waved her makeshift hammer at him. "And this isn't a dildo. He's my boyfriend, I'll have you know. The Hulk."

She'd been hoping to ruffle Rick's feathers a little, break that irritatingly superior demeanor. But he disappointed her. His face shut down again, going back to his blank expression from earlier. Giving nothing else away.

"And yes," she added, "I washed him. Just in case you were wondering."

"I wasn't."

"Apologies for waking you, Mr. Harrison," Lana said smoothly. "It's not usually so noisy around here. Aurora had a really stressful day. I'm sure you'll cut us some slack?"

"No worries," he said breezily, as if he hadn't just barged in here all pissed. "Glad there's no emergency."

He had a tattoo on the inside of his forearm, a stylized *K*. She wondered what it meant but wasn't about to ask.

He was judging her right now. She knew it. He was probably used to getting his way, doing multi-million-dollar deals in the boardroom. Or something else testosterone-heavy, where men swung around their metaphorical dicks. He probably drove a fast, sickeningly expensive car and was over-compensating for an itty-bitty micro penis.

Except one glance at the resting bulge in his sweatpants, and she could tell he had no insecurities in that department. Maybe he'd be as big as the Hulk when he got hard.

Her panties were getting damp. She had to stop looking at him.

With that thought, she turned around and started hammering again.

"We'll quiet down," Lana said, "I promise."

"I don't promise!" Aurora took another thwack at the nail, hitting her fingers with green rubber once again in the process. "Ow."

She looked back at Rick, whose face had wrinkled in disgust. "Please stop doing that. I'm going to get you a real hammer. Wait, okay?"

"Not waiting." *Thwack, thwack, thwack.*

Lana groaned. "If I had one single ounce of self-consciousness, this would probably be pretty embarrassing."

Chapter Six

*D*evon found a hammer in his things. He'd grabbed the tools on his way out of the Bennett Security office just in case he needed to make any fixes to doors, locks, or cameras in Aurora's building. He hadn't expected to be using them to rescue a vibrator from certain destruction. But if he could help out, he was happy to do it.

Even if it meant getting close, once again, to Bennett's sister. But the girl was clearly struggling with the trauma of what she'd seen. He cursed himself for being short with her when he first went into her place, but he'd been genuinely worried.

And he'd felt a little sheepish about not even wearing a shirt.

Devon grabbed a tee and pulled it on before heading back into the hallway. He sent off a quick text to the team back at the office, who'd no doubt seen him on the cameras. *Thought there was a problem, but false alarm. Handling it.*

He pocketed his phone and walked back next door.

"You could be slightly less antagonistic, Rory," he heard Lana saying.

"We don't owe that pompous jerk a damn thing. Screw him and the Tesla he rode in on."

He gritted his teeth and strolled back into the apartment. Aurora grabbed for the hammer, but he held it out of her reach. Fuck, she looked sexy. Sleek leggings that hugged her ass and legs. Her stomach bare, tops of her breasts rounded into view by her tight sports bra.

Which I shouldn't be noticing.

"I don't think so. You've done enough damage. Consider me your designated hammerer."

"You think I'm *drunk?*"

"No. But your friend mentioned you'd had a rough day. I might know a thing or two about that. People handle shock in very different ways."

"Oh, from your vast experience as a rich, entitled douchebag?"

He returned her glare. That was his cover story, sure. He should've been glad that she'd bought it. So why did her frown irk him so much?

Lana groaned again, hand over her eyes. "I'm going to make us some coffee."

"Just show me what you were doing so we can get this over with," Devon said.

Aurora handed him the drywall anchor. Thankfully, she'd gotten rid of the vibrator. A smile tugged at his lips, thinking of her waving that thing around. He had to admit, it had been kind of funny. Once he'd realized that she wasn't actually in any danger.

He tapped the anchor in, then hung the picture hanger. She pointed at the canvas she wanted, and he lifted it up into place.

"Thanks," she said begrudgingly.

He turned back to her, arms crossing over his T-shirt. "You're probably experiencing a surge of adrenaline right now. A mild sedative could help. You need to get some real sleep before the inevitable crash comes."

Her frown returned. "I don't need you to mansplain to me how I feel. Thanks for hanging the picture. We won't bother you anymore."

"Somehow I doubt that." He couldn't fight the grin anymore. Devon padded across the living room and let himself out.

HE MANAGED to get a few more hours of sleep before his alarm went off. There hadn't been any more noise from next door. He made a cup of instant coffee and sipped it while he checked the hall camera. No one had come or gone from Aurora's apartment.

In the hours since he'd arrived, he'd spent far too much time with her. Not exactly keeping his distance.

The calm now was a blessing, a sign that Aurora was resting. Maybe today would be easier. Uneventful, even.

So why did he feel the urge to go over and check on her? See how she was doing?

He showered, got dressed in jeans and a tee, and occupied himself by reading the latest technical manual on Bennett's favored surveillance camera system.

A low ding came from his computer—a notice that the motion sensor in the hall had picked up movement.

On his laptop screen, he saw Aurora emerge from her apartment with a small paper bag in her hands. He grabbed his keys, getting ready to follow her. But she didn't go toward the elevator.

Instead, she turned toward his place.

Devon went to his door. Aurora's face appeared on the monitor, showing the feed from his doorbell camera. She'd swept her hair into a ponytail. No makeup concealed the dark circles beneath her eyes. He wished he could wipe those shadows away. His palm pressed flat against the wood, knowing she was just on the other side.

He knew hardly anything about her yet, but he liked Aurora Bennett. She wasn't what he'd expected. In fact, he had the feeling she was the type of woman who would constantly surprise him.

It wouldn't hurt to be her friend, would it? Surely Bennett wouldn't have a problem with that. Devon didn't want to keep making her frown.

Ring the bell, he told her. *So I can answer.*

But after a moment of deliberation, she set her bag on the doorstep and left.

Once she'd returned to her apartment, he opened his door and brought the bag inside. The paper crinkled as he opened it. There was a pistachio muffin wrapped in plastic film, along with a note.

Sorry for the noise last night. Consider this a peace offering.
Your neighbor,
The Hulk

Chapter Seven

*A*urora spent the next two days drifting in and out of sleep. Lana ordered groceries and went down to the lobby to pick them up. Every time Aurora woke, she found her friend in the kitchen, cooking up a storm. All of Aurora's go-to meals, like chicken breasts and tuna salad and vegetarian chili, even a dish of baked macaroni and cheese. It was especially thoughtful, considering that Lana didn't like to cook.

But finally, Lana had to return to the office. She kissed Aurora goodbye on the cheek. "We're getting everything ready to make the arrest. Max has been helping track Crane's movements for us, so I'll keep you posted. You've got the police detail outside, keeping watch. The officers were hand-picked by yours truly."

"Do they know I'm the witness to Wolfson's murder?"

"No, only that there's a potential threat to this building. We're keeping the circle as tight as possible for as long as we can. But I left the number for police dispatch on the fridge; you call them if anything comes up."

"I know." She'd spoken to Max, too, and he'd promised he was giving the police the full support of his company, just as

Lana had said. Max hadn't mentioned the bodyguard again. Her brother was actually listening to her, giving her some space, and for that, Aurora was grateful.

"But remember," Lana warned her, "after Crane and his men are arrested, we'll have to move for the court to unseal the complaints. That means your identity as the witness will be revealed. We're going to delay as long as we can, since today is Sunday. But as soon as tomorrow, we won't be able to keep your identity secret anymore. So stay safe. Stay here."

"I've got it." She'd already been thinking about that. Aurora took a deep breath.

"Love you." Lana touched her cheek.

"Love you, too."

She left, and Aurora locked the door.

The penthouse level was too quiet. She hadn't heard a peep coming from next door. Rick Harrison hadn't shown himself again, not since Aurora left the muffin on his doorstep. She could only assume that she'd smoothed things over with him. She didn't like the guy, but she'd had to admit —after Lana made several highly reasonable arguments—that the man wasn't so bad as a neighbor. If she had anything heavy to lift, he'd be able to handle it.

And she could watch his muscles work again.

She remembered the flex of his biceps. That mysterious tattoo. The memory almost made her search for an excuse to ask him over.

Almost.

Later that morning, Aurora got a text from Lana.

Turn on Channel 3 News. It's happening.

She switched on the TV.

"—who I'm told has an update for us," the news anchor was saying. "Mary?"

The view switched to a reporter, who held a microphone at the edge of a crowd. "We've just received word that

Dominic Crane, a Los Angeles club promoter, has been arrested for the recent murder of local business owner Brandon Wolfson."

Aurora recognized the building behind the reporter: the West Oaks Police headquarters, just a couple of blocks away from Aurora's apartment.

"We expect Crane to arrive here in custody any minute. While Crane claims to run a legitimate business, he's previously been accused of money laundering, wire fraud, and criminal conspiracy. Up until now, he's been cleared of any wrongdoing. He's the younger brother of Warren Crane, the alleged head of the notorious Silverlake Syndicate, which has been active in the Los Angeles area for decades. Warren Crane is now behind bars at San Quentin Federal Penitentiary for tax evasion."

Aurora covered her mouth. Cold sweat ran down her sides. Lana had said something about Dominic Crane being a crime boss, but hearing the details made it all seem more real.

She still didn't understand why he'd want to go after Wolfson. What was it Crane had said?

You didn't just steal from me. You took my money and started a little business on the side.

Aurora had told Lana and the DA everything that Crane said. But they hadn't explained what any of it meant. Wolfson couldn't have been involved with some crime syndicate, could he?

Lana was at the district attorney's office right now, working hard on the case against Crane. And Max was probably at Bennett Security headquarters, consulting with his own investigators or conferencing in with police detectives.

And what am I doing? Aurora asked herself. *Hiding in my house. Just like I was hiding when those men killed Brandon Wolfson.*

She looked around at the penthouse apartment. Even after her recent redecorating, it still felt more like a hotel room than her home. That restless feeling was itching at her skin again. Like some unseen attacker was stalking her. Running her to ground.

She knew exactly what it was—*fear*. If she stayed trapped in this apartment, the fear she'd been avoiding for the last several days would crash down on her and swallow her whole.

On the TV, the reporter said, "I have confirmation that Crane and two of his associates are now in custody. Crane is in a squad car, being transferred as we speak to the West Oaks Police Department, where he'll be booked and processed for holding. I'm told they've added extra security because of Mr. Crane's high profile. In just a few minutes, we should see the motorcade entering this driveway. We should be able to catch a glimpse."

Soon, Crane and his men would be officially booked. Lana might have to release those court documents tomorrow. Then everyone would find out Aurora was the witness. She had a time-bomb strapped around her, a clock ticking down her last few hours of being able to leave this place.

Aurora grabbed a windbreaker and baseball cap from the hall closet. Her keys and phone dropped into her pocket. Then she was out the door.

SHE JOGGED past the squad car, trying to act natural. Lana had said the officer didn't know she was the witness. And thankfully, the officer didn't show any interest. She was just another resident.

The outside air was cool, smelling of the ocean. She was out. Finally, she could breathe.

She could already see the crowd gathered at the police station down the street. She kept her hat pulled down, though she couldn't imagine that anyone would be looking for her yet.

Everyone probably had their eyes on the news vans and reporters, who were swarming all over the sidewalk and into the street.

She just hoped that she wasn't too late.

Aurora watched for the Channel 3 sign. She spotted the reporter she had seen on television and got as close as she could to the woman. The other people on the curb jostled her, and she wrapped her arms around herself, scanning to her left and right.

Aurora was shocked by the size of the crowd. But West Oaks almost never had murders. Certainly not murders of wealthy men by L.A. organized criminals. Around here, this was a very big deal.

She couldn't help thinking about everything Lana and Max had said about the dangers she could face as a witness. But she was standing right in front of the police department, in front of at least a dozen cameras.

I'm safe, she repeated to herself. *I'm fine. Nobody knows me here.*

And she did feel like a bit of a badass for venturing out. She wasn't hiding anymore, and just that small victory had done a lot for her mood.

She wanted to see Dominic Crane in handcuffs and surrounded by police. That man and his henchmen had been haunting her dreams for the last several days. From everything Lana had said, this process could stretch out for weeks or months. Maybe even longer. But Aurora refused to live in fear.

Crane was the one who should be a prisoner, not her.

There was a flurry of activity on the street that ran along the far side of the police department building. A siren whooped, and a whole line of police cars came into view. "This is it," someone shouted. People started running and pushing for a better view, while officers held them back. She could see the mouths of the reporters moving, though she couldn't hear them.

A tingle ran across the back of her neck. She spun around, feeling watched. But she couldn't spot anyone who seemed out of the ordinary. Her eyes met different people in the crowd, but she didn't recognize anyone.

Don't be paranoid, she told herself. *You're okay.*

The first car rolled into the driveway behind the police department building, where the jail was located. She saw two people in suits sitting in the front seat. Then several more cars that held uniformed officers.

And then, smack dab in the middle, she caught sight of Dominic Crane. His dark hair falling past his chin, his large, elegant features. The man looked completely calm, as if he were being chauffeured to the airport and not heading in to be booked and charged.

This was the man who'd ordered the death of Brandon Wolfson. Aurora felt a surge of nerves.

After that, more cars pulled into the driveway, but Aurora got pushed out of position and couldn't see who else might be sitting inside them. By the time she got back to a good vantage point, the line of cars had all pulled in, and police officers were clearing the crowd.

Aurora followed along with the other people as they began to move down the block. She still had that uncomfortable feeling that someone was studying her.

She glanced across the street, and that was when she saw him.

There was a man staring straight at her.

She'd never seen him before. He was generic in every way, almost hard to describe. But his gaze didn't waver from hers, and she felt his animosity. Panic sent her heart up to her throat.

He took a step into the street. He was coming toward her.

She turned and ran, searching for some way to escape. Suddenly, the crowd had dissipated, and she'd ended up at

least half a block away from the police department entrance,
no officer in sight.

No, no, no. I never should've left the apartment. She took off
down the sidewalk, heading back toward the police headquarters. Then someone stepped into her path. She nearly
screamed, raising her hands to defend herself.

It was her neighbor. Rick Harrison.

"What are you doing here?" she sputtered.

He was out of breath, his expression full of concern. "Just
out for a jog. What's the matter?"

For a split second, she wondered how he knew that something might be wrong. But she figured she must've looked
terrified.

"There was a man. I thought…he might be following
me."

But when she turned to look, the man was gone. She
scanned the street, but there was no sign of him.

Rick's hand closed over her elbow, pulling her toward him
protectively. And she didn't even mind. She was glad to have
him beside her. His stoic demeanor—and his muscles—were
just what she needed right now.

"What did this man look like?"

"Never mind. He's not here anymore."

Was this like seeing the gun in Rick's hand the other day?
Just her imagination running wild? She had no clue.

Lana would no doubt tell her this had been a very dumb
idea. And it certainly hadn't gone the way she had hoped. She
had felt pure terror when that man crossed the street, coming
toward her.

But then, she tried to reason with herself. How would a
random man know that she was the witness to Wolfson's
murder? And even if he did somehow know, how'd he guess
that she'd be at the police department today?

Just in case, she was going to text Lana and tell her what
she'd seen. If that guy was actually after her, she wanted to

make sure that the police and the district attorney knew. But there was no point in freaking out about it now.

She just wanted to get back home.

"You okay?" Rick asked. "Is there anything I can do?"

"Would you mind walking me home? I'm ready to go back now."

Chapter Eight

*D*evon's heart tapped a rapid beat as he escorted Aurora toward her building. He had seen her leave her apartment and had raced to follow her. Not so close that she would notice, but also trying not to lose her. And she had certainly done her best to keep anyone from tailing her, getting herself lost in the crowd.

Once she'd gotten near the police department, he'd guessed what she might be doing. He'd heard that Crane was being arrested that morning. He couldn't believe that Aurora would take the risk of going near that guy, but Devon also had to admit that it took balls. If he could've looked into the eyes of the man who'd murdered his brother, he would have. But Devon would never get that chance. The man who'd killed Kellen had shot himself instead of being taken by the police.

He shook his head, trying to rid himself of the thoughts. That wasn't a good headspace. He was supposed to be focused on Aurora, not on himself.

Devon hadn't even intended to approach Aurora on the street at all. But then he'd seen the frightened look on her face.

"Have you ever felt like you couldn't completely trust your senses?" Aurora suddenly asked. He looked over at her. Her face had gone pale. "I mean, like you were so caught up in thinking about one particular thing that you started seeing it everywhere."

"Sure. After my dad died when I was a kid, I kept thinking I saw him from the window of our car. We'd be driving down the street, and I'd keep telling my mom that he was out there. Trying to find us."

Devon couldn't even count the number of times that had made his mother cry. After a while, Kellen had made him stop.

After his brother's death, the same thing didn't happen, though. Kellen had been his identical twin, so Devon already saw his brother's ghost every time he looked into the mirror.

Aurora was studying him with new interest. "I'm sorry that happened to you."

He shrugged. He hadn't told her for sympathy, just so that she could know she wasn't going through anything unusual. Yet he wasn't entirely sure what she had seen. Bennett was going to want to know more when Devon made his report later.

"You think you imagined a man following you?"

"Maybe. I really don't know."

If there could be somebody out there who was targeting Aurora, Devon sure as hell wanted to find out.

They reached the main entrance to the building and walked inside.

"Let's assume you really saw this guy, and he was following you. Did you recognize him?"

"No."

"You have no clue who he might be?"

She groaned. "I'm going to tell you something, because you live next door to me, and you should probably know what's going on."

"Okay," he said. Even though he guessed what she was about to tell him.

"I was a witness to a crime a few days ago. The murder at The Lighthouse Club."

She gave him the basic outline of what had happened, all of which Devon already knew. He forced his eyebrows to raise, trying to act surprised. But he didn't have to fake his concern.

He hated that she had gone through such a terrible experience. It wasn't right that she'd ended up in the middle of some kind of underworld dispute, when her only mistake had been planning a party for the Wolfsons. She'd just been in the wrong place at the wrong moment.

By the time she'd finished her story, they were standing outside of her apartment. "Have you told the police about seeing that guy today?" Worry burned in his gut.

"I texted Lana. She's a district attorney. I haven't heard back from her yet. But like I said, maybe it was nothing. Maybe I'm just seeing scary things all over the place because I'm…" She stared at the ground, her voice dropping to a whisper. "Scared."

Shit. He wanted to pull her into his arms. "I don't blame you. You went through something really fucked up. I'd be scared too."

"I really hope you're not patronizing me right now."

"No way. I wouldn't." During his time in the army, he'd learned that there's no such thing as being "fearless." Not unless you were out of your mind or hopped up on drugs. Real soldiers learned to manage their fear, not deny it or hide from it.

She glanced at her door. "Do you want to come in for a little while?"

Would that be professional? She wasn't in danger. But she was scared. *I'm making sure she's all right.*

"If you don't mind that I'm kind of sweaty from my run." *From chasing you down*, he corrected to himself.

Her gaze moved over him, making his skin heat. Her mouth quirked in a hint of a grin. "I kinda like you sweaty."

Was she flirting with him?

She was.

"Honestly," Aurora added, "I'd just rather not be alone at the moment. You happen to be here. Beggars can't be choosers."

He laughed, his ego promptly deflating.

She unlocked the door. Her keys clattered onto the kitchen counter, and she shed her windbreaker over a chair. "I'm sure this is not what you bargained for when you moved in. Police watching the entrances and a murder witness next door."

"Actually, you might be surprised."

"Oh yeah? Why is that?"

"I was expecting tight security," he improvised. "That's one of the perks of the building. Or so the property manager told me."

She rolled her eyes. "Yep. Bennett Security's signature service." Aurora sank onto a barstool, resting her elbows on the counter. "So, what's your deal? What do you do, exactly, over in that apartment of yours?"

"Aside from being a rich, entitled douchebag?"

She grinned for real this time, and the smile lit up her face. "Exactly."

"I manage a hedge fund." He knew his cover story by heart, and he hated it. Devon had no interest whatsoever in the stock market; Kellen had been the one with a head for investing. If Aurora asked questions about this supposed "hedge fund," he had every intention of deflecting.

"But aside from that?" he went on. "I grew up in L.A. I went to a military school for a while. I'm new to West Oaks." He had to be vague about his real background—not many hedge fund guys would've gone to West Point—but he wanted to tell her something true.

"I *knew* you had some kind of military background."

He shrugged. "Yeah, you got me. But civilian life was better for my family, so here I am."

"Family? What kind of family? Like a wife, kids…"

"Nope, I mean my mom and sister and niece. Those are all the ladies in my life."

She seemed pleased by his response.

"What about you?" he asked.

"Do I have a wife and kids? No."

He felt himself smiling. "I mean, how'd you end up here?"

"That's a long conversation." Aurora got up and went to the fridge. "You're probably thinking, no party planner in her twenties could afford this penthouse apartment unless she's got overindulgent parents who're rolling in dough. Right?"

"I was not thinking that." Not those specific words.

"Ha, don't think I've forgotten what you said when we met." She mouthed the words, *spoiled little rich girl.*

He cringed. "I'm sorry about that. I didn't really mean—"

"Don't worry about it. I *might* have been slightly bratty that day." She dug around inside the fridge, emerging with two beers. She handed him one and popped the top on her own. "But know that you're wrong. I'm not spoiled, and I'm not rich. My brother is, but that's not me."

"But you *do* live here."

"Yeah, because he owns the building! I just got back to town a few months ago. I needed a place to stay. Max loves that he can keep an eye on me here, which he could never do when I was away for college in St. Louis. He gets off on control, and he claims he just wants to protect me."

Guilt roiled Devon's stomach. He looked down into his beer. "But if you don't want your brother controlling your life, why'd you agree to live in his building?"

She scowled, and he held up his hands. "Not that I'm judging," he added. "Just curious."

Aurora sighed and closed her eyes. "I have reasons. But that's where the long story comes in."

He sat beside her and took a swig of his beer. "I'm listening."

"Max is a lot older than me. We grew up in West Oaks, but not in the nice part. He couldn't wait to get away. As soon as he turned eighteen, he enlisted. Left home. Then a whole bunch of shitty things happened at once."

She paused, so he asked, "Like what?"

Aurora took a small sip, not meeting his eyes. "My mom was a massage therapist, and my dad's a barber. They worked down here on Ocean Lane, serving the West Oaks 'elite.'" She added air quotes, showing her disdain for the word. Or perhaps for the people. "They lived paycheck to paycheck. Doing the best they could. But one day, the water heater flooded our house. Insurance wasn't going to cover all of it. There were some other factors, too. My mom wound up in the hospital with the flu, for one. But suddenly, we didn't have a house anymore."

She blinked rapidly, though Devon couldn't see any tears. "We lived out of the car for a while. Stayed with friends. My dad lost his job because he kept being late. It got harder and harder for them to dig themselves out."

"When did your brother find out?" Because he could imagine the man's reaction upon hearing about his family's crisis. But as a soldier, Max wouldn't have been able to rush straight to them in their hour of need. Devon had certainly been in a similar situation, and it was awful. He'd felt powerless.

"My mom broke down and told him a year later. They'd been able to fool him for that long. But things had been getting a lot worse. My dad built up some gambling debt, always trying to win back what we'd lost. And my mom... She started smoking way too much weed. Trying to dull the pain."

She spun the bottle cap on the countertop. "Max was so furious. The next time he had leave, he came home. Straightened things out as much as he could, arranged a different place for me to live. With Lana, the woman you met before. She'd been my babysitter. That relieved some of my parents' burden, not having to worry about me, but it was so hard for them. Needing their son to fix their mess, losing—"

She cleared her throat. "See, I told you this was a long story. Way too long. You probably have other things to do."

"No. I have nowhere else to be." *I'm all yours*, he almost said.

Her eyes met his. After another minute, she went on. "Fast forward to when Max left the army and came home. Started his security company, which took off fast. I was off in college, on scholarships and a bazillion loans, then went through a terrible break-up. Max offered to help, and I accepted. He's been incredibly generous with his money, and of course, I'm grateful for that. But he acts like an overprotective father more than a brother. It's too much."

"He must feel guilty. You were just a kid, and he wasn't around when you needed him the most."

"I don't want his guilt! You have no idea how many boyfriends he's chased away. How many times I found out from teachers that my 'dad' called, asking about my grades, and I knew it was him. In some ways, Max is the best brother anyone could hope for. But sometimes, he's pathological."

And I'm helping Max lie to you, Devon thought. *If you find out, will you hate me?*

He was afraid he already knew the answer.

Chapter Nine

*S*he couldn't believe she'd told Rick so much of her history. And he'd listened, his attention unwavering. Like he honestly cared. She hadn't even told her ex in St. Louis the entire story, and they'd been together for three years.

"Thanks for sitting through all of that."

His brows drew down over his hazel eyes. "I should be thanking you for telling me. I know it's not easy to open up."

"Somehow, it is with you."

Wow. She actually kinda liked this guy. It had nothing to do with the fact that he had money. His job as a hedge fund manager didn't even fit with the rest of him. Rick was down to earth, sincere. Assertive enough to keep things interesting. And the rocking body didn't hurt.

She hadn't felt this interested in a guy in a long time. Before her dry spell, she'd been with Justin, having boring sex for three years because she'd thought she loved him. All the while, she'd downplayed Justin's efforts to belittle and control her, which had left her isolated.

She practically needed her cherry popped all over again. Perhaps Rick Harrison was just the man to do it.

He was turned toward her on the stool. His knee bumped

gently against hers, then drew away. Her eyes strayed to his lips, and his mouth opened slightly.

Then her phone rang. It was Lana. Reluctantly, Aurora answered.

"I got your message," Lana said. "You were at the station when Crane arrived? What happened?"

Aurora told her friend about the man she'd seen outside police headquarters. "I can't even say why he bothered me. I'd never seen him before." She felt Rick tensing beside her. His knee brushed hers again. "It just seemed like he was watching me. Following me."

"Okay." It sounded like Lana was writing something down. "I'll make sure someone reviews the security camera footage around the station. I'll also have the sketch artist call you so you can work up an image."

"That sounds good." Aurora was relieved she'd called and that Lana was taking this seriously. Just like Rick had.

"You're not alone, are you?"

"Rick is with me. From next door. Turns out, he's not as douchey as I thought." She smiled at him.

"Good. I'd feel better if you stay with someone until we can check out this man you saw. And Rory—no more running off, okay?"

"Got it."

"Stay in. Have some fun. Bye." Lana's voice was teasing. *Have some fun with Rick*, she meant. Aurora was inclined to agree.

"Anything I can do to help?" Rick asked after she'd ended the call.

"Keep me company?" She pressed her knee to his again, and this time, he kept the contact. "I could use a distraction."

"When my mom's got too much on her mind, she likes to bake."

"You want to bake with me? Seriously?"

"Yeah. Why not?"

"Okay. Sure." This guy was too good to be true.

She pulled up a sugar cookie recipe on her phone.

His bossy side came out as they mixed the ingredients, but she found that she didn't mind it so much. He wanted to crack the eggs a certain way, measure out the flour just so.

"The recipe is right there," he protested. "They give directions for a reason."

"I guess I'm just not a rule follower."

"I gathered that much."

He was surprisingly comfortable in the kitchen, at least compared to what she would've expected from a guy who managed a hedge fund for a living. He must've had enough money to buy whatever cookies he wanted.

But he had grown up in a house where his mom baked for him. She found herself wondering more about his family, his childhood. He had told her so little about himself, and yet she had spilled almost her entire life story.

But every time she tried asking him a question, he brought the subject back to the moment.

So he didn't want to talk about himself. It wasn't a deal breaker. She'd give him time to open up.

Soon, the cookies were in the oven, and Aurora got out a new bag of powdered sugar to make the frosting. She started jabbing at the top with a knife, but then Rick pulled the bag out of her hands.

"You can't do it that way. You're going to cut yourself. Or spill it everywhere."

"It's fine." She tried to pull the sugar back.

"Hold on, you need to—"

"If you would just—"

The bag popped open. A puff of white exploded into the air. They both froze.

"My face is covered in sugar right now." His expression was solemn, his tone dead serious. "Isn't it."

She snickered. His face, his hair, his shirt—everything was dusted with white. "You're like a giant cookie."

Aurora leaned forward, her breasts bumping into his torso. Her finger swiped across his chin. Slowly, she stuck the finger between her lips and sucked.

"I knew you'd be sweet," she whispered.

His eyes focused on her, his gaze pure molten heat. His hands went to her waist. She tilted upward, right at the same moment that he moved down. His mouth stopped an inch away from hers.

His hands tightened on her waist, the rest of his body going still.

"Kiss me already," she said.

Then, finally, his lips brushed hers.

He pulled back slightly, then kissed her again. So gently. Each time their lips touched, they parted more, the hunger between them building. Like a car on a roller coaster, ratcheting upwards toward the inevitable release. With each kiss, she felt him giving in more and more to the moment. Relaxing into her.

He tasted like powdered sugar and mint. Rick's tongue licked into her mouth, and she groaned in response. Desire raced through her, dampening her panties, and beading her nipples. It was like they'd tipped right over the edge, and now the roller coaster was in free fall. Their hands were all over each other. He squeezed her ass. She rocked against his crotch and felt his length getting hard just for her. She made a sound of appreciation. He was going to feel so good inside of her.

"I want to ride you," she said, "right here on this floor."

Abruptly, he took a step back. "Okay, hold on. We can't."

"Pretty sure we can. We were doing just fine." She leaned forward again. His hands moved to her shoulders, holding her at arm's length.

"I mean, *I* can't."

All the heat and desire she'd been feeling vanished like

sugar dissolving into water. "You said you were single. I mean, you implied—"

"It's nothing like that. There's no one else. But this—" He gestured between them. "It can't happen."

"I don't understand." He'd seemed to like her. He'd been hard for her, so she couldn't imagine a physical obstacle on his part. And she hadn't hallucinated the chemistry in that kiss.

"Was I moving too fast?" she asked. "We don't have to sleep together yet. We can just go back to kissing. That was really nice on its own."

She took a step forward, and he shuffled back. "My life is…very complicated right now. You and I, we're in different places. This can never go anywhere, so… We shouldn't start."

He seemed like he was babbling. But as she replayed his words in her head, she started to get it.

He didn't think she was good enough for him.

"'Different places,'" she repeated. "Because you're this fancy finance guy, and I'm a formerly homeless party planner living in her brother's apartment?"

"What? No, that's not it. At all."

"Then what is it, exactly? How am I wrong?" *Please, tell me I'm wrong.*

But instead, he said nothing. The emotion drained from his face. It was like he'd suddenly put up a wall against her.

"I should go."

"Then do it!"

She never should've confessed so much to him, told him all that stuff about her childhood. Of course, a man like him wouldn't see past it. He probably felt sorry for her.

Most guys would've fucked her anyway and ghosted her later. So maybe she should be grateful. He was an upstanding variety of arrogant asshole.

But still an asshole.

Aurora went to her room, leaving the mess in the kitchen. The front door clicked shut, and she knew he was gone.

Chapter Ten

*D*evon closed his door and knocked his head against it. "What the *fuck* were you thinking?"

Okay, he had not been thinking. That was exactly the problem.

He'd put his hands all over her. His boss's sister. *Exactly* what Devon had promised Bennett he would never do.

But she'd smelled so good, felt so good in his arms. For those few fleeting seconds, he'd lost control. That kiss had been pure fire, burning him up from the inside out. He'd wanted to rip off her clothes, bend her over that countertop, plunge himself inside her, and fuck until they were both spent.

Shit, he was getting hard again.

Thank god he'd come to his senses before anything else— anything unforgivable—had happened with her.

Then he remembered the hurt look on her face right before he left, and his whole body clenched with guilt and regret. His erection disappeared. She thought that he looked down on her, which couldn't be further from the truth.

He really liked this girl. Why couldn't he have met her some other way? Why couldn't she have some other brother?

He had to go back over there, right now. Nothing inappropriate could happen again. He wouldn't let it. But he at least could come up with a better explanation for why. Something that wouldn't hurt her so much.

He put his hand on the doorknob, and then his phone rang in his back pocket. He dug it out.

His boss was calling. Shit.

"Lana told me what happened," Bennett barked from the phone. "Is Aurora okay?

"Yes, I just left her place. I followed her when she went out earlier, caught up with her. But she's fine now."

"Did you see this man that she mentioned? The one who she thinks was following her?"

"No, sir. I didn't."

"That's unfortunate." His disapproval came through, loud and clear.

Devon gave Bennett an update on everything else that had been happening, though he obviously left out a few details. But his boss wasn't going to let him off that easily.

"I saw on the camera that you were over in her apartment for a while. I thought we talked about you keeping your distance. What exactly were you doing?"

Devon's pulse spiked. Immediately, his head filled with images of Aurora. Her soft kisses. Her lips, whispering that she wanted to ride him.

"She was pretty upset. She didn't want to be alone. I wanted to make sure she was settled before I left."

Bennett was quiet. But then he said, "All right. I appreciate that. I'm working with Lana on tracking down this man that Aurora saw, but in the meantime, I don't want her leaving that building. Keep me posted on any developments. I need to go. We've got a situation here ourselves."

Devon was about to say more, but Bennett had already hung up.

The arm holding his phone dropped to his side. He looked

down at his shirt. He was still covered in powdered sugar, and his skin felt sticky with it.

He headed towards the bathroom, stripping off clothes as he went. He had to get cleaned up quick, and then he was going to figure out what the heck he was supposed to do.

The shower switched on with a hiss.

Devon turned up the volume on his security app, so he would hear if the team watching the cameras back at the office contacted him. He stepped into the spray.

The water ran over his head, down his shoulders and stomach. Washing away his tension along with the sticky sugar.

Devon pushed back the shower door and glanced out at his phone. All quiet. Everything was fine. Maybe he could spend an extra minute or two in here, getting his thoughts in order.

His mind started to wander again to the girl next door. Aurora.

She wasn't the spoiled brat he'd expected. Not by a long shot. She'd been through more in her childhood than most soldiers he knew. And yet, she managed to be brave and funny and sweet all at the same time. He smiled, remembering how she'd waved around that giant green vibrator the first night they'd met. The girl was shameless in the very best way.

And sexy. So very sexy. He recalled her soft mouth on his, the little purring sound she'd made.

His cock stirred. His smile vanished as the image in his mind shifted. Now she was on her back, sliding her sex toy in and out of herself. Moaning as it hummed inside of her.

Holy fuck, he was hard. And he couldn't stop the flood of dirty thoughts. Aurora, fucking her tight, wet opening with her vibrator. Aurora on her knees in her kitchen, unzipping his jeans. In his imagination, her tongue flicked out to lick his cockhead, right before she took him into her mouth. That mouth, hot and eager around him.

Devon groaned aloud, his voice rising over the patter of the water against the tiles.

He could never have her. But if he jerked himself off thinking about her, nobody would know. Certainly not his boss.

He closed his eyes and fisted his shaft. Water pounded against his back. His fingers squeezed and tugged at his length, his other hand reaching down to cup his balls. His movements sped up. His mind pictured Aurora naked on his lap, sliding up and down on his cock as she cried out with pleasure. Riding him, just like she'd wanted.

"Oh, fuck." And just like that, his orgasm thundered through him.

With every last stroke, he moaned her name and thought of how he'd make her shake as she came. Then he'd kiss her and hold her after, until every bad thing disappeared from her mind.

But by the time he'd washed himself off and gone into the bedroom, he was already getting hard again. One look at the bed, and he pictured Aurora lying on it. Somehow, he only wanted her more. Probably because his hand was a poor comparison to the real thing.

Not good.

"Get your head together. You're stronger than this."

Devon went to the computer and sat down. He pulled up a new notepad file and placed his fingers over the keyboard.

After Kellen died, Devon had gone through a few days where he'd hated the world, hated everyone who'd kept on living when his brother was gone, including himself. He ran for miles, pushing himself to his limits, screaming at anyone for the slightest infraction. His whole existence meant shit without his brother in it. He'd thought losing his father was bad. But this? It was indescribable. Intolerable.

Then his mother had asked him to come back home, and

a deadly quiet had settled over him instead. Days went by in a blink, days he couldn't remember.

Finally, he'd shoved his heartbreak aside, sat down on his bunk, and made a list.

He wrote down everything that still mattered: his duty to his family, his duty to his country. Friends he had made in the army and the fellow officers that he respected. His ambitions for his career.

And seeing it all on the paper, he'd known exactly what he had to do. His own feelings and desires meant nothing compared to family or country. But right in that moment, those two duties couldn't co-exist, either.

When he'd enlisted, he intended to give all of himself to his country. He'd lived by the Ranger Creed: move further, faster, and fight harder than any other soldier. But his mom and sister had lost too much already. He couldn't put his own world back together without his brother. That was impossible. But at least he could try to heal theirs.

So, he made the only choice he could. He'd asked for a discharge. And then, he'd worked his ass off for the army for the next year until his request was finally granted.

Sometimes, he still thought of what might've been. But he knew in his gut that he'd done the right thing.

Once again, Devon felt like he was at a crossroads. He couldn't figure out what to do. He needed to lay everything out again, and he'd see the right path.

He started to type. Words appeared on the computer screen before him.

Taking care of Mom, Ruby, and Haley, he wrote. His family still had to be a top priority. That much hadn't changed.

Next, he added, *Bennett Security*. Because he had a duty to his boss and his coworkers as well. They were counting on him.

But then he hit "enter" several times and typed the name *Aurora* at the very top. Even above his family, above everything else. Because no matter what, even if Bennett somehow fired him right now, Devon would still stick around until he knew that Aurora was out of danger. Or at least until he knew some other trustworthy person had taken his place.

Nor did he want to hurt her himself. He couldn't bear the thought that she was over in her apartment upset because of him.

Devon could almost see his brother shaking his head. *What about you, man?* Kellen would say. *You can't be the perfect employee and perfect son for your entire life. When are you finally going to acknowledge what you want? Because if you don't, it's going to catch up with you.*

"I want our family to be secure. I want Bennett to think his faith in me has been well placed. And I want Aurora to be safe and happy. *That's* what I want." Any other feelings on his part would stay out of the picture.

Could he manage to do all those things? He was going to try.

But the only way was to tell her the truth—the *real* truth. About who he really was, and who'd hired him. Bennett might be angry at first. Aurora definitely would be. But with the truth in the open, Devon would be far more effective as a bodyguard. Eventually, everyone would see that.

A notification dinged, jarring him back to the immediate present. Aurora had just left her apartment. The camera feed from the hallway showed her going for the stairs to the rooftop terrace. He exhaled in relief. She'd be fine up there.

Maybe he should go up and explain things to her right now.

No, he decided. They both needed space. Tomorrow, he'd give Max Bennett a heads-up, and then he'd tell Aurora everything.

He knew the remote team had their eyes on the building's cameras, but Devon needed something to do with his nervous energy. On his computer, he double-checked the various security points. A West Oaks P.D. squad car sat out front, yards away from the entrance. Just as it should be.

Next, he pulled up the camera feed at the building's back door.

He sat forward, his nerves instantly on guard.

There was someone leaning into the driver's side window, chatting with the officer inside. He checked the time. The next police shift change was supposed to be in one hour, not now.

Were they just shooting the shit? It wasn't protocol. Was it another officer? Maybe plainclothes?

I should call headquarters, he thought. *See if they know what's up.* Maybe he was overthinking it.

But before he could hit dial, the camera feed cut out. The overhead lights flickered at the same moment.

Devon shot to his feet. "*Fuck.*" He didn't know what was happening, but it wasn't anything good.

He hit a key on his computer that would send an emergency SOS to the Bennett Security office.

Aurora. He had to get to her. *Now.*

Chapter Eleven

*A*urora went upstairs to the rooftop deck. She had to get away from her apartment. Powdered sugar was scattered everywhere, and the place still smelled like Rick. Like his shampoo, and the faint masculine scent that was just *him*.

Rick's body had responded to her during that kiss. That much had been obvious. But she'd thought that he liked her as a person, too.

She couldn't believe she'd gotten things so wrong.

Aurora was a firm believer in second chances. She often didn't trust first impressions, because so many people had trouble being their true selves with strangers. She was always willing to give someone the benefit of the doubt, especially if they'd met under difficult or stressful circumstances.

But her first impression of Rick had been spot on. He wasn't completely irredeemable. He had enough integrity to tell her now that nothing could happen between them. But when they'd met, he'd seemed like the kind of guy who cared about status far more than she ever would. And about that, she had been right.

Why did she have such awful luck with men? Was it really so hard to find a nice, funny guy who wanted the same things she did? A guy who wouldn't make her feel worthless, like her ex, and like Rick had today?

The only silver lining was that Rick had distracted her for several hours from the danger surrounding her.

She just wanted all of this to be over. But that wasn't going to happen anytime soon. She hadn't even heard from the sketch artist yet, and the sun was starting to go down. So that would mean another night of uncertainty, not knowing if someone out there was searching for her. Not knowing if, or when, Dominic Crane's friends would be able to find her.

Did the Silverlake Syndicate know her name now? Did that man outside the police station work for them?

What if she'd been wrong to refuse Max's offer of a body-guard? Maybe she'd been too hasty. Too wrapped up in her own personal history with her brother, blinded to the reality of what she faced. Dominic Crane and his Syndicate buddies didn't care about her need to assert her freedom from her brother.

"They might really be coming after me," she said into the night. "What am I going to do?"

She hadn't actually believed that until today, when she'd seen that man on the street and been convinced he meant her harm. She was going to have to call Max, eat her own words, and give in.

You win, Max. You win.

Just then, Aurora heard a shout.

The noise had risen over the ambient hum of the waves on the beach and the constant patter of voices along Ocean Lane. It must've come from close by.

She scanned what she could see of the street in front of the building but spotted nothing unusual. The low overhang at the entrance hid her view of the squad car.

Aurora crossed the deck and went to the other side, which overlooked the alley at the back of the building. This was where Lana had pointed out the other squad car just a few days ago. Looking down, Aurora could make out part of the police car. A bar of emergency lights spanned the top.

But there was something going on. Some movement in the shadows that she couldn't see in detail, although she heard the echo of voices four floors below.

She leaned over the railing, trying to get a better view.

There was a slam that sounded like a door closing. And then she spotted a figure at the rear of the police vehicle. Opening the trunk, the person dumped something heavy inside, then shut the lid. The car drove away.

None of it made sense. What was that heavy thing? Why did the officer leave without someone replacing him?

Unease spread through her, a knowledge that something was off. But what should she do? Call the number for police dispatch that Lana had given her?

Yes. That was a good idea. Maybe there was an emergency nearby, and for some reason, they needed every officer to respond. Stranger things had happened, even in West Oaks. She pulled up the number on her phone.

Then she heard the quiet click of another door, but this one was much closer.

It was the door to the rooftop terrace.

No one was supposed to have access to this rooftop, except for her and Rick. Her heart fluttered. Had he come to see her? Maybe he regretted what had happened earlier and wanted to explain.

She couldn't see the entrance from where she was standing. She held her breath, waiting. But no one appeared.

Was someone else up here? Someone who didn't belong?

The entire world seemed to slow. Aurora's body felt like it was stuck in place, like she couldn't move. But she managed to take a small step to one side, ducking behind a large planter just as a figure stepped out onto the deck.

The man had a clean-shaven head and a close-cropped goatee. At first, she was relieved. It wasn't the man from outside the police station.

But he held something long and dark in his hand.

A gun.

"I see you back there." His voice was gravelly. Merciless. "I don't want to hurt you. I just want to talk."

She didn't believe him for a second. Every nerve in her body screamed with alarm.

She was trapped.

Suddenly, another guy lunged out of the shadows, tackling the gunman to the ground. They rolled across the deck, fighting over the weapon. Aurora gasped when she recognized the newcomer.

It was Rick.

Rick punched the other guy's face with two quick, vicious jabs of his fist. Blood spurted from the man's nose. With his other arm, Rick pinned the gun to the floor. The thug tried to buck him off. They rolled again, and Rick twisted his legs around the thug's waist, his arms tight around the man's head in some kind of chokehold. He clearly knew what he was doing.

Rick's foot kicked the man's gun away. Aurora dashed over and grabbed the weapon as it skidded across the deck. With shaking hands, she aimed it at the struggling man.

"Rick, get out of the way."

He spared only the tiniest glance at her. "Lower the gun, Aurora." His tone was completely calm. He was hardly even out of breath. "I'll be there in a moment."

The other man was struggling in Rick's vise-like grip. But Rick didn't release the pressure on the man's throat. The guy's face turned red to purple, then his head jerked. All at once, he went limp.

Rick tossed the guy to the side and vaulted back onto his feet. He fixed an intense gaze on Aurora, walking slowly toward her with his hands out.

"You need to hand me the gun. Can you do that?"

She could hardly breathe enough to respond, but she twisted the gun around in her hand and held it out, butt first. Rick took hold of the weapon. He stripped out the magazine, then stuck the gun in one planter, bullets in another.

It was only then that she noticed Rick had another gun, this one strapped into a holster by his armpit. He hadn't even drawn it.

"What the hell is going on?" Her voice was sharp with suspicion. He was not some hedge fund manager who had just happened to need a furnished apartment.

"No time. There are more intruders downstairs, and they've cut the camera feeds. I think they've tampered with our connection to the main office as well. We need to get out of here."

"Downstairs? But I have to get back to my apartment. I need my purse." She had left everything but her phone down there.

Noises came from behind them, and Rick pulled her down. She heard footsteps, voices. More people had just stepped onto the deck.

Then there were shouts. They must've found the other guy Rick had left lying there.

"Aurora, go." Rick pushed her toward an alcove, where the top of a ladder was visible. "Take the emergency escape route. The one that's just for the penthouse level. I doubt they'll know about it."

She nodded. There was a concrete-reinforced shaft with a ladder inside of it, leading to a special exit door. Max had reminded her after Wolfson's murder. The door would only open from the inside, but from the exterior of the building, it was completely concealed.

Rick was right. That was their best way out.

The voices were coming closer. "But what about you?"

"I'll catch up. Hurry."

She crawled toward the alcove, found the ladder, and started her descent.

Chapter Twelve

*D*evon crouched behind the planter boxes, peering through the foliage. Two men stepped cautiously onto the deck. One of them stooped to check on their fallen comrade.

He'd just meant to choke the guy out. But the man hadn't gone down easy, and Devon had felt something crunch inside the man's neck. The dude likely wasn't going to wake up again.

But that man had been going after Aurora with a gun. If Devon hadn't gotten here…

The thought made his blood run hot with rage, but he couldn't let that distract him. These bastards were the threat now, and Devon wasn't going to let them get past him.

They were spreading out. They didn't know yet where he was. That was his only advantage.

He had to direct them away from the emergency exit, where Aurora had gone.

Silently, Devon inched his way along the planters. He peered out again, checking on the position of the others.

It wouldn't be long now. He had only a matter of seconds.

One of the men started in the direction of Aurora's escape

route. Devon lifted his weapon and fired. His target went down, shouting. Blood spurted from the man's leg.

The other ran—a pale man with bright red hair. A bullet hit the planter next to Devon, sending out a shrapnel of ceramic shards.

Devon fired. But his shot only grazed the assailant, who had suddenly jagged to the side. More gunshots roared past Devon's ears. Pieces of the walls and the deck exploded into the air. Devon rolled, taking cover.

But the redhead was on him. For one harrowing split second, he looked up into the cold black circle of a gun barrel.

Click.

The gun was empty.

Devon's leg shot out, kicking the red-haired man in the knee. The guy collapsed, moaning. Devon stood up. He, unlike his opponent, had counted his shots. He still had several rounds left in his Glock 22.

"Whoever you are, you're dead," the guy said from the ground.

"I beg to differ. Stay down, and maybe you'll live."

Slowly, he nodded, his hands raised. Devon retrieved the man's pistol. Across the deck, the guy with the leg wound was whimpering quietly. Devon walked over to the wounded man, planning to disarm him as well.

Then, a movement on his periphery made Devon's body respond faster than his mind could think. The red-haired guy was barreling toward him. A desperate attempt, and it would be his last. Devon's trigger finger squeezed.

A dark circle appeared on the man's forehead. He fell into a heap.

Devon looked back at the man with the leg wound. "I hope you're smarter."

The guy nodded. Tears leaked from his eyes into his mustache. He already knew what to do. He gestured at his pocket, and Devon reached in to take the guy's weapon, keeping a gun on him the whole time.

"Consider this your lucky day. Don't be like your friends. Don't come after us."

The guy nodded again, his hands trembling.

"I'd call 911 for you, but I have no service. Guessing I have you and your friends to thank for that? But the ambulance won't take too long." Most of West Oaks would've heard the gunfire.

Devon left his phone on a planter and ran for the emergency exit. He raced down the ladder and found Aurora at the bottom of it. She was keeping herself together, but her pupils had dilated, and her movements were jerky.

"All those shots, I thought…"

"They disrupted the security system. Maybe even hacked it. So, I have no idea how far ahead of us they might be."

"But nobody else is supposed to know about this exit, right? It wasn't on the schematics."

"That's what your brother said." Her eyes widened at his mention of Max. But this was no time to start explaining. "They must have somebody on the inside. Either the DA's office, or Bennett Security itself. Because there's no way Crane's people should've been on you so fast. Until I know who we can trust, we need to get the hell away from here."

"What about the ones upstairs? Are they coming after us?"

"No." He didn't elaborate.

Aurora nodded, her jaw clamping down on the questions that were no doubt spinning through her mind like a hurricane.

"Stay here. Then follow me at my signal." Devon counted down in his head, then burst out of the exit door, spinning his body, and pointing his gun from his two to his ten.

But nobody was waiting for them. "Okay, let's go."

He grabbed Aurora's hand, and they rushed along the narrow passage in between Bennett's building and the next.

Duct work rattled over their heads. They reached a chain-link fence. But just before the barrier, he spotted a small steel door in the brick wall of the next building. It had an electronic keypad lock. He input the code Max had given him, and they went inside.

They were in a utility room.

Devon spotted the camera in the ceiling. Bennett had made a special arrangement with the owner of this building to do certain security updates. If someone at Bennett Security had betrayed them, or if the entire camera system had been compromised, then it was possible they would be spotted if the bad guys figured out which feed to check.

He lined up his shot and took out the camera lens.

He still had the two extra guns he'd taken from the rooftop. One he hid behind a water heater, and the other he stuck into his pocket.

Still holding Aurora's hand, he pulled her toward the other end of the room. They came out into a spacious, modern lobby. It was another fancy apartment building. The doorman saw them emerge and jumped up from his seat.

"Hey, what are you doing?"

Devon ignored the man. Through the glass doors of the building, he could see a crowd already gathering. This building had an entrance on a different street than Bennett's. He could only hope that the men searching for Aurora wouldn't be within sight.

They pushed out of the doors and melted into the crowd, moving calmly away from Ocean Lane.

"This way." Devon pulled Aurora across the street and into another alleyway.

She stopped, shaking her arm free of his grip, her face a mask of panic. "Where are you taking me? How do I even know I can trust you?"

"Because Max hired me. I'm your bodyguard. Now, let me do my job and get you the hell out of here."

Chapter Thirteen

*A*urora felt like she was watching a movie. This couldn't be her life.

Rick—except she realized now that probably wasn't his real name—was leading her through a series of alleyways, moving her away from Ocean Lane and from her home. She felt strangely calm, like none of this could really be happening. She had fallen asleep. She was dreaming.

Except a pragmatic, rational part of her, the part of her that was every bit Max Bennett's sister, told her that all of this was very much happening. She was in life-threatening danger. And her only hope seemed to be following this man she had known as "Rick Harrison" toward some unknown destination.

Rick spun around to face her. "Wait. Give me your phone."

"Why?"

"It's important. They could be tracking you with it."

She handed him the phone, thinking he'd hit some button, flip some switch. But instead, he dropped the phone onto the concrete and smashed his boot into it.

She screamed. "What are you *doing*?"

"Did you not hear me? They might've been tracking you. Now, they can't."

"What about your phone? Do I get to destroy it?"

"I left it back on the rooftop, emitting an emergency signal. I had no service, but even if I did, I have no idea who might've been listening in to a call. If the security system was compromised, my device could've been as well."

Oh my god. How is this happening?

He charged out of the alley and passed a kiosk, which was selling souvenir T-shirts and hats. Rick stopped to buy one of each, paying with cash.

"Here, put these on."

"Won't that make me draw more attention? I'll look ridiculous."

"Just do it." He shoved a hat down on her head. Grumbling, she shrugged on the shirt as they kept walking.

"Keep your head down. There are cameras all over this area, and I have no clue how much these people can access."

"You haven't told me where we're going."

"A friend's place."

"But—" She stopped herself from stating the obvious— that he'd said he was new in town and didn't know anyone.

He didn't really live next door to her, either. That had all been fake. A *lie*.

She'd nearly had sex with him just that afternoon. And she didn't even know this guy's *name*. Usually, she had slightly higher standards than that.

He changed directions suddenly, dragging her to a different curb just as a bus pulled up. It was a free local shuttle that ran along a main avenue to and from the beach. They boarded, sitting near the front with their heads down.

Aurora couldn't get her heart to slow down. She didn't want to keep holding his hand, but she also felt like she'd spin away from reality completely if he let go.

They didn't go far. The bus entered a hip neighborhood,

driving past small, overpriced bungalows built in the 1920s. At the next stop, he tugged her hand, and they got off.

Finally, after dragging her along several more blocks, the guy who probably wasn't Rick walked up the driveway of a white bungalow, through a gate, and into the back yard.

"Come on. Keep up."

He knocked furiously on the back door. When there was no answer, he stooped to snatch a key out from under a propane grill.

The key twisted in the lock. The door creaked open.

Feeling like she was sleepwalking, Aurora wandered inside. Not-Rick was inspecting each door and window, flipping latches and locks. The house was crowded and cozy, a single story, full of knickknacks and pictures of people she'd never seen.

"Where are we? Why is it so cold?" Her teeth were chattering together.

"It's not cold. You're in shock." He took a blanket from the back of the sofa and laid it over her shoulders.

"Wait. Wait. I don't even know your name. You're not Rick, are you?"

He blinked. "No. My name is Devon Whitestone."

She searched his face, and he looked the same as before. Yet she couldn't find any sign of the man she'd been getting to know the past few days. The man she'd started to like.

"And the hedge fund?"

He shook his head. She felt like such an idiot. He reached for her, his expression apologetic, but she shrank away.

"Don't you dare touch me. I'm pretty sure you saved my life, and I'm grateful for that. But you've been lying to me since the moment we met."

He turned away. In the kitchen, he took a cordless phone off its cradle and flipped through a notebook on the counter. "Thank god he has a landline," Devon muttered.

"You don't have anything else to say to me?"

Now he was dialing the phone. "Like what?"

"An apology?"

"I don't have time for that right now. I did save your life, but the saving is ongoing."

She sat on the couch, tipped her head back, and hollered in indignation. Not at him, really, but at this whole situation. She felt completely powerless—*lost*—and she detested the feeling.

"We need to find a way to reach Max." She had many mixed feelings about her brother, but he was the only person she trusted to handle a situation like this.

"That's what I'm working on." Devon held up a finger and spoke into the phone. "Chase? Hey man, don't say anything. Just listen. You saw the caller I.D., so you know where I am. Get here. Tell no one." He paused. "Yeah, it's bad."

Devon put the handset down and rubbed a hand over his face. "What a mess."

"Who was that?"

He walked into the living room. "Chase Collins. He's a police officer and my friend. I'd trust him with my life. He lives here."

"Okay." Aurora tugged the blanket tighter around herself. "He'll help us get in touch with Max?"

"Yeah. That's my plan."

"But what if…" Her voice cracked. "What if something's happened to my brother? Or Lana? What if those Syndicate people went after them, too?" *Because of me*, she thought. A lump balled in her throat.

Rick—no, *Devon*—knelt on the carpet in front of her. "That's very unlikely. But you know Max can take care of himself. And Lana seems pretty capable, too. They're fine."

Her lips were trembling, and her eyes stung.

"Hey, listen to me. You'll see them soon. But no matter what, I'm staying right by your side. Okay? Even if you're pissed off at me, I'm not going to let anything happen to you."

She choked back a sob. "I *am* still pissed. But would you just hold me for a little bit?"

He got up onto the couch and put his arm around her. Aurora sank into him, resting her head against his chest.

~

A CAR DROVE up and parked beside the house. Aurora sat upright, blinking. She'd fallen asleep in Devon's arms. He gave her a small smile as he stood.

A police officer burst through the back door. "Christ, Dev, there was shit all over the radio. Shots fired, fatalities. What is going on?"

Fatalities, Aurora thought with a shiver. Devon had said those men weren't coming after them. He'd killed them. He'd killed them to protect *her*.

Chase pulled Devon into a hug, pounding on his back. Then the officer spotted Aurora on his couch, and his eyebrows shot up.

"This is Aurora Bennett," Devon said.

"Bennett? As in Bennett Security? Your boss?"

"That's the one. There's a lot to explain, but first I need to call in. It has to be discreet, though. I'm not sure, but we might be compromised."

"We had units over at that building."

"They might've been injured. I hope to god it was minor. Aurora's the witness to the Wolfson murder. Her identity was supposed to remain secret, but there must've been a leak. Only a few people in the West Oaks District Attorney's Office, myself, and Max Bennett knew. Possibly some more, if anyone inside West Oaks P.D. figured out why you had units at Aurora's building."

"Shit." Chase was nodding. "Okay, I get the need for discretion. I'll get in touch with Bennett. But I'll need a little time to make sure nobody else is listening in. This is Dominic

Crane's men we're talking about, right? Silverlake Syndicate? Do you think they know who you are, Devon?"

"I'm not sure. If they've been watching her, they might've seen me with her. But I've been posing as her neighbor under a different name. Most of my coworkers didn't know what assignment I was working. But if Crane's guys have someone inside Bennett Security, they may have been able to connect the dots. That's why I couldn't go to my own place. If you can see to my mom and Ruby, get them somewhere safe until I know more, I'd appreciate it."

"You don't have to ask. It'll get done."

"I'm sorry about this, Chase. I wouldn't have brought you into it unless I had no other options."

Chase squeezed his friend's shoulder. "No, I'm glad you came here. I'm only subletting this house from my cousin. Not like I could afford it on my salary. But make yourself at home. Just stay safe, okay? I'll touch base with Bennett, and we'll figure out what to do. And Dev, if there were shots and fatalities at that building, there's going to be a shitload of official questions coming at you."

"I know." He took out the gun from his pocket, wrapped it in a dish towel from the kitchen, and handed it to Chase. "I took this from a guy on the roof. I fired it. There's another I left behind a water heater at the building next door to Bennett's. Can you get them into evidence as soon as you can?"

Chase tucked away the bundle. "Sure thing."

Aurora got up from the couch and walked over to him. "Thank you for everything you're doing. I'll pay you back somehow, I swear."

He waved his hand. "Don't mention it, really. I'm just glad my friend here was around when you needed him. He's the best guy I know." Then Chase glanced around his home, grimacing. "I guess I should pack up some things and stay somewhere else. I don't think this place is big enough for three."

"I'm not kicking you out of your own home," Aurora protested.

But Chase had already gone into the bedroom, where he picked up a duffel bag and started shoving clothes into it from various drawers. "I already told you, it's no trouble. Devon has backed me up before. He's an honorary cop, and we have to stick together." He flashed her a handsome grin. "Besides, this is my job, right? Protect and serve."

Chase went over to Devon, and the two men embraced again. "You take care of yourself, brother," Chase said.

"You, too."

"I'll head to your mom's as soon as possible."

Devon briefly closed his eyes, emotion floating over his face, before his expression turned stoic again. "Thank you."

Chase left, and Devon locked the door.

Chapter Fourteen

*A*fter Chase was gone, and Devon had checked the perimeter of the house again for weaknesses, he went back to the kitchen. Aurora was there, rinsing off a dish in Chase's sink.

"What are you doing?" he asked.

"I figured if I'm taking over the guy's house, I could help him out with some chores."

"I'm sure Chase will appreciate that. He's kind of a slob."

She shrugged. "I've seen worse. Often in my own apartment. Mostly, I just needed something to do. Some way to feel useful."

"I get that."

He went out to the attached garage and fetched the supplies that Chase always kept on a shelf out here. On the work bench, he disassembled his Glock, moved the magazine to a different shelf, and began to clean the metal parts. While his gun would end up in evidence at some point, too, he still had to have it ready to see more action. Plus, he needed something to do with his hands, and now that the tensest moments had passed, he didn't know what to say to Aurora.

She knew the truth now, but he hadn't been able to deliver the news gently the way he had intended. To say the least.

And if he told her now that he'd been about to confess everything earlier, there was no way she would believe him.

Aurora appeared in the doorway. "How long before Max gets here?"

"It will be a while, and I doubt he would come here himself. Too many eyes on him. As soon as he knows it's safe, he'll probably send someone to get you and take you to a more secure location."

"You wouldn't take me yourself?"

He would've thought she'd welcome the news that they'd be parting ways soon. "I'll do whatever my boss tells me. I usually work behind a desk."

"Could've fooled me." She vanished from the doorway.

When he came back inside, she was switching off the faucet and drying her hands on the souvenir T-shirt. "Was anything you told me true?"

"Some of it. I did go to a military school. West Point."

Aurora crossed her arms, laughing bitterly. "Army. I knew it. What about Special Forces?"

"No, 75th Ranger Regiment. I got out about six months ago. Been working for your brother for three. So, I am new to West Oaks."

She turned around and picked up a clean glass. Filled it at the tap. With her back still turned, she said, "And your mom? She lives in West Oaks, too?"

"She moved here at the same time as me, along with my sister and niece. From Los Angeles. They needed a new start, for a lot of reasons." He thought of Kellen but didn't want to get into that.

"Your father…"

"Died when I was a kid. Like I told you. He was a cop. I tried to be honest as much as I could."

"About a few details, yeah. But I shared my entire messed-up childhood with you. I wasn't holding anything back. Do you know how that makes me feel?"

He leaned past her to wash his hands in the sink. He'd worn gloves to clean his weapon, but his skin still felt grimy. Aurora took a step away, avoiding him.

"I never wanted to hurt you. I'm truly sorry for that. I was only trying to do my job, keep you safe." *Which I did*, he added silently. He turned off the water, shook off the excess, and leaned his hip against the counter, facing her.

"Your job?" She smirked. "I doubt that kissing me was in the job description."

He bit the inside of his cheek. A vein at his temple twitched. "It's not like I was chasing after you. You invited me into your apartment."

"You didn't have to say yes!"

Fury radiated from her. He leaned in, their noses just inches apart. "I was trying to be there for you. As a friend. Because you seem like a nice person." *I liked you*, he thought, though he doubted she'd want to hear it. "When we kissed, I stopped things before we went too far. I told you it couldn't happen."

"Yeah, after I'd already made an idiot of myself."

He'd said he was sorry. He was tired and stressed, and his nerves were completely ragged. He'd killed *two people* today. What did she expect him to do? Prostrate himself at her feet?

"I can't help that my body responded when you basically threw yourself at me."

Her eyes narrowed. "Your *body?*" Her arm jerked, and the entire contents of her glass splashed into his face. "How does your body respond to *that?*"

Devon sputtered, wiping his eyes. His shirt was soaked. Anger flared in his chest, breaking through his carefully managed demeanor. It was like Aurora knew every button to push to make him lose control.

He peeled off his wet shirt, tossing the sodden fabric aside.

His palms planted onto the countertop on either side of her, caging her in.

"I get it. You don't like me. You think I'm a lying son of a bitch. But I'm the only thing standing between you and a bunch of murderous gangsters right now. So it would help if you could play nice." He licked a stray drop of water as it cascaded over his lips.

She was breathing hard, breasts heaving. "Are you finished?"

"No. I'm *not*." He drew himself even closer, not quite touching. But the scent of her was heady in his nostrils, a mixture of flowers and spice.

"You're right, getting close to you was never part of the job. But the conversations you and I had? The kiss? That was all me. The *real* me. And when I told you I couldn't...*be* with you, it wasn't because I didn't want you."

Aurora arched her back against the countertop. She glanced down at his bare torso, the gaze turning molten. He felt the blood coursing through him, heading straight to his dick. *Down boy*, he thought. *Not going to happen.*

"But nothing has changed," he continued. "I'm still assigned to protect you. The kiss was a mistake—*my* mistake. You can call me an asshole if that makes this easier. Whatever you have to do to get through the next few hours. Then, I promise, you'll never have to see me again."

He pushed off the counter and stalked away from her, before his already shredded self-control could break altogether.

Chapter Fifteen

*a*bout a half hour later, the landline rang. Devon went to answer it. "It's Max." He held out the phone, his face impassive. "He'd like to speak with you."

Aurora held the handset to her ear. "Max?"

She had managed to keep herself calm for the last few minutes, surfing through Chase's cable channels. Devon hadn't spoken to her; instead, they'd been ignoring one another, which had saved her some further awkwardness. She could almost pretend she was back on her own couch, binging on home improvement shows and trashy reality drama.

But with her brother on the line, the overwhelming emotions of that day crashed back over her. She closed her eyes, fighting back tears.

"Hey, Rory. I hear it's been a rough day."

She was still angry that Max had lied to her. Had forced *Devon* to lie to her. But she was in no position to get snippy with him when his plan had saved her life.

"Not one of my best. I need to know what I'm supposed to do. How can I help fix this?" She wanted to get her testimony on the record so she could nail these monsters.

Max sighed. "I wish it were so easy. I'm doing all I can,

but things have been crazy over here. Somebody got into our system, and we're still trying to get to the bottom of it. What I really need is for you to sit tight. Officer Collins has been in touch with me, and it sounds like you're as safe at his residence as anywhere else. If I try to move you now, it will just be opening you up to more prying eyes."

"So I can't testify yet."

"No. Not yet. Lana is working on that."

"Is Lana there?" She wished her best friend could come to her, but that would probably just put Lana in danger. Too bad because it would've been nice to have a buffer between her and Devon.

The chemistry between them in the kitchen—Devon's shirt off, water dripping from his skin—it had been almost too much to bear. She didn't want to embarrass herself any more than she had already. He was attracted to her, sure, but not enough to break the rules. He'd made that clear. In fact, Devon preferred never to see her again if he could help it. There was only so much rejection a girl could take.

"Lana's here, and she wants to talk to you. But a couple more questions first. Officer Collins said you weren't hurt, but I'd like to hear it from you. Is there anything you need?"

"I'm fine. I mean, my phone is gone, I have nothing except the clothes I'm wearing… But, um, Devon took care of me." She glanced over. Devon was pacing across the living room, hands on his hips. He'd taken a quick shower and changed into new clothes. Some of Chase's, she assumed. The two men were around the same build.

"And thank god for that. I know you didn't want protection, but I followed my gut. I saw the aftermath of that firefight on the terrace. It was ugly."

"I didn't see much of it. I used the escape ladder."

"Good. You did really good. After you talk to Lana, I'll need to speak with Devon about logistics. I'm hoping that tomorrow I'll be able to relocate you, and Devon can get back to his usual tasks."

The sinking feeling in her belly surprised her. "Okay."

Her best friend came onto the line. Aurora sat on a kitchen chair, resting her forehead against her hand.

"Rory? Are you okay?"

"I'm in one piece."

"You have no idea how scared we were. Me and Max both."

"It was awful." Aurora heard Devon in the living room, still fidgeting. "When can I testify? I can't just sit here. Especially when you and Max could be in danger, too, but you have to stay visible. I have to *do* something."

"We're negotiating with Crane's defense lawyers, but it's complicated. This isn't the usual procedure. So far, they've been playing hardball."

"What does that mean?"

"Obviously, the Syndicate already found out your identity. But Crane's lawyers want to know *where* you are, which I am *not* going to tell them. And even if they agree to let you testify early, Crane's counsel would be there in the room too, questioning you. That's a defendant's right. But I'm not okay with that until we can be sure you'll be safe."

Aurora groaned, folding her arms, and dropping her head onto them.

"We're doing everything we can. It won't be long, I promise."

"Lana, did you know? About…Devon?"

"Hold on." Lana went quiet, and it sounded like she was murmuring something in the background. "Okay, I got rid of Max for a second, so I can talk to you as your BFF, and not Assistant DA. I had no idea until Max told me. Your hot neighbor Rick Harrison is really your *bodyguard?*" Her voice had gone up several octaves. "I mean, what the *actual fuck?*"

"I know. It's messed up." Aurora snuck a peek over her

shoulder. Devon's eyes briefly met hers, and then he disappeared into a bedroom. Yep, he'd definitely heard all of that.

"Especially because I kissed him earlier. It's so embarrassing, L."

"Wait, Aurora Bennett is embarrassed? Since when? You're the girl who was brandishing a vibrator at him a couple of nights ago."

"It's embarrassing because..." She was already speaking quietly, but now she lowered her voice to a whisper. "I thought he liked me. But he was only hanging around for his job."

He'd claimed to be attracted to her. That hard-on in his pants hadn't lied. But an active sex drive wasn't the same as *feelings*.

"Sweetie, you've been through far too much today. It's amazing you're keeping it together at all. Focus on your hot bodyguard all you want if you need to. Hell, kiss him again if that's what it takes to get through the next day."

Aurora snorted. "That would be a *no*."

"Whatever. But from everything I've been hearing from Max, Devon is a really good guy. I'm sure he's been doing his best, just like the rest of us. Don't waste any energy on embarrassment or feeling bad. You're too precious. And unless Devon is a total brainless dumbass, he already sees that, too."

She doubted that. But it hardly mattered. They'd be parting ways soon enough.

After talking to Lana, Devon took his turn with the phone. Aurora found some leftover pizza in Chase's fridge and ate it cold.

By then, it was getting late, and her body was slowing down. She could barely keep her eyes open.

Aurora stumbled into the nearest bedroom and fell right to sleep.

Chapter Sixteen

*D*evon woke up on the couch. The house was quiet, so he guessed Aurora wasn't up yet.

He got up, rolling his neck, trying to get the crick out of it. Chase had a shitty couch. But at least Aurora went to bed early and seemed to have slept well.

Devon let his mind go over everything Max had said to him last night.

Just before the attack on Aurora's building yesterday, Max's people had detected suspicious activity on their network —a brute-force attempt to access their databases. They'd immediately gone into defensive mode.

But that had also helped cut off Bennett's team from Aurora's building.

Unfortunately, Max couldn't yet rule out someone working from the inside. Or perhaps a vendor or someone who knew their office and its system. Max had their computer expert, Sylvie Trousseau, working on it.

While he'd had his boss on the phone, Devon had made sure that Chase was being taken care of. Max assured him that he put up Chase in a luxury apartment in one of his other buildings, complete with an on-site food delivery service. It sounded like Chase was going to be having a little TLC out of all of this, at least.

"You made me proud today," Max had told him. "You kept Aurora safe in the worst possible circumstances. Thank you. I'm not going to forget this."

"Just doing my job, sir."

"And you did your job damned well. I'm glad that I can count on you."

Would Max have said that if he knew what had almost gone down between Devon and Aurora? Maybe, after taking out three bad guys and getting Aurora out of there, Max would've forgiven him even that. But Devon wasn't going to test that theory. He couldn't step out of line again.

Even if Aurora was worth the headache of facing Max, which he suspected very well might be true, Devon could not afford to let himself get distracted.

Before now, the threat had been abstract. They hadn't known for sure that Crane would go after her, and certainly hadn't expected that her identity would leak so soon. There were a lot more factors at play than even Max had realized.

Now Devon had to expect another attack at any moment. If he was going to see Aurora safely through this, then he had to shove any interest in her way down deep.

By the time Aurora stumbled out of the bedroom, Devon had brushed his teeth and found some toast for breakfast.

"Morning. Chase has extra toothbrushes in his sink cabinet."

She mumbled something and disappeared into the bathroom.

For most of the day, they kept out of each other's way. Devon stayed in the kitchen, while Aurora watched TV in the living room. Devon kept staring at the phone, expecting it to ring with word of the pending relocation.

But no call came until almost dinnertime.

"Dev? It's Tanner."

One of the other bodyguards on Max's team.

"Just got word from on high. Max needs you to stay put at least until tomorrow. Everything status quo?"

Aurora stood up from the couch, arms crossed, watching Devon speak into the phone.

"Nothing to report. Is Max going to send someone to relieve me? There are guys with more experience. Like you."

"Can't risk it. Even I don't know where you are, so don't tell me. And I saw you during that defense workshop we all did. You can handle this. Call if you have any issues. We'll update you if anything changes here."

"Got it." He set down the phone. "We're stuck here another night."

Aurora groaned. "I guess I'll take a shower then. I was hoping to wait until I could get my own clothes to change into, but I feel disgusting."

She didn't look it. But Devon kept his mouth shut.

While Aurora showered, he dug into Chase's refrigerator for some dinner. They needed real food, not just toast and left-over pizza.

He found some tortillas, salsa, and ground beef. In a couple more minutes, the beef was sizzling in a skillet.

The water shut off in the bathroom. Devon was just setting their food on the table when Aurora came out, wearing a fresh, too-large shirt, along with a pair of pajama pants. Chase's clothes. She'd rolled them up at the waist and cuffs.

Aurora posed when she saw him looking, sticking out one foot. "Yes, I realize how silly I look. Does Chase own a washing machine?"

Devon pointed over his shoulder. There was a laundry set-up in the room behind the kitchen. She went to dump her clothes inside the washer.

"You made dinner?"

"We had to eat something."

"This looks great, thank you." Aurora accepted the plate

that he handed her, but then she said, "Wait, I need to say something. I came up with a whole speech while I was in the shower, and I better say it now before I forget it."

Devon braced himself for another lashing.

"I'm really grateful to you for everything you did yesterday. I couldn't remember if I'd said that yet. It was definitely the most frightening thing I've ever been through, and you were so calm. I'm scared to think what would've happened if you hadn't been there."

He opened his mouth, but she held up her hand. "And don't just say you were doing your job. At least let me thank you. Don't act like it was no big deal. Because it was for me."

"You're welcome. I did it because Max hired me, but also because I care about you." He quickly added, "As a friend. I wouldn't want to see you hurt."

She rolled her eyes. "Don't worry, I'm not getting any wrong ideas. I'm over that stuff from before. The kiss, whatever else I *might* have said…"

She did a wiggly little dance in her chair, like she was ridding herself of all those unpleasant memories. It was pretty cute, actually.

"I'm calling a do-over," she said. "We're good now."

"I'm glad to hear it. So, you're not mad at me anymore?"

"Mad? Was I mad? It's all getting fuzzy. That's the do-over magic at work."

He grinned. They ate dinner, Aurora complementing his cooking multiple times, noting that she wouldn't have expected either an army grunt or a hedge fund manager to have such skills in the kitchen.

"Actually, I was a lieutenant." His friends had loved giving him shit for it.

"My apologies, Lieutenant Whitestone." She saluted. "I should've known you weren't a 'Rick,'" she muttered. "And how did I believe that hedge fund story?"

"I barely even know what a hedge fund is."

She arched an eyebrow. "Don't play dumb. You went to West Point. Pretty sure you know *all* kinds of things."

Their eyes locked. His mind had gone straight into the gutter, and judging by the pinkness to her cheeks, she'd gone there with him.

Aurora broke the eye contact. "I do want us to be friends, but I have one condition."

"And that is?"

"That you don't lie to me anymore. Not even to protect me."

He screwed up his lips. "I guess I can do that. But it goes both ways—you have to tell me the truth, too."

"I haven't lied to you. About anything."

They were both quiet for a while. Aurora played with the last bit of tortilla on her plate. "Have you...killed anyone? Before yesterday?"

"Yes."

He didn't volunteer any information, and she didn't ask. He'd done what he had to as a Ranger, and he didn't think about it too much. Some of his friends had PTSD. But for Devon, it was just something that happened, and it made him neither upset nor proud. He would've avoided harming anyone if he could. But in those moments, he hadn't hesitated to act, and he had no regrets.

His kills weren't the memories that haunted him at night. Only the people he'd loved and lost kept him awake. His fellow Rangers who were killed in action. Kellen. His dad.

"I keep thinking that those men are dead because of me," Aurora said. "Like maybe they didn't want to be there, but they thought they had no choice. Or maybe they really just wanted to talk, like that first guy claimed on the terrace."

"They had guns. Those men would have killed you. Maybe hurt you in other ways first."

She pressed her lips together, swallowing. "I'm not saying

you did anything wrong. But you were defending *me*. If not for me, you wouldn't have those men's lives on your hands at all."

"It's not your fault. None of this is your fault."

She held his gaze, blinking back tears.

He was amazed at how little she had cried. Not because he thought she was weak. Just because any sane person would cry after the things she'd been through.

Aurora reached for his hand and squeezed. Immediately, she let him go, and he missed the feel of her skin. Missed it too much.

"Why don't you go to bed?" Devon stood and started clearing the plates from the table. "I'll clean this up. I'm sure you're exhausted."

Aurora glanced at the door to Chase's bedroom, which opened off the living room. "Wait. There's only one door here. Where's the room you slept in last night?"

"You're looking at it." He pointed at the couch.

Her eyes bugged. "You slept *there*? It's three feet too short for you. How did you even fit?"

He laughed. "I can sleep standing if I need to. There's only one bedroom, and it's yours."

"I'm not some spoiled little rich girl, remember? I've slept on sofas before. You take Chase's room."

He shrugged. "You can sleep wherever you want. But I'm not taking that bed."

"Fine, you know what? We could keep arguing, but neither of us is going to back down. We'll share the bed. You'll have your side, I'll have mine, and it will all be very platonic and professional."

She marched off toward the bedroom. And she was right —when it came to Aurora, there was no use continuing to argue. Devon hadn't known her long, but he'd learned that much. She could be just as stubborn as he was.

So they'd be sharing a bed. It wasn't such a big deal. He'd

bunked with fellow soldiers plenty of times. He could handle himself around Aurora Bennett.

Right.

He threw his clothes into the washer along with hers and set the machine going. Then he checked each window and door—yet again. Aurora was done in the bathroom, so Devon took his turn. He brushed his teeth for around eight minutes.

Yeah. He was stalling.

Finally, Devon went into the bedroom. Aurora lay in the bed, covers up to her chest, eyes staring at the ceiling. Her eyes darted to his.

"I changed the sheets. I was too tired to think of it last night."

"Cool. Okay if I turn off the light?"

She nodded, and the room plunged into darkness when he flipped the switch. Devon slid under the blankets, feeling the mattress give beneath him. He had worn a pair of Chase's shorts and a tee to bed. The sheets were cool and smooth against his legs. They smelled like detergent, but Aurora's scent was there too, slightly masked by Chase's shampoo.

Devon couldn't help turning his head, trying to make out the shape of her in the dark. He heard her breathing. She was so close. He wanted to reach past those few feet and pull her toward him. Sink his fingers into her long hair, which just a moment ago had been splayed across the pillow.

Enough. He had to stop. This wasn't like him, letting his mind run away from him this way. He'd already made the decision, and he knew what to do—usually, the follow-through was the easy part. But when it came to Aurora, he felt the urge to cross every line, just as long as it brought him to her.

He heard Aurora shifting against the sheets. Sitting up.

Every minute, the room was getting brighter as his pupils dilated. She was wearing that T-shirt of Chase's, and Devon balled his fists to either side of him, gathering the sheet in his fingers. He didn't like that so many things that belonged to Chase were touching her right now. He wanted to pull that shirt off her, cover her with his body, claiming her as his and no one else's.

But it wasn't even that he wanted to sleep with her right now. He wanted to hold her, to hear her breathe, and to feel her heart beating against him.

"Can I ask you something?" she said.

He turned onto his side, facing her. "Sure."

"What does the K stand for?"

"Oh." Unconsciously, he touched the tattoo on his forearm. "It's for my brother. Kellen. He was my twin."

"Was?"

He swallowed. "He was killed about a year and a half ago. He was in the L.A.P.D. Like our dad. There was a mass shooter at a grocery store, and Kellen was one of the units that responded. Didn't make it out."

A heavy weight settled in his stomach any time he talked about his brother. He felt it there now, like a chunk of iron pulling him down. Sometimes, it got so heavy that he didn't know how he'd ever stand up again.

"I'm so sorry. Is that why you left the military?"

"Yeah. My mom couldn't stand the thought that they might lose me, too."

"No wonder you usually work the desk at my brother's office."

He nodded. "I got the tattoo right after I learned about his death. I liked carrying something of my brother on my skin, so that the world could see. Otherwise, I'm not sure anyone would've known. Sometimes, I went weeks without saying his name. It was too difficult. But I didn't want anyone to think I'd forgotten."

She sighed, leaning back against the headboard. She had bent her legs, arms wrapping around her knees. "I thought my past was difficult, and I didn't even lose anyone. I kept going on and on about being annoyed at my brother for such petty reasons, when you..."

He couldn't stop himself from sliding his arm across the bed. His fingertip met her foot. He told himself that just that tiny bit of contact was enough, that it couldn't hurt. It was all he needed. Just to be able to feel that she was there.

"Your pain isn't canceled out by someone else's. If it worked that way, then no one could ever feel sad, because there is always somebody else in the world who has it worse."

Her hand covered his, their fingers entwining. "How do you do it? Stay so strong, even when you've been through so much?"

Fuck if I know. "I guess... I just keep looking forward. Focusing on what's next."

"That's a good strategy. But it sounds kind of lonely."

Devon wanted to disagree, but he'd told her he wasn't going to lie to her anymore.

"And what's the point of being lonely when someone's right next to you?"

She pulled his hand up to her mouth and kissed his knuckles. He almost laughed, the action was so prim.

Then her leg stretched out. Instead of touching her foot, his hand was now against her thigh. Her skin was so warm and smooth. Without his permission, his fingertips traced upward, following the curve of her hip.

She was completely bare beneath the T-shirt—no panties, nothing.

His cock sprang to life, instantly so hard that his head swam from the loss of blood. Every cell in his body screamed to keep going. He thought he'd break if he didn't slide his fingers between her legs. He knew she'd be wet. She'd open up for him, moaning. It would be so easy to pull down his shorts, push inside her, and take what she wanted to give him—

Devon rolled away and shot to his feet. "I'm not going to do this." He was speaking more to himself than to her, reminding himself of his duty. He walked across the room and wrenched open the door.

"Devon, wait."

He went out into the living room, shutting the bedroom door behind him. His fingers dug into his scalp, yanking at his hair in frustration.

The couch it is, he thought.

Chapter Seventeen

*A*urora woke early in the morning, determined to keep herself busy. When she got to the living room, Devon was already up, reading some kind of sports magazine from Chase's coffee table.

"Want eggs?" He didn't look up. "They're on the stove."

So, they were pretending that last night didn't happen, apparently.

She went to the kitchen and served herself breakfast. Eggs, toast, jam. Aurora sat at the table to eat. Devon tossed down his magazine and disappeared into the bedroom. She heard him breathing rapidly. He was doing push-ups. But he'd gone where she couldn't see him.

Was he avoiding her?

Devon *had* touched her last night. She hadn't forced him to do it. But to be fair, she'd started it. She really hadn't intended to get so hot and bothered. Around Devon, her body had a mind of its own.

It made no sense. Finance guys didn't usually do it for her, and military men certainly didn't. Such alpha men had a tendency to tell everyone else what to do. That wasn't her thing, in or out of the bedroom.

But this man turned off her rational brain and turned on…everything else. *It's because of the stress of all this,* she thought. *Some kind of biological imperative to mate with the man most likely to keep you alive.*

It would fade. At least, she hoped this urge would fade.

She'd thought she wanted him when he was Rick Harrison. But Devon Whitestone wasn't just a sexy guy next door. He was kind, thoughtful, smart… Infuriatingly honorable. He was the strongest person she'd ever known, not just physically but mentally, too.

A knocking sound came from behind her. She jumped up from the table.

There was a shadow visible through the shade hanging over the back door. Someone was there.

"Devon!"

He came in, sweat shining on his face from his workout. "Shit," he muttered. He grabbed for the gun that he'd hidden in the kitchen cabinet.

"Hide. Get ready to run if we need to."

Fear ran through her like electricity. *Not again,* she thought. Aurora dashed into the living room, crouching down behind a tall bookcase.

She could just barely see Devon. He crept toward the back door, his gun at the ready. The knocking continued, speeding up. Then slowing down again. It was strange.

Devon dropped the gun to his side, straightening. "It's Morse code." Without warning, he crossed to the back door, unlocked it, and threw it wide.

"You nearly gave me a heart attack," he said to the person outside.

"Ha," a female voice responded. "I don't believe that for a second. You haven't had an elevated heart rate since the first time you put your hand under a girl's shirt. Which was, what —a few weeks ago?"

"Very funny. Get in here." Devon shut the door. The lock clicked back into place.

Aurora emerged from the living room. A petite woman stood in the kitchen. Her strawberry-blond hair was trimmed into a blunt bob, and she wore chunky pink plastic glasses. She smiled and waved.

"Aurora, this is Sylvie Trousseau. Sylvie, Aurora Bennett."

Sylvie stuck out her hand. "I've been dying to meet you! Max talks about you all the time. I just wish we were meeting under different circumstances. How are you doing?"

So this woman knew everything that was going on. And she knew Max.

"Sylvie works at Bennett Security with me. She's our lead data analyst and computer expert. But what are you doing here, Sylv? I thought it wasn't safe yet for Max to send anyone."

"Don't worry, I followed all the protocols to lose any possible trails. I got here clean."

"Are you here to take me to a safe house?" Aurora wasn't sure if she wanted the answer to be yes or no.

"Not yet, I'm afraid. And Max wouldn't send me." Sylvie set her large tote bag in the kitchen and started unpacking it. "I was in charge of the remote team watching Aurora's building. That was a shit show. We had an attack on our system, which cut you off from us. I'm really sorry about that. Your brother's keeping the details of your situation to a very limited group, for obvious reasons."

She brought out a laptop computer, opened the lid, and waited for it to boot up.

"So, he's still not sure if someone inside Bennett hacked our system?" Devon asked.

"I've been up most of the night, trying to get to the bottom of it. Max is livid. He sent the other two members of our team home, pending my investigation. Someone definitely tried a brute-force attack, and it looks like it came from the outside. But I don't think they reached anything sensitive. It wasn't all that effective."

Devon grinned, crossing his arms over his ample pecs. "And that's how Bennett knew that you couldn't be involved?"

"Damn straight. Because he knows if *I'd* set up the hack on our system, nobody would have even realized anything was wrong. I'm way too smooth." She leaned over to type a password into the laptop.

"But you could have done a sloppy job on purpose," Aurora pointed out. "As a misdirection."

Sylvie's eyebrows lifted. "Damn, Whitestone, you'd better watch out for this one. She's one sneaky lady."

"You have no idea."

Laughing, Sylvie said, "You make a good point, Aurora. Luckily, Max knows me well enough to trust that I'd never put anyone he loves in jeopardy. No matter what."

There was so much about her brother's life that was foreign to Aurora. For all her years in St. Louis, Max had downplayed his business ambitions to her. She hadn't even realized his true level of success until returning to West Oaks. And then, once she was back, she'd let old resentments keep her distant.

She'd met a few of his army buddies who worked for him now. But Aurora had only visited the Bennett Security office once, right after she moved here. Maybe, if she'd made a point to understand her brother's company, she'd have met Sylvie or Devon before. Maybe she wouldn't have been so resistant to the whole bodyguard idea in the first place.

"Anyway," Sylvie went on, "I'm pretty sure the disruption of security at Aurora's building was a separate operation. More localized. But it was all coordinated. Stage an attempt on our main office databases as a distraction. Then go after the real target—Aurora herself. Your building's alarm system is designed to fight back when it detects interference. The bad guys probably got a glimpse of our camera feeds, which caused the cameras to reboot exactly as those men breached the building."

"Which is why the cameras went off," Devon said.

"And someone took out the police officers guarding the exits," Aurora remembered. "Do you know yet if they're all right?"

"Just knocked out, thank heaven," Sylvie said.

"Good. But that happened right before they came after me on the terrace. Because they saw me go up there on the camera before it switched off?"

Sylvie grimaced. "It's a big loophole in our security, and I'm pissed we didn't see this weakness before. You can bet I'm going to be writing a patch on that a.s.a.p. But this plan was sophisticated. It took a lot of people and a lot of money."

Aurora felt a shiver go down her spine. "Dominic Crane. And the Silverlake Syndicate."

Sylvie opened up various windows on the laptop, typing what Aurora guessed was code. "That's right. But the Syndicate had help. Someone told them your identity, Aurora, and where to find you. *And* how to circumvent our security. It had to either be someone inside our company—which I'm really starting to doubt—or it came from the government side. West Oaks P.D. or the District Attorney's Office."

It couldn't have been Lana. But how well did Lana know her boss, the DA? And if the leak truly came from the police—

Aurora's legs were like jelly. She had to sit down. "Could they find us here? Chase is West Oaks P.D."

"Chase wouldn't tell anyone," Devon said. "There's no way."

Sylvie agreed. "We're keeping tabs on him, discreetly, just in case. It's possible the Syndicate has learned Devon's identity by now."

"I was afraid of that, and that's why I told Chase to get my mom and sister to a safe location."

"Exactly, we know. We're taking good care of them," Sylvie said. "The only worry is that someone could make the connection between Chase and Devon, given their friendship, but that's less likely. Devon's only lived in West Oaks a few months. And Chase's name isn't officially on the title for this house since it's a sub-let from his cousin."

Aurora breathed out, trying to relax. "So, what do we do?"

"Stay hidden. Everyone knows you're the witness now because it's public knowledge. But nobody except a handful of people knows where to find you. I'm going to help make sure it stays that way. Which is why I've come bearing gifts."

She turned the laptop toward Aurora. "Ta-da. This is for you. A completely secure terminal with its own internet hotspot and VPN—that's a virtual private network—to mask your whereabouts. You can communicate with your contacts, but nobody can trace you."

Devon leaned a hand on the table, looking over Aurora's shoulder. "Nice. This is perfect, Sylv."

"Don't worry, I brought one for you, too. So, you can reach Max and your family, and nobody has to take turns." She elbowed him affectionately in the side, and Aurora felt a twinge of annoyance. Exactly how well did they know each other?

"But don't think you can start binging Netflix and playing video games. Max wants to go on the offensive."

"How?" Aurora asked eagerly.

"I'll tell you all about it. But first, let me set up Devon's machine. I'm guessing you'll want to take a minute to check your email and your social accounts, Aurora? If it were me, I'd be dying to."

Aurora sat down at the computer and opened the internet browser. Thankfully, she remembered her password for her email, so she could log-on. Usually, she didn't get very many email messages from friends. But since yesterday, there were dozens. The word had gotten out about her being the witness to Wolfson's murder, so there were plenty of panicked subject lines asking how she was. She guessed that they must've also heard about the attack on her building, given the urgency in their wording.

Not many friends from St. Louis had written, though. They probably hadn't heard the news out of Southern California. Then again, after her break-up with Justin, most of their joint friends had dropped her.

Pushing that thought away, she got onto her Instagram account. She drew a blank on that password, so she had to reset it using her email. And she couldn't access the full app on the computer, but she was able to see and respond to her messages.

A few more friends had been checking on her there. She sent off quick responses, assuring them that she was safe and in a secure location. But she just didn't have the energy to write more, or to reply to all the old high school classmates that she hadn't even spoken to in ages.

She spotted a message from her ex, Justin, and promptly deleted it. She didn't need his mental games right now.

A message came in while she sat looking at the screen. It was Nadia, Brandon Wolfson's wife.

Aurora, is that you? Nadia had written. *It says you're active. Just want to make sure that you're all right.*

The poor woman. She'd already lost her husband, and now all this new drama.

She responded to Mrs. Wolfson's message, asking for a reminder of her phone number, and then called using FaceTime.

Nadia appeared on the screen. She was an attractive woman in her late forties, with gray-blond hair and unlined skin. Usually, she had impeccable makeup and clothes, but right now she looked like she'd either just gotten out of bed or hadn't gone to sleep. A loose jogging top, no makeup.

"Aurora, I was so terrified after I saw the news. Thank god, you're okay. You aren't hurt, are you?"

"I made it out just fine. I'm in a secure location. But how are you doing? I can't imagine how terrible this has been for you." It had been less than a week since Brandon's murder.

"For you and me both. I can't even begin to talk about Brandon right now. I'm just so sorry that you got dragged into this, whatever it is. I don't understand it. Just a few days ago, you and I were planning my birthday party for next weekend, and now Brandon…"

The woman wiped away tears.

Aurora folded her arms on the table. "I'm so sorry."

"Some of my friends still want me to have the event. But I don't know. It would be so hard to see everyone."

"That's true. But it might also be nice to have them around. I'm really missing my best friend right now." Though she knew her own situation was hardly comparable, since she hadn't lost anybody that she loved.

A small line creased Nadia's forehead. "You don't think it would be terrible? Having a party so soon after Brandon died?"

"Don't think of it as a party. More like a support group."

Nadia's eyes squeezed closed. Tears fell. But she smiled. "You're something, Aurora. Thank you. Maybe…it might be nice to have an event to look forward to. Do you think the caterers are still available? I haven't spoken to anyone in days, paid bills, nothing."

"I'm sure it'll be fine. I can send them a quick email and check for you. Same with the florist and the baker." They'd missed the final deposits with all the chaos lately, but Aurora bet she could get the party back on track.

"Really? Are you sure?"

Aurora had already done so much of the planning. And having some work to do gave her a glimmer of hope. Eventually, this would all be over, and she could get back to living her life. Doing everything that she loved.

And what about Devon? she wondered. They had talked about being friends... But that was too much to think about right now. Not on top of everything else.

She ended the video call and sent off a few emails about Nadia's birthday party.

Sylvie came out of the bedroom, where she had been setting up Devon's device. She closed the door behind her, leaving him in the other room.

"He's going to call his family. I'm sure they must be worried."

Aurora nodded. She'd gotten the impression that he was close to his family, especially after his brother's death. So of course, Devon wanted to reassure them.

"I'm surprised Max let you give us access to our email and everything. I would've thought he might not trust me to keep our location a secret." Aurora shrugged. "Maybe it's not fair to call him paranoid, given everything that's going on, but he's always been overprotective. Like he thinks I'm so stupid, I'll mess everything up if I'm left to myself."

"Oh, no. This was Max's idea. He can be a little intense, I'll give you that. But he knows what he's doing. If he's over-protective, it's only because he cares so much about you."

"How long have you worked with him?"

"Three years. Max is a great boss. The best I've ever had. I can imagine it might be a little stifling to have him as a brother, but all I can say is, he lets his employees have some free rein. He listens to our ideas. He's always open to hearing different opinions."

"This is Max Bennett we're talking about? I guess he's different at work than he is with family."

Sylvie laughed. "Maybe so. Family's always complicated. Mind if I sit?" She grabbed a chair and pulled the laptop toward her. "So, we got a ton of video footage from around

Ocean Lane the other day. When you saw the guy watching you near the police station?"

"Right."

"Lana Marchetti said they had a detective going through it, but without a more detailed description, the police haven't made any progress. And of course, you haven't had a chance to work with the sketch artist, since you've been a touch busy, and we'd rather keep you separate from the police side of the investigation for now. So, Max thought you should take a look yourself. See if you can spot him."

"My brother did? Really?"

Sylvie smiled wryly. "I told you, Max is all about giving us a chance to prove ourselves. Does that sound good to you?"

"Of course! I've been dying for some way to help."

"I'm sure you have. I just need to log in to the secure remote server, and I'll be able to access the footage they've compiled."

While Sylvie went through the various levels of passwords and authentication, Aurora said, "It's interesting to hear a different perspective on Max." She drummed her fingers on the table, trying to be nonchalant. "What about Devon? How well do you know him?"

Sylvie tilted her hand back and forth. "Enough to know he's one hundred percent reliable. And enough to worry about him because the man never takes a break. He's the only person who works as hard as Max." She barked a laugh. "Or me. Devon's the one we call if somebody is sick or needs the night off. He has no social life, far as I can tell. But he always insists that he's fine. He's as empathetic as they come. But that man's got his own emotions on lockdown."

That sounded like Devon. "So...no girlfriends?"

"I've never seen him with anyone, and from that look of concentration he's usually got, I'd guess it's been a long time for him. If you know what I mean. A guy that wound-up?

When he finally loses control, it's going to burn down the neighborhood."

Aurora's skin heated, thinking of the kiss they'd shared. Devon—though he'd been "Rick Harrison" at the time—had indeed lost his perfect control for a few blissful seconds. The two of them had almost combusted before he'd shut it down.

But what would happen if Devon finally let go of all his inhibitions? That would be something to see.

"Don't tell him I said any of that!" Sylvie begged. "He'll give me so much shit."

"Do you ever date guys in the office?"

She made a face. "Nah, Captain America isn't my style, and my office is full of them." Her voice dropped to a whisper. "I go for the bad boys."

"Oh, please tell me you're seeing someone scandalous. I haven't gotten any since my ex in St. Louis. I need to live vicariously."

"Ha, I wish. The problem is, I want a bad boy on the outside, and a sweetheart within. Which is some kind of mythical beast, far as I can tell. But enough about me. Let's find that dickwad who was following you and nail him to the wall, shall we?"

Sylvie cracked her knuckles and placed her fingers on the keyboard.

Chapter Eighteen

*D*evon's sister answered his video call. Her face loomed on the screen, way too close to the camera.

"Finally!" Ruby was her usual self—perfectly groomed, plucked, and styled. "What in the world is going on? Chase shows up at our house, claiming that we're all in danger, except he can't explain why. And then he says you're mixed up in it."

"Are you with Chase right now?" Devon had thought Chase was in some luxury penthouse of Bennett's. "Where are you?"

"Oh no, you don't get to ask questions. I want to know why I had to pack our mother and my baby up in five minutes and flee for reasons nobody has yet explained."

He gave her the short version: that he was on a bodyguard detail, protecting an important crime witness.

Ruby sat back. She looked like she was in a hotel room, with a plush headboard and fancy wallpaper behind her. The baby must've been asleep in a different room because she didn't bother to keep her voice down.

"You were supposed to be taking some days off. And

instead, you're on bodyguard duty? That sounds really demanding."

"I'm sorry, I really don't mean to worry you and mom. This assignment wasn't supposed to be quite so—"

"You think I'm worried about me and mom? Okay, mom has been completely freaking out. She'll be plenty relieved to know you're all right. As am I, even though I *still* don't feel like you've told me what's really going on. But I'm a lot more worried about *you*. You've been working yourself to the bone. You're exhausted. Just look at you." She gestured at the screen. "You look like shit."

"Gee, thank you."

His sister huffed. "Part of me wants to call up that boss of yours and tell him to quit working you like this. It isn't right."

He was worried she would do it. Ruby was just as stubborn as he was, and a whole lot louder. "It isn't Mr. Bennett's fault. This case blew up in a way that none of us expected. I've been taking on extra shifts because that's what our family needs right now. It's been hard, but I know it won't be that much longer until I have the money for Mom's down payment, and—"

"See, there you go about the down payment again. Devon, I've told you that isn't your responsibility."

"Then whose responsibility is it?" He said this matter-of-factly. He didn't want to hurt her feelings. She hadn't asked to get accidentally pregnant, or for her boyfriend to desert her. But they all had to be realistic.

Devon had been there when his niece was born. He stood by Ruby in the delivery room, squeezing her hand, talking her through the contractions. He was the first person in their family to hold Haley. The nurses had handed her to him, and he'd brought that tiny bundle over to his sister in a hospital bed. That very day, he had promised he would do whatever he could to support them. He wanted Haley to have every opportunity. He wanted his niece to have her mom around.

"I've been looking at job opportunities," Ruby said. "There's a salon on Ocean Lane, really high end. I've already had an interview. They loved my portfolio."

Devon was shaking his head. "But you said you wanted to be home with Haley. If you want to go back to work, then of course I'll try to make that happen. But with the daycare costs, I thought we decided that it just didn't make sense."

They both knew their mother would want to take care of Haley all the time, but the arthritis in her hands simply made that impossible.

"No, Devon, *you* decided. But I never did. I never agreed that the cost of me staying home would be you completely burning yourself out. I'm not even talking about your job being dangerous. So don't even go there with me. Forget about whatever guilt trip Mom has put you on since Kellen died."

Devon tried to cut in, but his sister wouldn't let him.

"Do you *want* to be a bodyguard?"

"For the long term? I...don't know. I like some things about it. I'm not bored anymore. But I can't—"

"Dev, if you want to be a bodyguard, that's fine. If you even want to re-enlist, I sure as hell would miss you, but I'd be happy for you. What I can't stand is to see you sacrificing everything you need, all your ambitions or dreams, based on this idea that you have to provide for me and mom. I'm going back to work, and I'm going to figure out some way to afford Haley's daycare. But I'm not going to let you do this to yourself anymore."

He hardly knew what to say. That had all come out of nowhere. Ruby slumped back on the bed, like she'd just relieved herself of a burden.

He'd just wanted to do the right thing by his sister. But when had doing the "right" thing become the wrong one?

"We can talk about this more later," Devon said. "After I get home."

"And when will that be? You can't protect anybody if you haven't been taking care of yourself."

"I'm going to get some rest now, Ruby. Okay?"

"All right, Devon. Goodbye."

After he finished talking to his sister, Devon got back to work.

He found Sylvie and Aurora chatting around the dining table. They quieted as he walked through, doing his usual checks of their perimeter. Everything was calm, just as it had been since they'd arrived. He wasn't about to let his guard down, of course, but they'd managed to keep a tight lid on Aurora's new location. They really seemed to be safe here.

He went back into the bedroom, and he heard the women laughing about something. He wasn't sure what that was about, but they seemed to be going over video footage. So Devon figured he should make himself useful as well.

He logged onto Bennett Security's secure server and accessed the camera footage from Aurora's building. Max and Sylvie had already been reviewing these images for clues about the men who'd come after Aurora. Along with Devon, they'd reconstructed the chain of events.

For the tenth time, Devon traced through the attack, minute by minute, hoping to spot some clue they'd missed.

A van had pulled up to the building's service entrance around five p.m., sporting the logo of a plumbing company. The garage security guy stopped them, asking about an appointment.

Meanwhile, men on foot approached the squad cars at the front and back of the building. Devon had seen one of them on the camera feed, leaning into the window and chatting with a police officer. Apparently, he'd been posing as a concerned citizen who'd just witnessed a mugging.

At exactly 5:05, a device inside the plumbing van set off a small electromagnetic surge, just enough to overload the building's electricity. The men chatting with the police officers had struck, pulling guns on both the police officers and the security guy inside the parking garage.

That was when Devon had seen the camera feed cut out, and the lights had flickered.

Within minutes, Crane's men had swarmed out of the plumbing van and into the stairwells of the building. It was an extremely sophisticated attack. Thank goodness no police, building staff, or residents had been killed.

But Devon was sure there was something else he'd missed. Someone casing the building. An unexpected delivery person, an uninvited guest. Crane's men had gone after Aurora so quickly. They'd come so close to finding her. Hurting her. Devon was pissed at himself for not stopping them sooner.

What did I miss? he asked himself. *And how am I going to spot these assholes the next time they come around?*

Chapter Nineteen

Sylvie loaded the camera footage on the screen. "We've compiled the feeds from all the streets surrounding West Oaks P.D. from the morning that Dominic Crane arrived in custody. Max has some serious connections with the city departments. Unfortunately, the quality is all over the place. I've already spent several hours looking over the feeds, as well as running them through some of our analyzers, looking for factors that are out of place."

"You have software that does that?"

Though maybe Aurora shouldn't have been surprised. Max had always loved gadgets and computers. She remembered one Christmas when she bought him a remote control car, and he fitted it out with a camera and microphone to spy on Lana's neighbors. He had ended up on the good side of the law, for the most part, but her brother definitely had a devious side. She had to give him that.

"Oh, you have no idea. These algorithms are scary, they're so good at predicting things. And the stuff we've got is nothing to the real code that people like the NSA or the FSB have going." Sylvie was shaking her head, and Aurora got the sense that she was more disappointed she didn't have access to such sophisticated software, than angry that governments had such power at their fingertips.

"The problem is," Sylvie went on, "that neither my eyes nor the algorithm could identify anything with all the chaos going on that day. Here, look at this."

She opened one recording and scrolled forward to a certain timestamp. "See? There you are."

Aurora saw herself on the steps of the police headquarters, craning her neck to look across the street. "You knew just where to find this image."

"I have a good memory. I told you, I've already been spending too long staring at these recordings. But anyway, you seem to be looking for someone right here. Is that when you saw the man you thought was watching you?"

"Yes, that's right when I first saw him, I think. The police car with Crane in the back had just passed by. And I kept having a strange feeling, like eyes were on me. Then I turned and saw him."

She remembered how their gazes had met. He'd been too far away for her to see the color of his irises, but she'd had the inexplicable impression that his eyes were ice blue. "His hair was kind of in between brown and blond. He looked like guys I've seen a million times before and, also, somehow completely unique. It was the strangest thing."

"Interesting. Some people have those kinds of faces. The government actually recruits them as operatives because they can move unnoticed. But he also wasn't behaving like anyone else in the crowd. Which you picked up on. That's impressive."

"I don't know. Maybe it's just that trademark Bennett paranoia." Aurora tried to shrug off the terror that crept up her spine. Whenever she stopped and really pondered the fact that there were mobsters—murderers—searching for her right now, she felt like she was going to have a panic attack.

"And you pegged Devon as a bodyguard the minute you met him, right? Or so I heard."

"Yeah. I guess."

Sylvie seemed to sense her anxiety and put a comforting hand on Aurora's arm. "We can take a break if you want. I know how difficult this can be. Just say the word."

"No, I'm fine. Let's keep going."

"Okay, I'm going to show you the feeds from the other side of the street from approximately the same time. Tell me when you see the guy."

Aurora studied the videos one by one. It was a painstaking process, reviewing the various angles and trying to take in so many details at once. All those faces, cars passing, most of it in black and white.

Then her eyes landed on a man with medium hair and a medium build. Both handsome and unremarkable. And she knew.

She pointed at the screen. "That's him. He's the one." She'd definitely seen him that day outside the police headquarters.

But there was something else about him, too. A recognition that tugged at her memory. What was it? Why did she feel that she knew him from some other place?

If she did, that might help explain why she'd noticed him in that crowd. But where could it have been?

She tried to remember, but it wouldn't come, and she chewed the inside of her cheek in frustration.

Sylvie did something with the computer, capturing a zoomed-in image of the man's face. "Great job. I'll get this out to Max right away, and hopefully, we can track this guy down."

"But we don't know for sure that he had anything to do with Dominic Crane, or those men who came after me."

Devon stepped into the doorway of the bedroom, leaning against the frame.

"We can't take anything for granted in this investigation," he said. "Sylvie is right. We need to follow every possible lead. And speaking of, I just found something else that I want to look into. A black Escalade that drove past Aurora's building a couple of times, both the day before and the morning of the attack. My gut says there's something not right about this guy. Think you could help me out, Sylvie? Maybe you've seen this SUV on one of the other feeds? It has damage to the grill, kind of distinctive."

Devon brought his laptop over to the dining table and set it down. He showed them the black Escalade, running through the two different recordings of the vehicle outside of her building.

More chills ran through her. She hated the idea that someone had been tracking her, watching her, when she'd had no clue. It was one thing for a secret bodyguard like Devon. She'd been annoyed and even hurt that he'd lied to her. But the realization that these creeps had been keeping track of her for hours, maybe even days... Maybe ever since the night she'd witnessed Wolfson's murder? It was too much to take. She felt her chest tightening, her lungs struggling to breathe. She crossed her arms, hands balling into fists.

"I'll see what I can find." Sylvie's fingers started flying over the keyboard faster than Aurora could even track. Various windows opened and closed, the feeds racing forward and back. She had no idea how Sylvie could make sense of it.

"One of you want to whip up some food?" Sylvie asked. "This might take a while."

Aurora went into the kitchen. Devon followed close behind her. "You doing okay with all this?"

"Sure."

She appreciated that he'd asked, except his voice sounded all wrong. He was being rough and formal, like he was really just some bodyguard. Like they hadn't been getting to know each other and agreed the evening before to be friends.

She had known he was upset at her for taking things out of the friend zone once again last night. But apparently, he no longer even wanted that.

She felt him watching her with those hazel eyes, waiting patiently for her to say more. Her body was so aware of him. The way his bulky muscles shifted, the angle of his chin. His scent was like catnip to her lady parts, making her tingle in all sorts of frustratingly pleasurable ways. If he didn't appreciate her "throwing herself" at him, as he'd accused her of doing, then maybe the guy should get a clue and step back.

She got bread and sandwich supplies from the refrigerator. Finally, Devon walked away.

Aurora made a ham and cheese sandwich for Sylvie, who accepted the food without taking her eyes off the computer screen. She took a bite, and then shouted, covering her mouth at the last minute before crumbs sprayed onto the computer.

"I've got it!" She switched around the windows. "This is another angle of the SUV going past Aurora's building. Like Devon already found."

Sylvie showed them a head-on picture of a black Escalade, driving down Ocean Lane in the late morning the day of the attack. That was the same time Aurora had left her building.

"But now, I've found where he goes next." Sylvie tracked the car as it drove around several detours that had been set up as a perimeter around the police building in anticipation of Crane's arrival.

Sylvie pulled up the next feed, following the Escalade from one camera to another. It parked at a curb, and the driver got out. He had medium-brown hair, an average build. Aurora held her breath.

Turn around, she thought. Even though she was already sure she knew what she'd see.

On the video, the man shut the door. Walked over to the meter and plugged several coins inside. Then jogged across the road, facing directly into the camera.

Sylvie whistled. "Well, well. The plot has definitely thickened."

It was the same man. But unlike when she had seen him outside the police department, he was wearing a dark blazer.

All at once, the memory flashed into her mind.

The strobe lights flashing over the dance floor, light glinting in the champagne flutes. The devil horns and angel wings floating through the crowd. She could hear the thumping music, the heat of all those bodies rising in the air…

The "Angels and Demons" party at The Lighthouse Club. Before Brandon Wolfson had been murdered.

She remembered his eyes. Ice blue.

"He was at the party the night Brandon died."

Chapter Twenty

*D*evon put his hands on his hips, staring down at the computer screen. A nondescript man had just stepped out of the black Escalade in the video. Sylvie froze the image as he walked, the edges of his blazer flying back.

I see you, Devon thought, leaning forward. He didn't know how this guy was involved, but Devon wasn't going to let him anywhere near Aurora again.

"So, this guy was at the party," Devon repeated. "Was he on the guest list? Do you know his name?"

Aurora's shoulders tensed. "If I did, I would have said so. I didn't even really notice him fully the night of the party. Not in any specific way. I think he was just one of the guests. The Wolfsons invited hundreds of people, and there wasn't a formal list. It wasn't like they sent out engraved invitations. That wasn't their style."

"But could he have known that you were in Wolfson's office at the time of the murder? Maybe he saw you. Maybe he was nearby."

"It's possible. But I really don't think so. Otherwise, why wouldn't he have told Crane and the others I was inside? And if he was just one of Wolfson's friends, then he would've been screaming his head off."

An edge had snuck into Aurora's voice. She was stressed, and Devon could certainly understand why. He wished he could wrap an arm around her. Comfort her. But that wasn't something the typical bodyguard would do. And he had sworn to himself that he would be nothing but professional from now on.

Which shouldn't be this difficult, he scolded himself.

"Take your time," Devon said. "You only just remembered him. Try to picture him. Maybe you'd seen him with the Wolfsons before? Perhaps they introduced him to you?"

Aurora made a sound of exasperation. "I don't remember!"

"Hey, it's all right." Sylvie stood up from the table. "I'll let Max know. This could be a big lead in the case, so you've both been super helpful."

Devon paced across the room as Sylvie chatted with Max on her phone. Aurora sat on the couch, pulling her knees to her chest and staring at the wall.

He had to force himself to stop looking at her. It was like she had a gravitational pull on him, and he had to exert serious effort to stay away.

Sylvie finished her call with Max. She came over to Devon, tapping a finger on her lip. "This guy isn't a known associate of the Silverlake Syndicate. His face is definitely not in any of the photos Lana provided us."

Aurora looked over. "How can you be sure already? I must've gone through a hundred of those photos after Wolfson's murder."

"Sylvie's got a photographic brain." Devon tapped his forehead. "Comes in handy."

His coworker just shrugged. "And I don't think this guy was there during the attack on your building, Aurora. He's not

in any of that footage. All the other attackers have been identified as members of Silverlake."

"I've never seen him, either," Devon said. "So, we don't
know where he's from."

"Or what he wants," Sylvie added.

That was true. This man hadn't done anything outwardly
threatening, apart from Aurora's impression that he was
following her.

Aurora got up. "I could ask Mrs. Wolfson. He was at her
party. She should be able to identify him."

Devon met Sylvie's gaze. "Let's wait to see what Max
thinks. I'm sure he'll want to use every possible method to find
this guy and see how he's involved. But we have to be careful."

Devon went to the front window and peeked out between
the curtains. The street was quiet, no cars driving by. Past the
line of houses, a water tower with "West Oaks" emblazoned
on its side poked into the sky. The afternoon was passing by
fast. They'd spent hours so far poring over the video footage.

Devon let the curtain fall back into place. "What do we
know about Dominic Crane so far? He's the head of the
Silverlake Syndicate. But he hasn't been for long. Before, it
was his older brother, who's in prison now. Right?"

Aurora walked into the kitchen. "That's what I heard on
the news. And we know that Brandon Wolfson was involved
with Crane somehow. When he and Wolfson were talking in
the office, Crane said that Wolfson had been stealing from
him. And that Wolfson had been running a competing
business."

Max had mentioned this to Devon, too. The police were
considering the business relationship between the two men,
and they assumed so far that the murder was in retaliation for
some kind of perceived betrayal on Wolfson's part. Of course,
Wolfson's wife had adamantly denied that her husband was
involved in anything criminal.

"A club like The Lighthouse would have had a lot of cash

coming in," Sylvie said. "Which would have made it a perfect place to launder money."

"That's what I assumed, too." But Devon shook his head. "Does this other man, the Escalade driver, work for Crane secretly? Was he the one who told Crane that Wolfson was cheating him?"

"Or did he work for Wolfson," Aurora suggested, "as part of this competing business? And if he did, what could he possibly want with me?"

Sylvie stood up, yawning. "I'd love to keep hanging out with the two of you, trying to puzzle through all of this. But we've been at it all day, and I gotta admit, I slept about two hours last night. I'm going to check with Max one last time, and then I'm going to start on my way home. Don't worry, I'm going to follow all the protocols, but that means it's going to take forever to get back to my place and into bed."

Sylvie gave Aurora a hug. Devon walked her to the back door, checking through the windows carefully before letting her out.

"You sure you don't want to take the car back?" he asked. "Like you said, it's going to be a long way."

Sylvie had told him she'd driven a car here but parked it on the next street. It was a means of escape in case Aurora and Devon needed it. Courtesy of Max.

"No, I don't mind the bike ride." She fastened the strap of a helmet beneath her chin. "Why else do we live in Southern California, if not to be outside on an evening like this?"

She picked up the bicycle where she had stowed it near the back gate. "I really like Aurora. Shame it took until this crisis for us to meet Max's sister. Some deep history there, I think?"

"Yeah, no kidding. She's...something else."

Sylvie's eyes twinkled knowingly. "Both of you take care of yourselves. And each other. I'll be sure to call ahead next time I'm heading over—or if Max is." Her brows lifted, like she was saying more and wanted him to read between the lines.

With a jolt of guilt, he wondered what Aurora had been telling her. About the kiss? About sharing the bed last night?

Sylvie would never say anything to Max, of course. But he liked Sylvie and didn't want her to be disappointed in him.

But she didn't seem mad at you, a voice said in his mind. *If anything, Sylvie was encouraging you and Aurora to get closer.*

"Don't get any ideas," he muttered as he closed the door behind himself, locking it.

"What?" Aurora asked.

"Nothing."

Once again, they were alone. The minutes ticked by with agonizing slowness. Toward night. Toward that single bed.

Devon parked himself on the couch, one of the laptops perched on his knees. "Get yourself some dinner if you want. I'm going to go over some things. I'll be here for a while."

"I'm not hungry. I'll just take a shower and go to bed."

He didn't say anything.

"Are you coming? Or are you going to sleep on the couch again, and be completely exhausted tomorrow, like you were today?"

"I'm not exhausted."

She snorted. "Right."

Aurora grabbed some clothes from the bedroom and went for the shower. But in the doorway, she spun around. "Don't think I'm not aware of what you're doing."

"And what's that?"

"You're shutting me out. Ignoring me."

"I think this is smarter. I was completely inappropriate previously, but it won't happen again."

She held up her hand. "I get it. I can handle rejection, or...whatever this is. But refusing to even look at me? After what we've been through? It's kind of a dick move."

She vanished into the bathroom, the door slamming behind her.

Chapter Twenty-One

*A*urora closed her eyes, letting the spray massage away the tension in her shoulders.

That man was so impossible. One minute, he was so kind to her that her heart ached from the attention. And the next? He pushed her away.

She'd never craved anyone this intensely. Her skin longed for his touch. Her lips yearned to kiss him again. How was she supposed to spend another night in the same house with him without the slightest possibility of physical contact?

He obviously wanted her, too. But he was torturing them both by trying to be "honorable." Following his "rules." The guy was so tightly wound, she half expected to see a wind-up mechanism jutting from his back, like a toy soldier.

Aurora had seen a few cracks in that armor he wore. The kiss in the penthouse apartment. The way he sometimes looked at her, and his touch on her hip last night. But he seemed to have no trouble shutting down his feelings.

Sylvie was right. The day that Devon finally, completely lost control, the lucky woman would probably be sore for a week afterward.

But dammit, she thought, *I want that to be me.*

If Devon were totally uninhibited, what would he want to do to her? What would he let *her* do to *him*?

Desire pooled in her lower abdomen, her clit pulsing with need. That sexy man was going to drive her insane. Was his dick as gorgeous as the rest of him? Was he cut, uncut? Long? Thick?

A groan snuck out of her throat as she imagined him stripping down. Showing off for her, while fierce need glowed in his eyes. No inhibitions, no control.

How would his hands feel? How would he smell? How would he *taste*?

"Oh god. Why do I do this to myself?" Close proximity to him had only made her cravings worse. His refusals only made her want him *more*. Which was a little screwed up, to be fair. But he'd admitted that he wanted her back, so it wasn't like her feelings were one-sided. She wasn't some creepy stalker.

Though, if she'd had the chance to spy on him getting undressed—yeah, she'd probably do it. *I'm pervy for him. I can't help it.*

The hot water ran in rivulets down her breasts, along her stomach, and between her legs. She slid her hand down along the same path, taking a moment to tug at her pert nipples, pretending that it was Devon's mouth on her instead. She whimpered, needing more.

Her fingers lowered. Caressed the hot wetness at her core. She moaned louder. *Devon. Yes. Oh*— She widened her legs, imagining him beneath her. Behind her. Every possible way.

But when she stepped to the side, her foot slipped out from under her. She yelped. Suddenly, she was careening downward, grabbing for any kind of traction. Her fist closed on the shower curtain.

"Help!"

She landed halfway out of the shower, water spraying everywhere.

The door flew open.

Devon stood there, mouth hanging open. His eyes moved over the scene.

The shower curtain—ripped.

The walls—soaked.

And Aurora, completely naked, sprawled all over the place.

"Holy fucking—" Devon grabbed a towel and lunged forward, both trying to cover her and get her upright at the same time. "I thought you were dying."

Of embarrassment, maybe. "I'm very much alive."

Leaning past her, he turned off the water. "Are you hurt?"

"I don't think so."

"What happened?"

"I—um—" *I was touching myself and thinking about you?* "Slipped. You probably don't want to know what I was doing."

He coughed like he was choking. "You *sure* you're not hurt?"

Aurora wrapped the towel around her. The cloth rubbed against her nipples. "I landed on my hip. It aches, but I think I'm okay."

"Let me see."

"I'm sure it's fine."

"But I should check."

A minute ago, she'd have been happy to strip down and show him any part of her. But his brusque tone infuriated her. Like her near nakedness didn't faze him at all, except for some mild discomfort. *This is inappropriate*, he was probably thinking. Just like he'd said before.

Oh yeah? I'll show you inappropriate.

She let the sides of the towel fall. The fabric barely covered her breasts and between her legs. Didn't hide her ass at all. She twisted, showing him her hip and an eyeful of butt cheek.

He swallowed audibly. "Looks like it'll bruise." Gingerly,

his fingertips brushed her hipbone. Poked. Prodded. "Any pain?"

"A little." *And a whole lot of something else.*

"Might want to ice it." His fingers disappeared behind his back, like he couldn't move them away fast enough. "Be careful. The floor's wet."

"Yeah. I noticed."

He reached for her shoulders, as if to steady her, and then pulled his hands away again. The room barely fit the two of them. He still stood there, back straight, eyes dancing around like he didn't know where to rest his gaze. Or maybe he was surveying the damage to the walls. Anything but survey *her.*

Yet, he wasn't leaving.

"I'm sorry for messing up the bathroom. I swear I'll make it up to Chase. And his cousin. If he has tools around here somewhere, I can fix the curtain rod."

A smile ghosted across Devon's face. "I've seen you doing home improvement. It didn't go so well."

She huffed. "That was a bad example. I'll have you know I am *very* handy when I have the proper tools. I can take care of things myself."

"I have no doubt." He snuck a glance down at her towel. He'd tried to be quick about it, but she saw.

Cracks in his armor.

She shrugged one shoulder. The towel fell a little more, revealing another inch of side-boob. His eyes strayed along her body again.

"I take care of things myself a lot. Actually, that's what I was doing in the shower when I fell. Touching myself. Since nobody else around here is willing to touch me."

Devon's nostrils flared, teeth biting into his lower lip. "Aurora, you *know* what I want. But…"

Just like that, the entire mood in the room shifted. His chest moved as his breath quickened. Heat surged through her body. Her clit throbbed again, craving contact.

"No, I don't know. Tell me."

He took a step closer. As he advanced, she backed up against the counter. "I should probably go. Definitely should go." His voice was husky.

"Uh-huh."

"This is a very bad idea." Every word seemed to take effort. Like he was trying to speak while holding his breath. "So, I'm asking you to please get dressed…before…I…"

"Before you what?"

She let her towel fall onto the tile. He groaned, so low the sound came from his chest. Aurora looked down at herself, seeing what he was seeing. Bright pink nipples jutting outwards with arousal. Full creamy breasts. The smooth curves of her hips. Trimmed dark-blond hair between her legs.

Next, her eyes moved to him, noting the straining bulge in his jeans. He shifted, trying to adjust himself in his pants.

But he made no move to touch her.

Aurora planted her hands on the countertop and lifted herself onto it. "I told you. I can take care of things myself. But I don't mind if you watch. That's not against your precious rules, is it?"

"Aurora, don't."

She spread her knees. His hazel eyes widened, pupils blown as he stared.

Chapter Twenty-Two

*H*oly. Fucking. Hell.

Aurora was perched on the bathroom counter, completely naked, her long hair spilling across her shoulders. Her legs spread so that he could see *everything*. She tilted her pelvis like she wanted to make sure he had a full view.

And oh yes, he definitely did.

Her gorgeous pink folds, her glistening opening. All of her, spread out for him.

His dick was as hard as granite, swelling against his zipper. Sweat beaded on his forehead and upper lip. It took every ounce of self-control to remain in place, unmoving, instead of launching himself at her.

They couldn't do this.

They really shouldn't do this.

He had a job to do. He was getting paid to watch over her. Max had warned him twice not to touch her.

Devon had already walked away from her more than once. He could do it again. So why wouldn't his legs move?

Maybe it's okay. I'm not really touching her, he reasoned. He wasn't doing anything at all.

He was just…looking.

Her hand lifted. She squeezed her breast, pulling at the nipple. "Do you like what you see?"

Another groan came out of him. The sound was so guttural, so animal, he barely recognized it.

Her lips spread in a wicked grin. Her back arched as she basked in his attention.

Next, that naughty hand of hers trailed between her round, perky tits, down past her belly button, and straight into the wetness pooling at her core. She played with herself, teasing her clit, letting her dampness coat her fingertips.

He could smell her, sweet and spicy, and so turned on.

"Fuck," he whispered, dragging the word out. His mouth watered. He was losing his damn mind. He couldn't take this. His balls ached with fullness, and his cock throbbed to be set free. *Stand down*, he told himself. *Your clothes are staying on.*

Hands off her. You can't touch her. You swore.

But his body had other ideas.

It was like the entire universe had collapsed down into this room, this woman. This single moment. Nothing else even existed.

His hands slid underneath her, clutching the smooth, bare skin. She made a sound of surprise as he palmed her ass and pulled her to the very edge of the counter. He licked his lips in anticipation.

He'd keep his dick in his pants. But he had to taste her. Had to make her come—on his tongue, in his mouth.

He bent over. She cried out as his tongue met her slit.

"Oh god, Devon. Yes. I want this. Please."

Her wetness spread over his tastebuds. She was every bit as sweet as she smelled. She moaned as he kissed her folds, and the sound was pure lust.

He'd gone down on plenty of women—not a ton, but enough—yet the experience had never been this intense before. With her gorgeous body open to him, laid out like a feast for every one of his senses, he couldn't remember his own name, much less why he hadn't stripped her down until now.

Aurora gasped when he lapped at her clit, then closed his lips around it. He found a rhythm, alternating between licking and sucking, adjusting the pressure based on the intensity of her moans. Fucking her with his tongue.

He nearly came in his pants, but he managed to stay focused on her.

He loved the sounds she was making. Little pants and gasps as her pleasure rose higher and higher. Her fingers wound into his hair, and her hips bucked against his mouth.

He slipped a finger into her. Then another. Her wetness dripped down his hand and across his palm. Her taste was intoxicating. He drank her in, his cock so hard it was painful. His free hand reached down and squeezed his erection through his jeans.

Come for me, baby.

He fucked her with his fingers, flicking his tongue over her clit again. Aurora screamed as she came, her hips thrusting. His tongue didn't stop laving until she quieted.

He stood up, licking his lips, wiping his chin. She panted, legs sprawled, a look of pure, exhausted release on her face.

"You," she whispered, voice needy. "I want to see you. Please."

Aurora reached for the button on his jeans. He had to help her push his zipper down. Distantly, some part of him said he wasn't allowed to do this. His dick was supposed to stay in his pants. There were rules. Someone had told him.

But nothing existed for him but her. That, and his own need.

He yanked down his boxer briefs. His cock sprang free, longer and fuller than he'd ever seen it,

"There you are. Devon, you're incredible."

He fisted his length, squeezing the base. Precum leaked from the tip.

"Let me see you stroke yourself."

He swirled his thumb in the moisture at the head, then licked his palm for more lubrication. He started working himself. His pace quickened, like a sports car going from zero to eighty. His fist was tight, fast, rough. His body was desperate to come. Devon was racing something. Racing the thoughts spinning inside his own brain. Trying to outrun the reality that waited just outside this moment.

Aurora watched him as he jerked. A smile grew on her lips. Her hand went to her own sex, fingers swirling around her clit, ready again already. Like she couldn't get enough. That was all he could take. "I'm going to—" he choked out, but he was already spurting onto her stomach, groaning as the orgasm tore through him. His fist pumped a few times more as he emptied, drawing out every last bit of pleasure from his body.

His knees gave out. Devon sat hard against the floor, chest heaving as he caught his breath.

He looked up. Aurora grinned down at him from the countertop. "That was fun."

Devon didn't say anything. All he could do was blink at her.

What. The fuck. Did I…just…do?

"You *did* like it, right? You came hard enough. I've got the evidence to prove it." She slid down from the counter, grabbed the towel, and wiped herself off. "You're freaking out right now. I can tell. Say something."

He managed to stand up, trying to get his dick back in his pants. "I…"

"Devon." Her voice was both teasing and warning. Her hand touched his chest, which was still covered by his T-shirt. "Don't you dare say that was a mistake. Don't run away from me again."

He'd eaten out Aurora Bennett. The sister of his boss. The boss who'd fire him—maybe even seriously maim him—if he found out.

But god, she had tasted good. And Devon had come so hard he was lightheaded.

So maybe it was worth it.

She lifted onto her tiptoes to kiss him. He felt her fingers on the waistband of his jeans. She pushed them over his hips, along with his boxer briefs, her hand coming to rest on his ass cheeks. She gave them a squeeze, humming appreciatively.

His cock stirred, the traitor.

"Now the shirt," Aurora whispered. "No fair that I'm the only one naked."

This was the moment. His one last chance to undo what he'd just done. Or at least, mitigate the damage. But all the walls he'd constructed to hide how he was feeling—all his perfectly honed control—had already crumbled into dust. Broken irreparably when he'd tasted her and heard her moaning in answer.

There was no going back. Not from this. Not from her.

Chapter Twenty-Three

*H*e still hadn't said anything. Indecision played across his face.

Please don't leave, Aurora thought. *Stay with me. Be with me.*

Devon stepped out of his pants and kicked them aside. He gathered the bottom of his shirt into his hand and yanked it off in one smooth movement. And now his body was finally, gloriously, on display. The torso and arms she'd seen before— the light dusting of dark hair across his chest and down his ridged stomach, the tattoo on his inner forearm. She ran her hands over his pecs, feeling the taut muscle beneath. His skin was soft, hot under her palms.

But this time, she could see how that trail of hair led down past his belly button and to his crotch. His cock was half-erect. Thick, cut, and roped with veins.

Aurora wanted to keep staring at the rest of him, but Devon yanked her against him, lifting her up in the air. Her legs circled his waist. One of his hands supported her, while the other cupped the back of her head. Their mouths collided. His kiss was unrelenting, his tongue stroking hers. His teeth nipped her bottom lip. Then he moved to her neck, carrying her out of the bathroom and into the bedroom.

He dropped her roughly onto the bed. She bounced on the mattress and propped herself on her elbows. Over six feet of pure, sexy masculinity stood over her. His eyes were like two dark flames, his gaze burning her skin with need.

Then Devon got onto his knees in front of her. His hard-on bobbed from the movement, but he ignored it. "Lay back for me and spread your legs. I need to taste you."

"But you already…"

"Once wasn't enough."

After his near silence in the bathroom before, his sudden talkativeness triggered a rush of wetness between her legs. "Oh, say something else. Devon Whitestone talking dirty just became my number-one fantasy."

His lips slid into a lop-sided grin. "Hmm, maybe later… After you come on my tongue again." He pushed her legs apart. She moaned as his head lowered. He started slowly, that talented tongue tracing circles around her clit. She was sensitive from his prior attentions, but the gentle motions began working her back towards the edge.

He licked her faster. Soon, the pleasure was building. So close. Her need was almost unbearable. "Don't stop," she panted. "God, yes."

His eyes flicked up to hers. A smile broadened on his mouth as he flexed his tongue, changing the pressure. And then she was over the edge, shaking, calling his name.

She was still catching her breath when he surged upward. His mouth crashed onto hers. His weight pressed her down, deliciously heavy. He rocked his hardness against her thigh.

"Please tell me you have a condom," she said.

He cursed. His weight disappeared, leaving her cold. She watched him scour the room, opening drawers and checking cabinets. But it was the perfect chance to admire him. His leg muscles were sculpted. Shapely calves, broad thighs. Round, tight ass.

Okay, now she was getting impatient.

"Thank fuck." Devon held up a shiny foil package. "I'm going to owe Chase after this."

"You and me both. Come here." She got up from the bed and grabbed the condom from his hand when he got close. "It's your turn to lie down."

"Look who's bossy, now?" A grin drew up at the corner of his mouth.

"Is that okay?" She bit her lower lip, more out of anxiety than an attempt to be sexy. Her ex always got annoyed when she wanted to take charge during sex. Sometimes he'd even lost his erection, saying he felt emasculated. Just because she wanted a little bit of control in bed. Or at the very least, give and take.

But Devon seemed intrigued. "I guess it's only fair." His hand rested on her waist, and his eyebrow arched flirtatiously. "What are you going to do to me?"

"Straddle you. Fuck you."

His eyes burned again, two pools of liquid flame.

"Pretty sure you can't make me."

She studied his body again. He was so much bigger than her, had so much power coiled up in those muscles, ready to strike. Fight and defend. The thought of this man underneath her made her legs weak. "I've already made you do all *kinds* of things."

Something flickered across his face. Guilt, hesitation. She cupped his neck, pulling him down into a kiss. "Don't think about anything outside of this room. It's just us."

"Just us," he repeated. His erection pressed urgently against her.

Now or never, she thought, nervousness and anticipation blooming in her belly. She wanted this so badly. To set the pace, make him come undone beneath her. Devon was as alpha as any man she'd ever met. Yet he also made her feel safe enough to show him this side of herself.

"You owe me a ride, cowboy. You're going to do what I say. Now *lie down.*"

Chapter Twenty-Four

$\mathcal{D}$evon stretched himself out on the mattress. His hand circled his erection, but she shook her head.

"Hands off. That's mine."

Aurora got onto her hands and knees on the bed, then crawled toward him. She straddled his thighs and tore open the condom wrapper. The latex rolled onto him in her deft hands. Using protection had never turned him on so much.

She backed away to kiss a line along one thigh, then the other. The kisses progressed upward along his stomach. His chest. But she wasn't letting any part of herself touch him where he needed it most.

"You're making me crazy," he growled.

She laughed, and her mouth slanted down onto his. He kissed her back, vigorously. Sucking her tongue and lips. Nipping at her neck.

Aurora straightened. Carefully, she lined up her opening over his tip. He felt her heat.

"Do you want me?"

"Yes. Now." He could no longer manage more than single syllables.

She started to lower herself onto him, inch by inch. He

had to squeeze his eyes shut. She was so tight. He held onto her hips, wanting to thrust into her. But she grabbed his hands and pushed them back to the bed.

"Your arms had better stay here. What happened to all that self-control?"

You destroyed it, he thought.

Aurora trailed kisses down his throat. "I'm going to fuck you when I'm good and ready."

Finally, she'd sank herself all the way to his base. She started to move, undulating her hips against him. His cock slid partway out of her, then home again, over and over. She licked her lips, looking down at him. It didn't take long for her to speed up, her features tightening as she enjoyed him.

He'd never seen anything so beautiful, so impossibly sexy as this: Aurora spread over him, using his cock with abandon, taking whatever pleasure she wanted from him. All he had to do was sit back and watch. She wasn't trying to dominate him, really. At least he didn't feel particularly submissive. But he understood that she wanted to be in charge of her own pleasure. And he fucking loved it.

"Squeeze my nipples," she commanded.

"Yes, ma'am."

He rolled the little pink nubs between his thumbs and forefingers. She tipped her head back, crying out. Devon groaned. One more scream out of her like that, and he wouldn't be able to hold back his orgasm.

She pushed her hands into his shoulders for more leverage. His hips lifted off the bed, meeting her, and she didn't complain. They moved together in perfect sync. "Devon," she gasped out, and then she shuddered, her movements turning staccato.

When he was sure she was finished, he bucked himself into her slick wetness. He didn't take his eyes off her as he came, pumping into her until he was spent.

They sprawled onto the bed side by side, panting. For a few minutes, he couldn't move.

Reality started to come back. But not the panic or the guilt. Their chemistry was too strong. Aurora was like a drug, and he'd resisted for as long as he could. Now, he was hooked.

Distantly, he thought of the danger outside. The men who'd come after Aurora. They were still out there, searching. Plotting.

Devon would die before he let them touch her. The rest of it? His job, her brother? He couldn't deal with that right now.

He left briefly to get rid of the condom, and then he was back next to her, pulling her close. She turned so that he was behind her, curving around her. He lay a path of kisses along her shoulder to her ear.

"You're a firecracker," he whispered to her.

She smiled lazily. "You're pretty smoking yourself."

"I need to go check on things. But I'll be right back, okay?"

She rolled over, eyes worried. "Promise?"

He stroked her cheek. "I promise. I can't wait to get back here." She grabbed his hand and kissed it. She looked so sweet there on the pillow. He was already looking forward to the next time he'd have her, wondering what position they should choose.

He was in so much trouble. But he still had a job to do, regardless of how badly he'd screwed up.

He'd just have to find some way to do both—protect her and have her. Because there was no way they could go back to whatever they were before. They'd already crossed the point of no return.

WHEN HE CAME BACK to bed, she was dozing. He slid in beside her. She smiled, eyelids fluttering.

"Everything looks good out there. Nice and quiet."

"Mmmm."

Her body was small but firm. He loved the way she fit perfectly against his side.

"Are you okay?" she asked sleepily.

"Better than okay." The last time he'd gotten laid, he'd still been in the army. And though he'd liked that girl and showed her a nice time, she hadn't meant nearly as much to him.

"You're not going to flip out over what we just did?"

"Flip out? Me? I'm way too cool under pressure."

Her head popped up to smirk at him. "If someone's pointing a gun at you, maybe. But if a woman kisses you?"

"This was a weird situation. You have to admit that." And there were still so many complications. He pulled her back down against him and ran his fingers through her hair. "But I don't regret a single second of it."

"Good," she whispered. The word was full of self-consciousness.

"Do *you* regret it?"

"Not at all. Especially now that I know you don't."

An image flashed through his mind of her on top of him. "I loved how demanding you were. Just in case you couldn't tell."

Her fingers tightened on his arm. "I'm glad. Not all guys are into being told what to do. My ex wasn't."

He ignored the surge of jealousy caused by her mention of another man. "Then he must've been insecure. I like it when you're bossy." He trailed a hand down her back and rested his palm on the curve of her rear. "This ex of yours. He's the reason you moved back to West Oaks?"

"Sort of."

Devon didn't want to hear about her with someone else. But he could tell that she needed to talk about it. Clearly, this past relationship was weighing on her mind. "What happened?"

She heaved a sigh. "Justin was my college boyfriend. He was the quarterback of his high school football team, but he chose to go to school on an academic scholarship. He was pre-med. Great on paper, obviously. I didn't realize at first how arrogant he was. My friends and my interests were never as important as his. He would poke fun at my classes. Like my major wasn't serious enough. He usually didn't seem controlling. He was more manipulative than that. He liked to take care of me and spoil me. Buying me gifts and taking me on surprise trips. I thought it was so sweet. But my senior year, after he started medical school, he got a lot worse. He was always belittling me for wanting to be a party planner, even though I loved the internships I was doing. He didn't like when I talked about what *I* wanted. Either inside the bedroom, or out of it."

So that explained her hesitation earlier about taking charge. Her jerk of an ex must've shamed her for it.

"I finally realized that Justin's attempts to 'take care' of me were really about *him*. He wanted to control me, as if I was an extension of him and not a separate person. And I actually let him do it. For *years*. I barely had a life separate from him in St. Louis. Not my own apartment, my own car, my own credit cards. Not even many of my own friends."

"That's hard to picture. The Aurora Bennett I know is no pushover."

"I know! I think he gave me just enough leeway that I felt assertive, but he always had the final say on anything that mattered. But eventually, I told Justin I wasn't happy, and he responded by setting up this elaborate marriage proposal at our college's homecoming game. As if I wouldn't be able to refuse if he just blinded me with an empty romantic gesture. But instead, it finally opened my eyes. After I left him, I had nothing. I could've struggled on, I guess, but I didn't even know who I was in St. Louis. Coming back home made so much more sense."

"And you felt like Max was doing the same thing? Trying to control you?" Devon stroked her back, and she melted against him.

"*Yes.* He was always protective when I was a kid, maybe because he's so much older. I know that Max loves me. He's been an ideal brother in so many ways. But I can't lose myself again."

"I get that." He closed his eyes, nestling his head into the pillow. Aurora's fraught relationship with her brother made a lot more sense now. He recalled his promise not to lie, and he hadn't. But Devon had still held back a key piece of information.

Aurora might need protection physically since some ruthless bastards were after her. But she needed no protection from the truth.

"There's something I should probably tell you. Max ordered me not to touch you."

She sat up. "Wait. He what?"

"When he first asked me to take on this assignment. I'm sure he was worried about someone taking advantage of you. He made me swear I'd keep my hands off you... And he implied he'd fire me if I didn't."

Which Devon had been trying not to think about. It wasn't Aurora's concern. He absolutely didn't want to worsen her relationship with her brother. But he was sure that Aurora would want to know.

"Fire you? Unbelievable. Un-freaking-believable."

"Honestly, if it was my sister? And I was hiring some of the guys I was in the army with? I'd have made them swear not to touch her, either." He wasn't going to argue Max's case further. He'd already tried that, and Aurora wasn't disposed to listen.

"You're telling me not to be angry?"

"No. I wouldn't dream of that. But I *would* like you to

know that normally I'd never do this. Sleep with someone I was hired to protect."

Her scowl lessened, and the corner of her mouth ticked upward in a smile. "Are you saying I'm special?"

"Very special." Devon hooked his arm around her waist, drawing her against him. He kissed her forehead, her nose. "After this is over, I'd like to take you out. Keep getting to know you. That was what I hoped I might do before— assuming I could get Max's blessing—but then…"

Her leg draped across his hip. "I was too irresistible."

"Damn right."

"So, you like me?"

"Yeah, I do. A lot." His body was reacting to her, showing her just how much he liked her.

"I like you too, Whitestone." She rubbed herself against him. This girl was insatiable. Maybe as insatiable as he was. Now that he'd given in to his craving, the carnal urge to fuck was overpowering.

Then she pulled away, sitting up again. Her expression had gone back to serious. "Let me handle my brother. He'll probably be mad, but I'll make sure he doesn't take it out on you. Until then? We'll keep this just between us."

"I can live with that."

She crawled on top of him and captured his mouth in a kiss. Devon reached for another condom.

Chapter Twenty-Five

$\mathcal{I}$n the morning, Aurora woke to over two-hundred pounds of man snoozing beside her. She propped her head up, just watching him. Devon was sweet all the time, but he was especially cute when he slept. Although she wasn't sure if he would object to being called "cute."

But Devon had already surprised her by not being what she expected. Maybe "alpha" men weren't really the problem. Some of them just gave the others a bad name.

She didn't know what they were going to do about Max, but they would figure that out later. Right now, she was too content to dwell on her brother and their issues. Even amidst the awfulness of the past few days, she was happy. In fact, she couldn't remember the last time she'd felt this bubbly inside. Not just happy, but completely alive. That was probably the adrenaline talking, but she also knew that Devon had every-thing to do with it.

She was sore between her legs, and she relished the feeling. They'd been up half the night. When it came to fucking, Devon's body *was* like a wind-up toy, ready on command. But he was passionate and attentive, too.

Maybe they would have met eventually, at some coffee

shop on Ocean Lane, or at her brother's office once she went for another visit. But as crazy as it seemed, maybe it was better meeting this way. In times of crisis, a person's true personality showed through. She and Devon already knew each other better than she'd ever known her ex, Justin. Which was depressing, in a way, because she'd been with Justin for so many years. It revealed to her how much she had grown.

Perhaps the universe had a sense of humor. Her life was in danger, and her fledgling career was in jeopardy. Yet she'd also met Devon right at the moment that she was most ready to be herself.

A phone rang.

The day before, Sylvie had left behind a burner phone for them. It sat on the dresser, jangling and buzzing.

Devon stirred beside her, snapping almost instantly awake. Before she could even get up, he had already launched across the room and answered the phone.

"Devon here."

Aurora had to cover her mouth over her laugh. Whoever he was talking to, they had no idea that he was buck naked right now. Or that she was covered in only a thin sheet right behind him. After a minute or two, it became clear that the caller was Sylvie.

"When will the car arrive?"

His eyes met hers. So Max was getting them out of here, apparently. Aurora felt ambivalent. She wanted to go some-place more secure, especially if that meant Devon wouldn't be in the direct line of fire. But she had also started to think of this cozy house as their place. She had no idea how many other people would be around them in one of Max's safe houses.

"Yes, we'll be ready." Devon punched the phone and set it down. "Sylvie said the car will be here in about an hour. She and Max are confident that nobody inside Bennett Security was involved in the attack. They think the leak came from somewhere inside the police department. They want to get us to a safe house."

To Aurora's disappointment, Devon was already pulling on clothes. "Max is sending one of his armored vehicles to get you."

"And what about you? You're coming with me, right?"

His face twitched, hardly betraying anything. "I'm going to take the car that Sylvie left on the next street and follow at a distance. Tactically, it makes a lot of sense. We need multiple vehicles to address a threat if we're followed."

Aurora couldn't remember where she had left her clothes. Oh, the bathroom. That shower seemed like forever ago. "But I haven't even fixed Chase's curtain rod yet."

Devon grinned at her. "We'll figure that out later. I think I owe Chase a full house cleaning."

No kidding. Aurora set about getting dressed and gathering up her extremely few belongings. Then she tidied up as best she could, pulling off the sheets from the bed and gathering up the towels to put in Chase's washer. Her stomach felt too unsettled for breakfast, so she sat down at her laptop to check her email.

Sylvie had written to both her and Devon during the night. Once again, it looked like Sylvie had been working instead of sleeping, even though she had claimed to be getting some needed rest.

Sylvie's message said that she had tracked down the license plate on the black Escalade. Unfortunately, it belonged to a Ford Taurus stolen from an airport a month ago.

Devon came up behind her. "You saw the message from Sylvie? Figures that the plates were fake. The car itself was probably stolen, too. Doesn't get us any closer to identifying our mystery man."

"The only real connection we have is Mrs. Wolfson." Aurora saw another message from the woman in her inbox, asking questions about the birthday party. "It would be easy for me to ask her."

He mentally debated. "All right, go ahead. It'll save some time. This safe house switch will take most of today to get settled."

She typed out the email, attaching the photo Sylvie had saved. She sent a copy to Jennifer Scoville, Brandon Wolfson's assistant, as well.

Devon squeezed her shoulder and leaned down to kiss her. She was glad to see that he hadn't completely gone back into bodyguard mode.

"I know you're eager to help with the investigation," he said, "but the most important thing right now is that we keep you safe. Lana needs you to testify if she's going to make her case. I'm sure Mrs. Wolfson would prefer that, too."

"You're right." Aurora still wrestled with being the subject of so much effort and attention. She didn't enjoy feeling like cargo to be shuffled from one location to another. Especially with no control over who was with her. But there was more at stake here than just her feelings. She owed it to Lana and everyone affected by the murder to get her testimony on the record.

Lana had warned her that the Syndicate might want to retaliate against her, even after she'd testified. But it was less likely. Witness retaliation was actually pretty rare overall. But if Max thought she needed a bodyguard going forward, Aurora was willing to discuss it.

The sooner all of that happened, the sooner she could get back to her life and figure out how to fit Devon into it— whether he was her bodyguard or not.

∾

THEY SAT in the living room, ready to go. The two laptops were packed into a bag at Aurora's feet. Devon had his gun strapped into the holster at his shoulder. Periodically, he glanced through the gap in the curtains to check the street. Aurora had wanted to sit next to him, but he had told her to stay farther back from the windows.

"Will it be much longer?" she asked. "It feels like we're in a time warp."

"It's only been five minutes. They're not due quite yet."

Chase's landline rang. Devon jumped up to answer it. "Hello?" He paused, looking confused. "Hello? Max, are you on your way?"

He hung up the phone. "Nobody there."

Aurora fidgeted nervously. "Is it important? Is Max okay?"

He glanced at the burner phone, which hadn't rung or received any new messages at all. "Maybe it was a wrong number. It was probably nothing."

She bounced her heels against the floor and her fingers on the couch cushion. Aurora wanted to get up and pace, but she had a feeling that Devon would find that distracting. His body had a tension to it that she hadn't seen since they'd first arrived at this house. He was on edge. And that made her anxious, too.

"I'm going to go check the back. Stay here." He walked across the house toward the kitchen.

Aurora thought of Lana, who was probably sitting in her office right now. Aurora's parents were traveling on Max's dime, and they probably had no clue that any of this was going on. Not that they'd been too concerned with her for years, anyway.

Aurora hadn't been envious of their vacation before since she hated to be so out of touch. She didn't like the thought of being stuck on some boat in the middle of the ocean, completely at the mercy of the weather and someone else's itinerary. But now, a trip to a faraway place didn't sound so bad. Maybe she and Lana would go on a cruise together once this insanity was over.

Or maybe she and Devon. Was it weird to want so much time with him already, when they'd only known each other a few days?

He was still in the kitchen, carefully checking the view from each of the windows.

Aurora heard a car engine. "I think they're here."

Devon strode toward her. When he got to the front window, Aurora was right at his elbow. The curtain flipped back by a centimeter under his fingertips. She caught a glimpse of something black and shiny.

Then everything started happening at once.

Devon screamed at her, "No! Get back!" He pushed her and she fell to the carpet, his weight rolling over her.

The world exploded into a storm of splinters and broken glass.

Chapter Twenty-Six

Rapid gunfire shattered the calm of the living room. Devon shielded Aurora with his body. His ears rang with the noise as his mind worked, trying to strategize.

He had caught a single glimpse of the black Escalade before the shots rang out. It had been just enough time to save them from being riddled with bullets. But now, Devon had to find a way to get Aurora out of the zone of danger. He didn't know if it was one person in that car or more. If several attackers might be flanking them even now, approaching them from the rear and sides of the house.

What would they expect Devon and Aurora to do? Were they trying to flush them out of hiding? Would they be waiting outside to pick them off once they showed their faces?

He had to choose. Stay or go? Neither option was ideal.

The gunfire paused. Then another burst strafed across Chase's living room. That settled it. Devon was going to get Aurora deeper into the house. Then, he could decide what to do next.

"Go towards the bedroom. I'll be right behind you."

Aurora crawled forward. Devon pulled the gun from its

holster and crawled along after her, keeping his head as low as possible.

Like always when he was in a crisis, a preternatural calm had fallen over Devon's mind and body. As if the rational part of him had fully separated from any trace of fear.

He and Aurora reached the bedroom, which faced the side of the house. At the window, Devon carefully stood to one side of the frame, keeping himself out of sight. With his gun at the ready, he checked one direction, then the other. No sign of any activity. He could see a neighbor next door in her kitchen, speaking into a phone with a panicked look on her face.

The gunfire had stopped, and he heard tires squealing. Perhaps it was just a drive-by, and the attacker was already driving away. The police would be here soon, which hopefully meant the attacker was already on his way out of the neighborhood.

But Max and Sylvie still hadn't determined whether someone inside the police department had leaked Aurora's identity.

Aurora was cowering on the floor, shaking. "What are we going to do?"

"I want to put some distance between us and this house, and then I'm going to contact Max. His car is still on the way. I'm going to have them pick us up." They could've gone for the car that Sylvie left behind, but Devon wanted the backup of more bodyguards. Briefly, he held Aurora's hand in his. "I'm going out the window first to make sure it's safe. Then you're going to follow me. Can you do that?"

She nodded, her eyes unfocused.

Constantly checking for assailants, Devon pushed aside the curtain and lifted the window sash. He vaulted over the sill and dropped onto the grass below. He pivoted left and right with his gun raised. When he was sure it was clear, he waved for Aurora.

She climbed out. "What now?"

"We're going to cut across some of the neighbors' yards." Most of the houses around here had low fences, so they were easy to climb over and provided a wide view of the surroundings.

Several frightened faces stared at them from windows as they passed, moving as quickly as they could from one property to the next.

At one point, someone burst out of his back door, shouting questions. But Devon didn't even slow. He didn't aim the gun at the neighbor, but he did make sure it was visible as they hurried onward. The guy quickly vanished back into his house.

They reached the next street. Devon told Aurora to get down while he scanned for threats. He didn't see any sign of the black Escalade or its driver. He had to assume it was the same man that they'd seen on the video footage. But he kept an eye out for anyone looking suspicious.

There was a sedan a block down, and Devon saw a woman and children inside. He ducked out of sight until the car had passed, more out of concern for innocent bystanders getting caught in any crossfire. Then he pulled Aurora up and they ran across the road to hide behind a hedge.

Devon pulled out the burner phone and dialed the only number that was programmed into the contacts. Max answered on the first ring.

"We heard there were shots fired at your address. Is Aurora all right?"

"No injuries. I've gotten her to the corner of Water Street and Birch Lane."

"Got it. I'm in the car. We're seven minutes out. Don't go anywhere if you can help it. We're coming to you."

As the minutes passed, Aurora's breathing got more and more ragged. Devon wrapped an arm around her and rubbed her arm. "Max is almost here. We're going to get through this."

She hugged him back and buried her face against his shoulder. "Chase's house—"

He almost smiled. "Don't worry about that. We'll take care of Chase, okay? But only after we take care of you."

"And you. I'm not going anywhere without you. No exceptions."

"Yes, ma'am. You're in charge."

"Damn right, I am," she murmured against him. Then Devon's smile faded. Dread surged through him.

The black Escalade had just turned onto the street.

"*Fuck,*" he said quietly.

Aurora lifted her head. "What?"

"Aurora, in about five seconds, I'm going to need you to climb that fence there and take cover behind the house. It's very important that you stay out of sight of the road."

"Why? What's happening?"

He held her close to him, partly to keep her from moving and giving them away. But mostly, he just needed to feel her and remind himself exactly what was at stake. This wasn't just a job anymore. He was going to do anything it took to get Aurora into her brother's car.

Devon glanced at his watch. Only two minutes had passed since he hung up with Max. Five more minutes until they would be here.

And that Escalade had almost reached them. Devon imagined the choreography in his mind. They would stay out of sight until the Escalade passed. But once it did, if the driver looked into his rear mirror, he would have a clear view of them where they currently sat.

So that meant a brief window when Aurora had to run for it, and Devon had to create a distraction. He didn't want to risk drawing gunfire toward an innocent person's house. But if Devon himself stayed out in the open, the asshole would keep his attention exactly where Devon wanted it.

"There's no time," he told her. "Right now, you just have to do what I say. I know you don't like it, but—"

"You just promised we were going to stay together. When I run, you're not coming with me, are you?"

Devon handed her the burner phone. "When Max calls, tell him where you are. It'll be like the rooftop terrace. I'll meet up with you." He would draw the Escalade away from her, then take Sylvie's car to catch up.

Tires rolled along the pavement, going much too slow. The driver had probably been circling, searching for them. The man assumed they were still on foot, which meant he might have even seen them running from the house. They would have to act quickly. This guy, whoever he was, wasn't stupid.

Devon felt the panicked energy in her body, just as clearly as if it were his own. "I need you to trust me. Now run."

At the same moment, black metal appeared in his peripheral vision. The SUV had just driven past.

Aurora darted the few yards to the next fence and swung her leg over.

The Escalade's tires screeched. It had stopped in the middle of the road. Devon was already racing toward the vehicle. He saw a glint of light against metal as the driver raised his own weapon.

Devon squeezed off a shot. The rear window of the vehicle splintered into a spider's web around the bullet hole. He crouched behind the bumper, then lunged out to fire twice more. He withdrew just as a bullet dinged off the fender.

Devon risked a quick glance in Aurora's direction. She'd disappeared over the fence.

The engine revved to life. Had the man seen her? Was he going after her? The driver probably hoped to cut her off at the next street.

He wouldn't stop until Aurora was lying in the dirt. Silenced.

Surrender is not a Ranger word, Devon thought. *He'll have to kill me if he wants to take her.*

The driver took another shot in Devon's direction, like he was thinking the same thing. The SUV peeled away. Devon ran after it, exchanging fire. Bullets widened the hole in the rear windshield.

He felt something pierce his left arm, as sharp and sudden as a bee sting. The vehicle rounded a corner and disappeared.

Pain rocketed up and down his arm. *I'm shot*, he realized. *Dammit. I don't need this right now.*

"Devon!"

Aurora appeared, running toward him. She grabbed him around the waist. Her eyes stared in horror at the growing patch of red on his shirt.

"Aurora, what are you doing here? If he sees you, he'll turn back around and come after you."

"Then let him. I'm not leaving you."

They ran for the cover of the hedge. Devon sank down onto the grass. His sleeve was now soaked with red. It was more than just a scratch. A lot more.

Devon ripped a strip off his T-shirt with his teeth. "Give me a hand?"

Aurora helped him tie a makeshift binding around the wound, cinching it tight. "Where's the phone? I need to get you to a hospital!"

"I'll be fine. You get out of here before that asshole comes back. Please."

She wouldn't listen. He debated picking her up and forcing her to move. But he couldn't carry her like this. He could walk beside her, but he'd be slow. And in a few minutes, if he didn't stop the blood loss, he'd be useless in a fight.

They heard a car speed onto the street, tires screeching. It had to be the Escalade. He had come back for them.

Devon checked his gun. Three bullets left. He pulled a

spare magazine from his holster and replaced it. "Aurora, *go.* I'll hold him off." *For as long as I can.*

Aurora's eyes were wide. "Not without you."

There was only one thing Devon could do—stop the car before it reached them. The engine gunned as the car sped down the road. He looked out from behind the tree, taking aim at the approaching black SUV.

His finger curled on the trigger.

But it wasn't the Escalade at all.

The vehicle skidded to a halt. Max Bennett jumped out of the passenger side, holding a shotgun. Another Bennett Security bodyguard—Tanner—got out of the back. They raced over.

"Max! Help him!"

Max gathered his sister and pulled her toward the car. Tanner hefted Devon into a standing position.

"Looks like you made one hell of a mess, Whitestone," Tanner said.

"You have no idea."

Chapter Twenty-Seven

*T*he car raced out of Chase's neighborhood. Some beefy guy was sitting in between her and Devon.

"He needs a hospital," Aurora said.

"Tanner is a field medic." In the front seat, Max had his phone to his ear and was alternating between speaking to Aurora and shouting commands into the device. He was telling Sylvie to check surveillance footage for the black Escalade. They had to find out where it had gone.

But Aurora could only think about Devon. He'd been shot. He was bleeding. Her stomach had lodged right in her throat. *Please let him be all right.*

Devon was too quiet. She leaned around Tanner. "What's happening?"

Tanner was doing something to Devon's arm. "I applied a quick-clotting agent from my kit. Looks like the bullet went straight through. He's in some pain, but it doesn't look too bad. I'll bet he's had worse."

Devon nodded slightly. "This is nothing." The muscles in his jaw bulged like he was clenching his teeth together. His eyes found hers, and Aurora saw so much strength there. She wished that she were the one checking on him. Holding him.

He'd taken a bullet trying to protect her. She had to do *something*.

She'd had every intention of running as far and fast as she could, just as Devon had instructed. But when she'd heard those gunshots, she'd frozen. She just couldn't leave him behind. And when she'd actually seen him get hit?

Her heart had burned with the knowledge: *my man is in trouble*. Though Devon obviously wasn't her man, not after such a short time together. They were barely even dating. And she obviously didn't have the right training or abilities. But in the moment, none of that mattered. Nothing could've stopped Aurora from going back to help him.

Max turned around. "You're sure the Escalade driver was the same guy you saw before?"

"Um, yes." Aurora had to tear her gaze away from Devon.

Max's face made a funny expression, glancing from her to Devon and back again. Did he see something there?

"Definitely the same guy. I think I saw him at the 'Angels and Demons' party, too."

"And Sylvie said he wasn't part of the Syndicate. So, what the hell is going on?" Max slammed his palm against the dashboard. "And how the fuck did he know where you were? As of this morning, nobody except the people in this car—and Sylvie—knew where you were."

And Chase and Lana, Aurora thought, but she didn't think it would help to say it.

Tanner had tensed beside her. Aurora didn't know the guy, but he seemed to be doing everything in his power for Devon, so she was disposed to like him.

Max shook his head like he was shaking off the thought. "Once we get back to the office, we'll reassess."

"That's where we're going? Your headquarters?"

But Max didn't answer. He'd sunk down in his seat, apparently deep in thought.

"You'll be safe there," Tanner murmured. "You'll have

half a dozen bodyguards and all of your brother's tech to protect you, not to mention bullet-proof glass and steel-reinforced doors."

"I wasn't thinking about me. What about medical facilities? Devon needs a real doctor."

"We've got one on call. We'll take care of him."

Aurora reached past Tanner and put a hand on Devon's leg. Tanner's eyebrow arched, but that disappeared when she scowled.

"I'm really okay," Devon whispered. "I just wish I'd stopped that bastard before he got away."

Tanner chuckled. "You're lucky the bullet hit your left arm. That right hand's your closest friend."

Devon used the hand in question to flip Tanner off.

Aurora could hardly sit still. She stared out the window, jumping at every black SUV that passed. They wound through the streets of West Oaks and then onto the freeway, where the ocean appeared, glittering in the distance.

Around ten minutes later, they pulled into the driveway of a brick building. This was the far edge of the waterfront, past the nightclubs and boutiques of Ocean Lane and the touristy beaches. Here, the waves crashed directly onto rocks and tossed foam into the air.

The driver swiped a keycard against the reader, and a heavy metal door opened. Inside, they parked in a garage among a handful of other cars. Bright lights flooded the space, making every corner visible. Although the vehicles were average, it looked more like a car showroom than a typical parking garage.

Max breathed out, fixing the shotgun back into a special case below the dashboard. He pushed open the passenger side door. "Lock down the building," he said to the driver. "Tanner, take Devon to the infirmary and have the doctor contact you directly when he arrives."

Aurora got out on shaky legs. Immediately, she rounded

the car to the other side, where Tanner was helping Devon to stand.

Max reached for her arm. "Aurora, come with me. This place might look secure, but I'd feel a lot better if you were upstairs in my office."

"I'd rather stay with Devon. I want to make sure—"

"Whitestone can manage just fine without you. Can't he?" Her brother regarded her, scrutinizing her response.

Devon's sharp gaze warned her. She was giving too much away.

"The guy got shot trying to protect me. Don't I owe him a little concern?"

Max put a firm hand against her back, ushering her toward an elevator. "True. He made all of us proud. I take care of my people, Aurora, and Devon will be no exception. Now let's get you upstairs. Lana is waiting."

As the doors slid open, she couldn't help glancing back at Devon. He was settling into a wheelchair that someone had brought down. He didn't look in her direction.

The elevator whisked her and Max to the main floor. They walked out onto polished concrete. One side of the massive space was all windows overlooking the ocean. The view was spectacular, just sky and water stretching away from the horizon, and Aurora paused for a second to take it in.

We will get through this, she thought, repeating Devon's words from earlier. Her heart tugged, wanting to know where he'd gone. Whether he was in pain. But Max gestured for her to follow him.

While the front half of the main floor was pure windows, the back half was an ocean of computer screens. They showed various camera feeds, metrics, databases. Far more information that Aurora could begin to process. Desks occupied the open workspace, with a dozen employees chatting or poring over the data on their screens. They all looked up as she entered.

Sylvie dashed over and gave her a hug. "Thank god you're okay! I'm so sorry, Aurora. I'm trying to track the guy who attacked you. I swear to you, I'll find him."

"I know."

"If I'm the one that led him to you, if he followed me…"

Aurora didn't want her to blame herself for the attack. "I can't imagine that's it. I have faith in you. You'll figure it out. But could you check on Devon for me? I'm really worried."

"Of course."

"I'm up this way." Max waved her toward an open-riser staircase made of more glass and steel.

Aurora said goodbye to Sylvie and followed her brother.

Max's office was perched above the others, with glass walls overlooking his employees beneath. So much money must've gone into building this. Max had to be proud of it. But her brother had always liked to show off a bit, even when they were younger and had nothing. Max would deprive himself to save up for one nice pair of shoes or a trendy coat. It was like he wanted to prove to the world that nobody could keep him down. Her brother had liked to portray a careful image. Strength, prosperity, ease. Even though their lives had never been easy, especially his.

"Aurora!" Lana ran out of Max's office and wrapped her in a bear hug. "I was so scared!"

Tears stung Aurora's eyes as she returned her friend's embrace.

"Get in here," Lana said.

They sat together on the couch. Max came in behind them, closing the door. From Aurora's seat, she could still see the gorgeous ocean landscape, but the workspace and its busy screens had disappeared from view.

Lana rubbed the knots between Aurora's shoulders. "You're sure you're okay? Do you need anything, like maybe some tea?"

I need to know how Devon's doing, Aurora thought. She

remembered what Devon had said—he just kept looking forward. That was the only way to cope. Aurora needed to do the same.

"Water would be great. And maybe some coffee?"

"I'll call downstairs. Someone will bring it up, cause this place is *fancy*."

"No kidding." She got up and paced.

Max stopped her, putting his hands on both sides of her face. "We're all thanking our stars that you're safe. I should've brought you back here the same night of Wolfson's murder."

"I wouldn't have wanted to be stuck here, anyway."

He smiled wryly. "I'm sure you wouldn't. But I underestimated Crane. I'm not going to let that happen again. The guy who went after you is staying ahead of us for now, but I've got my best people on it."

"And Chase Collins? It was his house that got shot up."

"I'll do whatever I can. Even write him a check and help arrange contractors."

She was glad about that. So many people had been affected by this mess. "There must be something I can do. Max, if I have to sit here like some princess in a tower, I'll lose it."

"You'll manage. The sooner I shut all of Crane's people down, the sooner this will be over." He strode toward the exit, already thumbing his phone. "I'll be back later."

The door clicked closed behind him. Through the glass, Aurora could see him jogging down the stairs.

Aurora threw up her hands. "You see how impossible he is? He doesn't listen to me!"

Lana shook her head, and Aurora suspected she was annoyed at both brother and sister. "Sometime, you two need to sit down and have a candid discussion. But this is not that moment. There's way too much going on. Speaking of—come back here. Slow down and breathe." She tugged Aurora to the couch. "Tell me honestly. What are you feeling right now?

This office is soundproof, by the way. Scream if you need to get it out."

"I'm tempted." Aurora dropped her face into her hands. "My head is spinning. Last night was possibly the best night of my life, and today was in the top five for the worst."

"Last night? What do you mean? Wait…"

Aurora looked up.

A devious smile had spread across her friend's face. "Do you mean *Devon*? You and the hot-neighbor-who's-actually-your-hot-bodyguard?"

Aurora shushed her. "Quiet. Max probably has listening devices in here."

Lana made a face. "No, he doesn't. We're fine. Now you have to tell me *everything*."

This topic was the perfect distraction. Once Aurora got going, she kept finding more to say about Devon. How easy he was to talk to, how kind, how he'd lost so much, yet had such an open, generous heart. She didn't kiss and tell, not in any detail. A jealous part of her wanted their sexiest moments all to herself. But she hinted that Devon was every bit as good-looking with his clothes off. And every bit as strong.

Lana nudged her arm. "You really like this guy."

"Yeah. I think I do. I know it's fast, but Devon is amazing. He did lie to me about his identity, which pissed me off, as you know. But I understand now that it wasn't his choice." Aurora frowned as she thought of her brother. "And do not defend him," she added when Lana opened her mouth. "Max actually threatened to fire Devon if he touched me. So, you can't even hint to Max about what you know."

"I'm not getting in the middle of you two. These lips are sealed." Lana glanced at her watch. "Well, sealed about you and Devon. I have a conference call in twelve minutes."

"You do?"

"With Dominic Crane's defense counsel. He called before you arrived, just after the news broke about the second attempt on your life. Which can't be a coincidence. Usually, I'd be in my own office over at the judicial center, but with you in danger and Max consulting on the case, I've been camped out here."

Aurora felt a surge of fury. "Tell them I won't be intimidated. I'm going to testify, no matter what."

"You could tell them yourself. Jump on the call with me. Make them squirm." Lana tapped her fingertips together like she couldn't wait.

"Tempting. But actually, I'd rather spend my time a different way."

"Do you need a shower? I brought some of your clothes here."

"Ugh, yes. You're the best, thank you. And then, I have an idea to get this princess out of her tower."

"Is this idea going to make Max furious with me when he finds out?"

"Probably. But I'll be furious with you if you don't help me, so…" This wasn't true, and they both knew it. But Aurora really did need her best friend's help right now. That was the only way she could stage the escape attempt she had in mind.

Lana groaned. "All right. Tell me what to do. But we'd better make it quick because I am *never* late for a conference call."

Chapter Twenty-Eight

*T*he doctor finished bandaging Devon's upper arm. He'd already cleaned the wound. Apparently, the bullet had gone through the soft tissue, causing minimal damage. Otherwise, he would've been on his way to the closest hospital for surgery.

"I'm prescribing antibiotics," the doc said, "as well as pain relief as needed. Can you make it with just ibuprofen, or do you need something stronger?"

"Ibuprofen is fine." Devon felt like he'd been hit by a truck, but he wanted to keep his head clear.

"Whitestone is our resident martyr," Tanner said from the corner. He was sitting in the visitor's chair, legs sprawled casually.

Devon flipped him off again with his right middle finger. The doctor chuckled. "I'll leave you to it, then. The paper I gave you has the instructions for keeping the wound clean. Call if there's any sudden redness, swelling, or fever."

"Thank you."

The doctor stripped off his gloves and left.

Tanner stood up, stretching. "You got lucky. That was

some serious shit. You must be looking forward to getting back to desk duty."

"I'm sure my mom is looking forward to that." Devon had asked Tanner to send off a message to Ruby and their mother, just to confirm that he was all right. For the second time in just a few days, he'd been in the line of fire. He couldn't imagine how his mom must be feeling right now.

"But what about *you*?" Tanner asked. "Desk duty not so exciting anymore?"

"Doesn't matter what I think."

"Mother-freaking-Teresa." Tanner shook his head.

Devon certainly hadn't enjoyed getting shot. Yet, for the first time since he'd started at Bennett Security, he felt completely alive. He'd been using all his skills and training. He felt like he'd been serving his highest purpose—protecting an innocent person. Just like his dad, and just like Kellen. That made Devon prouder than he'd been since leaving the service.

This is where I belong, he thought. *Protecting people.* Not selling expensive security systems to the wealthiest residents of West Oaks. And not sitting behind a desk. Those roles were important, too. But Devon belonged out in the field.

Did that matter, though? Nope. Nothing had changed. He still had his mom and Ruby to think of.

And Aurora. She was a new element in his life. He'd spent just a few days with her, and he only wanted more. He didn't know how to make everything work.

"What's Bennett's sister like?"

Devon shrugged, looking down at his feet. How could he possibly answer that question without giving his feelings away?

"Smart. Seems nice."

"Yeah, she seemed *real* nice." Tanner grinned and ran a hand over his beard. "I've only seen her once around here, and it's no wonder Bennett tries to keep her under wraps."

Devon's hackles raised. "Careful," he said through his teeth. "She's the boss's sister."

But Tanner just laughed. "Something tells me I'm not the one who needs to be careful."

Someone knocked at the infirmary door. "Everybody decent?"

Tanner opened the door. Sylvie came in, holding cups of something steaming.

Aurora was right behind her. "Hey, how are you feeling?" Her hair was damp, and she'd changed clothes. Jeans and a cropped tee had never looked so good. His heart rate jumped at the sight of her.

He had it so bad for this girl.

"I'm all patched up. It wasn't too bad." Devon sat up against the pillows, ignoring the throb of pain in his injured arm. Aurora had stopped at the end of the bed. He couldn't take his eyes off her.

"Whitestone could've lost three-fourths of his limbs, and he'd still say it 'wasn't too bad,'" Tanner scoffed.

Sylvie handed one cup to Tanner and set the other by Devon's bed. "Lattes, fresh from the fancy coffee maker in the break room. But you know, Tanner, I meant to grab you one of those cookie things. We should probably go back to get it."

"We should, shouldn't we? I guess we'll have to leave these two alone."

"Aurora, I gotta take care of this cookie situation and get back to work. My break time is almost over. I'm sure you can take care of our patient?"

Tanner made another snide comment under his breath, and then finally, they were gone.

Aurora came over and sat gingerly on the bed. "Are you in much pain?"

"Nah." He pulled her closer with his good arm, tucking her into his right side. "We both made it here, and you're in one piece. So, I can't complain. Although I still think you should've run when I told you, instead of coming back for me." That had worked out fine since Max had ended up finding them instead of the attacker. But it had been pure luck.

"I'm not that great at following orders. If this thing between us is going to last beyond today, you'll have to get used to it."

No kidding. "I'll do my best."

She settled her head against his pillow, looking back at him. "The past week I've seen some really terrible things. But watching you get hurt might be the worst."

"I had to protect you. I would've done a lot more."

"I know." Her fingers brushed his forehead and his temple. She pressed a gentle kiss to his lips. Her mouth was tender and kind and sensual all at once. His body was far too wrecked at the moment to get turned on. But his heart and his spirit felt replenished just having her near.

"I just wish I could make everything better," she said.

"You already are."

"Can I get you something to eat? Or rub your feet? You take care of other people all the time. Me, your family." Her kisses ran along the side of his neck. "I want to take care of *you*." She touched his inner thigh, making her meaning clear. Briefly, he imagined Aurora kneeling between his legs, her sweet lips wrapped around his cock. He liked that idea a lot.

"I will definitely take you up on that later. For now, just having you beside me is all I need."

Aurora was the best possible medicine. He'd never felt anything like this for a woman before. Like she was water, and he'd never realized until now how thirsty he was. His need for her scared him, and it was so much more than sexual.

"Okay. I'll stay right here all day if I can. Lana distracted my brother so I could get out of his office, and Sylvie set me up with a phone so she can tell me if Max is heading to the infirmary. So, we don't have to worry."

"Then I won't."

They kissed a while longer, and then just sat with their foreheads together. His thoughts strayed to darker places.

"What's wrong?" Aurora asked. "You're frowning. Do you need pain meds?"

"I was just thinking of Kellen."

"Your brother. Oh, Devon. No wonder."

His K tattoo was on his left arm. The doctor had given him a sling to keep his arm steady, so the ink was hidden. But he felt it there on his skin, a reminder of the twin he'd lost.

"I've never been shot before. They said Kellen died instantly. Didn't suffer. But when I realized I'd been hit earlier, I thought immediately of him. If he'd felt the same kind of impact and knew what it meant. How much time he had, what he might've been thinking."

Aurora's palm caressed his cheek. "He would've thought of you. How could he not? You're his twin."

"Maybe." Devon and Kellen had fought sometimes. They'd each battled to be "man of the house" after their father died. And in the months before Kellen died, Devon had been busy with missions. They hadn't spoken nearly enough. They'd taken the future for granted.

"The weird thing is that I feel even closer to Kellen now. Does that seem strange?"

"Because you've experienced the same thing he did?"

He nodded. "I've wondered, ever since he died, if he would've made different choices if he'd known what was coming. If he knew he'd have to make the ultimate sacrifice, would he have chosen a desk job? Or some other career altogether that was less dangerous? After today, I think I know the answer: he would've done it all the same. He was willing to give up everything to help other people. And that made his life even more precious, for every minute that it lasted."

Devon blinked back tears, and Aurora's eyes were shining. He couldn't believe he'd said all that. He'd avoided speaking about Kellen, even with his family, ever since that terrible day.

But with Aurora, the words had flowed effortlessly. And it felt damned good to have said them.

"You must miss him so much."

"Every fucking day." That did it. The tears overflowed, streaking down his cheeks. Aurora wiped them away. "I just wish I could live the way he did. Kellen knew the risks, but he lived with purpose. It's what I used to—"

He stopped when he realized what he was about to say. Devon used to have that sense of purpose in the army. But he'd lost it. He loved being near his mom and sister, of course, but he'd lost a part of himself.

"You used to what?"

He shook his head. "I was just thinking of the past."

He missed his unit, but overall, Devon didn't mind civilian life. Yet he wished he could find that sense of purpose again. Consulting on security systems wasn't enough. He wanted to face down the kind of danger that he'd seen today. He wanted to be a bodyguard.

His mom would never be okay with it. But maybe Ruby would, given their recent conversation.

And what about Aurora? Could she deal with dating a bodyguard who risked his life? What about settling down with a guy like that?

Settling down? a voice mocked in his head. *You are so far ahead of yourself.*

But he couldn't help it. Aurora snuggled against him, and he looked down at her, imagining waking up to this view each and every day. Then heading into work to protect the vulnerable. It wouldn't be a bad life.

But it was pure fantasy.

Aurora's phone buzzed in her pocket, and they both jumped. She got off the bed. "Hello?"

It's Lana, she mouthed. She gasped as she listened. "I'll be right up."

"What happened?" Devon asked when she ended the call.

"Lana spoke to Dominic Crane's lawyer. Crane says he had nothing to do with the attacks, and he wants to talk to *me*."

Devon sat forward, which made the pain in his arm flare. "No way. That can't possibly be safe."

"It'll happen by video. I don't have to leave the building. Lana hasn't told Max yet, but she thinks it's a good idea. I *do* want to know what Crane has to say for himself."

"Should I be there with you?" Devon didn't want Crane thinking about Aurora, much less looking at her, even on a screen. How could they possibly trust the word of a mobster and a murderer?

"I'd like that, but it's probably not wise." Aurora reached for his hand. "You should get some rest. And Max…"

He understood what she meant. The more time that Devon and Aurora spent around each other, the more likely that Max would notice their closeness. Devon wanted to tell Max the truth at the right time, and this wasn't it.

"I'm not very good at resting."

Aurora kissed his cheek. "Then consider this an order. Take a nap."

He threw up a salute.

She grinned. "I'll see you later."

It wouldn't be easy to stay in this bed, out of commission, while Aurora dealt with Dominic Crane—even if it was only through an internet connection. But he *was* tired. As soon as Aurora was gone, he felt his eyes closing. For the first time in a while, he couldn't keep his exhaustion at bay.

Chapter Twenty-Nine

Aurora went back upstairs. Max spotted her as she stepped out of the elevator. "Where have you been?"

"Checking on my bodyguard, the guy who got *shot*." She didn't like how defensive she sounded. But she'd live with concealing her feelings for the moment if it made things easier for Devon.

Max nodded begrudgingly. "I've been planning to get down to the infirmary, but it's been hectic up here. How is he?"

"The bullet didn't cause much damage. The doctor finished, and Devon's resting."

"Thank goodness." Her brother hooked an arm around her shoulders. "Lana told me the plan for the video meeting. You sure you want to do this? You don't owe Crane a damn thing."

"But if I can help end all this, I have to try. I refuse to be afraid of him."

Max sighed. "And that's exactly why I worry about you. You *should* be afraid of a man like him. But Lana is in favor of hearing him out, so I'll go with it."

They went up to Max's glass-box office. Lana was waiting.

"Crane appeared before the court yesterday, and the judge granted our request to deny bail. A huge victory. So today, his lawyers are at the jail in a meeting room. They've asked to talk, but I've got to tell you, they're being super cagey and weird. Even this video meeting they want is way beyond what's normal. But I have the feeling it'll be enlightening, at the very least."

"Do I have to say anything?" Aurora asked.

Lana tucked a stray lock of dark hair behind her ear. "It would be better if you don't. The district attorney has given me full authority to handle this case, so I'll do the talking. I don't think Crane's lawyers are playing games with us—this is way too risky for them—but if it's not productive or you aren't comfortable, we can end the call at any time."

"Okay." Aurora sat on the couch by Max's desk, trying to calm the butterflies in her stomach. "Where will the screen be? Are we using your phone, Lana?"

Max laughed. "We've got better equipment than just a phone." He hit a key on his computer keyboard. "Are they on the line?"

"Hold on." Lana's thumbs typed on her phone screen. "Yes. They're on the line."

Suddenly, one of the glass walls of the office turned opaque, and a different room appeared on a huge screen. A skinny man in a tan suit sat behind a table. Dominic Crane stood beside him, glowering at the camera in his prisoner jumpsuit. She'd built him up so much in her mind that she'd forgotten how young he was. Early thirties at most. He looked more haggard than the last time Aurora had seen him. But Crane still retained that air of royalty that she remembered. Thick, wavy hair, alabaster skin, and darkly beautiful features. His drab clothing didn't make him any less imposing.

Max's fancy wall screen made it look like Crane was standing right before her. Aurora suppressed a chill. This was the man who'd been trying to kill her. Because of Dominic

Crane, Devon was lying in an infirmary bed recovering from a gunshot wound.

That thought chased the fear away, leaving only seething anger.

Lana stood up, walking toward the screen. "Hello Mr. Sandford. Mr. Crane."

The two men nodded back.

"I thought the attorneys for Mr. Crane's co-defendants might be joining us?"

"No," Mr. Sandford said. "I've been in touch with them, but given the circumstances, I decided this meeting should just be us."

"And what circumstances are those?"

"The recent attempt on Mr. Crane's life."

Max slammed his hands on his desk. "Are you kidding? Crane's life? What about my sister being chased and shot at this afternoon? She was nearly killed for a second time. She's being terrorized!"

"That's exactly why I wanted us to speak," Crane said. "I had nothing to do with—"

Sandford held up his hands. "Everyone, please. This will be far more efficient if we refrain from emotional outbursts."

Max's fists were so tight, his knuckles were turning white. But he exchanged a glance with Lana and said nothing more. Neither did Crane.

Aurora didn't like sitting there silently after they'd been talking about her. But she had no idea what was going on here. Someone had tried to kill Crane? And it had sounded like he was about to claim no knowledge of the attack on Aurora. She couldn't understand it.

"What attempt on Mr. Crane's life?" Lana asked. "That's a shocking claim, and this is the first I'm hearing of it."

Sandford folded his hands on the desk. "Early this morning, someone here at the holding facility attacked him. They're refusing to talk. But—"

"I don't give a fuck about that," Max said. "What does Crane know about a black Escalade? Does the driver work for him?"

Crane shook his head. His face remained placid. "Why? Is that the vehicle that went after you, Miss Bennett?"

"Don't you speak to her."

Aurora jumped up from the couch. "*Enough*. All right? I can talk for myself."

Lana was shooting her warning glances. Aurora was supposed to let Lana handle this. But she couldn't just sit quietly while they discussed her.

The only person to actually address Aurora so far was Crane himself. Wasn't that messed up?

"Yes, someone driving a black Escalade tried to kill me today. Did you send him?"

"No, I did not."

"But why else are these people after me? You're trying to stop me from testifying about Wolfson's murder. I won't be intimidated."

Lana put a hand on Aurora's arm.

"And I wouldn't dream of trying to silence you," Crane said smoothly. "When the truth is known, I'm sure that I'll be exonerated in court."

She didn't see how that was possible. But Crane spoke with such confidence that she was tempted to believe him.

"How? I know what I saw in Wolfson's office."

Sandford leaned over to whisper something to Crane, probably a warning not to respond. But Crane wasn't listening any more than Aurora was.

"I didn't order Wolfson's death. Why would I? The man owed me money." Crane ignored his lawyer's horrified expression. "But if someone did, Wolfson deserved it. He was a betrayer and a human trafficker, nothing better than scum."

Aurora opened her mouth in shock. Brandon Wolfson? A human *trafficker*? That couldn't be true.

Sandford waved his hands over his head. "Not another word on that subject. We're not discussing Wolfson."

Lana looked amused. "Then let's get back on track, shall we? I appreciate the insight into your defense strategy on the murder charge, but I'd love to know why your client needed to speak to my witness."

Crane leaned forward toward the camera. "Because I am *not* trying to kill Miss Bennett. I run a lucrative promotion business, and certain people are jealous enough to resort to murder and deception to oust me."

"Promotion business?" Max scoffed. "Don't you mean gang of thugs and criminals?"

Crane tilted his head back, looking down his nose. "We invest in and promote restaurants and nightclubs like The Lighthouse. Brandon Wolfson stole some of my investment to run an unsavory business on the side. But Wolfson had more allies than I realized."

Lana cut her hands through the air, halting the conversation. "Hold on a moment. The men who invaded Aurora's apartment building were known associates of yours, Mr. Crane. Members of the Silverlake Syndicate. Like you. And you expect us to believe you didn't order that hit?"

"It's the truth. It's possible someone else who knows me got overzealous."

Max hit a few keys on his computer. A smaller window popped up on the large screen—the still image of the driver of the black Escalade from the surveillance footage. "What about this man? Have you seen him before?"

"Never."

Max rubbed a hand over his jaw. Aurora knew her brother's mannerisms. He remained skeptical, but he was considering Crane's claims. Could the man be telling the truth? Lana had said that the Escalade driver wasn't a known member of the Silverlake Syndicate. Something much bigger was going on here. Something that none of them understood.

Crane went around to the front of the table, sitting on its edge. They couldn't see Sandford behind him at all. "The fact is, Miss Bennett and I are both targets. Someone wants to get rid of me *and* stop Miss Bennett from testifying. Which means that we should be working together."

Sandford leaned his head to one side, trying to get back into the conversation. "That's why we want to arrange to get Miss Bennett's testimony on the record right away, as a sign of good faith."

Lana pointed at the man. "If you're spinning me some kind of bullshit about a preliminary hearing—"

"I'm talking about the procedure you requested, Ms. Marchetti. We're willing to agree."

Aurora exchanged a glance with her best friend. This was great news, right? As soon as Aurora testified, there would be no reason for anyone to come after her. At least, she hoped not.

"But Aurora will be testifying *against* you, Mr. Crane," Lana reminded him. "You're sure about this?"

The man shrugged one shoulder, unconcerned. "As I said, when the truth comes out, I'll be vindicated. Miss Bennett's testimony is only one side of the story." He inclined a head at Aurora. "But no matter what, I don't put pressure on women. That's not how I do business."

Again, she felt like he was in the room with her, instead of merely on a screen. But this time, Aurora wasn't unnerved by the impression. If he didn't mind her testifying, then he had to be telling the truth. His version of it, anyway.

Lana crossed her arms. "But what about Crane's co-defendants, Mr. Sandford? They'll have to agree, too. They're entitled to object, and to question her when she's under oath."

"Of course. I'm confident I can get them on board."

"All right. But what do you want in exchange for all this cooperation? Don't even think about immunity. Not unless you're willing to give up a lot more."

Crane spoke over his lawyer. "Get the judge to reconsider his decision to deny me bail. Whoever is trying to kill me, they have the best chance of getting to me here in holding."

Lana nodded. "I think I can get the district attorney to agree to that. With conditions, of course, including electronic monitoring."

The lawyers spent a few more minutes discussing logistics and schedules, then ended the conference. Aurora exhaled, sinking back against the couch. They'd scheduled her testimony for the day after tomorrow at the courthouse.

"I can't believe that Crane wasn't behind those attacks," Aurora said. "Assuming we believe him."

Max grunted noncommittally.

But Lana looked thoughtful. "I'm inclined to accept what he says. It makes sense, honestly. I've been hearing rumors from my friends in the L.A. District Attorney's Office. There's discord within the Silverlake Syndicate. Dominic took over less than a year ago, and some people aren't happy about it. They see him as weak compared to his older brother. He has a reputation for avoiding certain income streams—human trafficking, underage prostitution, sales of the most dangerous opiates like fentanyl. Crane has been focusing the Syndicate more on high-level financial and property crime."

Aurora recalled Crane's claim about Brandon Wolfson. "He said Brandon was involved in human trafficking. If that's really true, then maybe Brandon was working with Dominic Crane's enemies within the Syndicate."

"Exactly. That fits. He's managed to maintain control until now, but his enemies must see his arrest as an opportunity to get rid of him."

"But if some members of the Syndicate want Dominic out of the way," Max reasoned, "wouldn't they *want* Aurora to testify? She's your star witness against him."

"True. I don't understand that part of it. We don't know exactly who's behind this conspiracy or what they want."

The driver of the black Escalade had something to do with it. And they still didn't know who they could trust within the police department, aside from Chase Collins.

Aurora stood up. "But once I testify, it won't be my problem anymore. Right? These people will leave me alone."

"That's my hope." Lana pulled her into a hug. "The danger will be far less urgent, *especially* with Crane's assurances. We're really close."

Aurora couldn't wait to tell Devon. A few more days, and this craziness might be over. Then they could go on that date they'd talked about. Max's disapproval would be their biggest worry.

Chapter Thirty

*D*evon woke to an unfamiliar room.

"You're up." Aurora was beside him on the bed. "Hi."

He rolled carefully to his side to face her. His arm ached, but not as sharply as before. He had vague memories of Tanner pushing him in a wheelchair. Someone coming to change his bandages. Then he'd slept for a long time.

But he didn't remember this room, and he didn't remember Aurora being there.

She was lying on top of the blankets. A glance at the window told him it was early in the day. "Where are we?"

"Max's apartment."

Which took up the entire third floor of the Bennett Security building above the main office.

Aurora sat up, resting against the headboard. "You've been asleep at least twenty hours. It's almost ten o'clock. I stayed in a different room overnight, but as soon as Max left, I came to check on you and found you still sleeping. I hope you don't mind."

Aurora seemed shy, which he hadn't seen from her before. His eyes moved to the door. "It's locked, right?"

"Yep. And nobody else is in the apartment. Just us."

Devon wrapped his uninjured arm around her waist and pulled her closer. "I like waking up to you. I'd kiss you, but I probably don't smell that great."

She slid beneath the covers and rubbed that gorgeous little body against him. She wore leggings and a different crop top. "You smell good enough to me." Aurora tilted her head, looking down at his lips. "So why don't you go ahead?"

He didn't need any more invitation than that. Devon closed the distance between them. He kissed her deeply, enjoying the minty taste of her mouth. Just a few thin layers of clothing separated them. His dick swelled in response to her. She hummed in appreciation when she felt him pressing into her leg.

"Good morning to you, too."

Reluctantly, Devon pulled back before she could take things any further. "I really do need to get cleaned up." He hadn't showered since before he'd gotten shot.

Aurora grumbled, but she scooted off the bed to help him stand.

"I'm okay. After a shower and some breakfast, I'll be good as new."

She pointed to a plate on the dresser. "There's a bacon and egg sandwich. Max sent it for you."

He devoured the food. Someone had left a stack of clean clothes at the foot of the bed. He picked them up and headed for a door, but Aurora steered him the other way. "This is the bathroom. The other door leads to the living room and the kitchen, and the million other rooms Max has in this place. Have you been up here before?"

"In Max's apartment? No. Definitely not." They all knew that their boss had a place on the upper floor of the building, but he didn't usually invite employees here. This room had a nice view, and the furnishings looked expensive.

"How about you tell me what I missed while I get cleaned up?"

"I can do that. Especially if I can take a peek while you're in the shower. Sexy." She winked at him.

"Maybe later. After I wash the grime off me?" He appreciated that she'd said he was sexy, but Devon felt like crap.

Aurora stayed in the bedroom, and he left the bathroom door cracked open. It was all marble tile, from the floors to the walls to the counters. He laid his clothes down and stripped off his hospital-quality pants. His bandages looked fresh enough, but the rest of him wasn't anything to get excited about. Hair matted on his head, a dark scruff on his chin.

The first thing he did was brush his teeth.

There was a shaving kit on the counter, and he poured shaving cream into his palm. "So, you met with Dominic Crane?"

"Yes, yesterday afternoon. It was really surprising, actually." She told him how Crane disavowed any knowledge of the attacks. "He's agreed to let me testify early. Lana said it's happening first thing tomorrow morning. Crane insists that he'll be found innocent."

Devon ran the razor over his chin. "He says he didn't order Wolfson's death?"

"Yep. And he claims that, even if he did, it was somehow justified because Wolfson's a terrible person. Involved in human trafficking and stuff like that."

He cringed. "That's disgusting. But so is Crane. Do you think he'll get away with it?" He glanced at her and saw her shrug through the crack in the door.

"The guy is extremely confident. Maybe he thinks a jury will come out on his side? Or he has some other kind of contingency plan? Crane's pretty convincing."

Devon didn't like how impressed she sounded. "But what about the Escalade driver? Is he one of Crane's enemies? Or his friends?"

"We don't know."

Devon didn't trust Crane for one minute. Maybe the guy didn't order the hit on Aurora, but there was a lot more he wasn't telling them.

"I want to be there tomorrow when you testify." Their eyes met through the doorway.

"I'd like that. I'm sure Lana or Sylvie can arrange it. Now hurry up in there, before I decide to jump into the shower and join you."

The offer was tempting. But the dirt of several days was still on his skin, and that idea weighed on him. His mind wasn't in the right place to focus on Aurora just yet.

Devon got in the shower. The hot water washed away the last bits of tension he'd been carrying. The bad memories and associations that gunfire triggered inside of him. Thoughts of lost comrades, Kellen, his dad. He imagined all that pain draining away beneath his feet. He always carried those remnants of the past with him. But they were usually tucked away out of reach. Where they couldn't hurt him.

By the time he switched off the shower valve, he was refreshed and alert. Devon pulled on the new pair of sweatpants. Drops of water ran from his hair and along his bare chest.

"Feeling better?" She'd pushed the door open wider and leaned her shoulder into the doorframe. One hip was cocked playfully.

"A hell of a lot better. Help me with my bandage?"

Aurora stepped into the bathroom. As she replaced the bandage on his arm, her eyes swept over him. She bit her lip. "I hate that you're hurt," she said, voice husky.

"Not hurting right now."

"I missed you."

"Missed you, too."

Devon spun her so that she was up against the countertop.

The ache from the gunshot wound was far away, a faint reminder of the fact that he'd almost lost her.

He took her mouth in a bruising kiss. His hesitation from days before had vanished. He couldn't get her close enough. His hands lifted her up, and she wrapped her legs around his waist. Her fingers dug into his wet hair, careful to avoid his injured shoulder.

Mine, he thought.

Rationally, he knew that Aurora didn't belong to anyone. And he'd never been a possessive type of guy. But some primal, animal part of him felt like he'd already claimed this woman as his own. No one else's. He wouldn't let anyone else touch her. He'd keep her safe and satisfied for as long as she'd let him.

How had he known her for just a few days? He felt like he'd known Aurora for so much longer than that. As if he'd been waiting for her all his life.

Soon, Aurora was gasping for air. "Wow, that must've been some shower."

"I feel like myself again. Maybe better."

A faraway voice reminded him of the risk. He was in his boss's apartment right now. But the lock on the door promised a few minutes of freedom. He couldn't tamp down the need inside of him.

All of her. He had to have all of her, *now*.

"Want you." With the blood rushing away from his head, he couldn't be more eloquent than that.

"But we don't have a condom. And I probably shouldn't dig around the apartment to find one."

He bit down on a growl of frustration. "Then at least let me taste you." He set her down on the countertop, meaning to slide her leggings off, but she shook her head.

"As much as I'd love a replay of the bathroom scene at Chase's house, I have other plans for you. Sit down on the chair in the bedroom."

"I'm not in the mood for you to boss me around." Right now, Devon needed to be in charge. He had way too much adrenaline pumping through his veins for anything else.

But Aurora only smiled, refusing to cave to his demands.

"On the chair," she whispered, and somehow that quiet, commanding voice was impossible to ignore.

This woman was undoing him. Taking him apart, piece by piece. But damn if it wasn't a good way to go.

Chapter Thirty-One

*S*lowly, Devon eased into the upholstered chair by the window. His erection bulged in his sweatpants. He looked more than a little pissed, though his mouth curved upward at the corners. His eyes held a challenge. If she wasn't careful, he'd wrest control of this moment back from her.

But Devon was clearly the kind of man who gave more than he took—in every aspect of his life, sex included. If she had to force him to sit back and receive pleasure, then she'd do it. She wanted to focus only on him. His body, his orgasm.

Aurora knelt in front of him. "Remember? I told you I was going to take care of you."

"You don't have to."

"But I want to. So, take off your pants."

A chuckle snuck out of his chest. "How can I argue with that?" He lifted his hips, hooked his thumbs in his waistband, and shucked the sweatpants to the floor. His cock sprang free, pointing at the ceiling.

"There you are." Her mouth watered. Aurora rested her hands on his thighs. The muscle felt like steel beneath her palms. For several seconds, she just took in the sight of him. By any objective standard, this man was gorgeous. Droplets of water were scattered over his shoulders and broad chest from the shower. His damp hair stood at wild angles.

In the window behind the chair, waves crashed onto shore. There was no way anybody would be able to see inside, not from this angle, and not with the sun so bright. But Aurora still felt a delicious tingle at having Devon naked here.

She climbed up his legs, running her hands over his eight-pack and pecs. Her mouth scattered kisses over his skin, enjoying the tickle of his chest hair. He reached for her, but she took his hands and placed them on the arms of the chair.

"You know the rules."

"They're not *my* rules." There was that challenge again in his gaze. Heat that seared through her. Part of her did want to lie back and let him take whatever he wanted. But that would have to wait until she showed him just how grateful she was. He'd saved her *life*.

And yeah, she got off on the control, too. She had to make him scream her name. Why should he get to have all the fun?

Straddling his legs, she peeled off her own shirt and bra. Her nipples hardened as he stared unabashedly at her breasts. God, she loved the way he looked at her. Like he couldn't get enough.

Aurora leaned forward to trail kisses down his neck and collarbone. Reaching his chest, she paused to lick one of his nipples, then the other. He groaned, grinding his pelvis against her. But she didn't stay there long. Her feet lowered to the floor, and her mouth kept moving down over the ridges of his stomach.

Just as her mouth was about to reach his hard-on, she leaned forward and rubbed her breasts on either side of him instead. His cock jumped.

"*Ughn*," he moaned.

Finally, she returned to her knees and took hold of him at the base. She swirled her tongue around his tip. Salt and musk met her tongue. His taste and smell were heady, pure masculinity. The fingers of her other hand caressed his balls.

Her tongue moved over him from his sac to his tip.

"Jesus." Devon threw his head back. "You're good at this."

She had a brief flash of unwelcome memory. Her ex Justin, frowning after she gave him head, asking how many times she'd done that before. Implying that she was just a little *too* skilled for his comfort.

Aurora liked sex. Until Justin, she had never been shy about that. She'd had a decent number of partners—those Max didn't manage to scare away in high school, and then plenty more as she'd embraced the freedom of her freshman year of college. Justin had made her feel guilty about it. As if her sexual history was something she needed to apologize for to soothe his ego.

But Devon seemed to be enjoying himself without the least bit of self-consciousness.

Her mouth closed around him, and she took him deep. His hand lightly touched her head, more of an encouragement than a command. She swallowed around him. He was moaning her name, and she'd never heard anything so sexy.

It didn't take him long. He shook as he came, hand tightening in her hair. She took every last drop, giving him one final lick as she sat up. Devon had practically collapsed into the chair. His chest moved as he panted.

"Come here."

Aurora climbed into his lap. Devon's right arm circled her, and his mouth landed on hers. His tongue parted her lips, no doubt tasting the saltiness his cum had left behind.

"Thank you," he murmured. "That was…beyond words."

"My pleasure."

"Pretty sure it was mine."

He nuzzled into her neck, holding her close. She felt a wave of relaxation and calm, as if she'd been the one to get off. But giving him pleasure had been nearly as satisfying. And snuggling up with him after? She couldn't imagine anything better. This man had already sunk beneath her skin. Her heart was in serious danger. It would be so easy to fall for him. Fall for his kindness, his bravery, his generosity. His incredible body and those soulful hazel eyes.

Okay, maybe her heart wasn't just in danger. She was already in free fall, and only Devon could catch her. Her rational mind warned that it was too soon to even think a certain four-letter word. But her heart was beating out the message loud and clear.

Should she say something? Or would that freak him out?

She sighed, and a wrinkle appeared between his eyebrows. "Are you okay?"

"Yes. I think so. But, well..."

Devon tensed. At the same moment, she heard footsteps out in the living room. Then a rough knock. "Whitestone? You awake?" And before she could do a thing, the door burst open, and her brother stood in the doorway.

There was no hiding what they'd been up to. At least Aurora was in Devon's lap, hiding some of his nakedness, and her own bare chest had been turned away from the door.

Max's eyes widened, his face instantly reddening with shock. "What the *fuck* is going on here?"

"The...the lock!" she stammered. "I locked the door!"

Max turned around, facing away from them, though he didn't leave. "The lock on this room is broken. Both of you get some clothes on." His voice was strained. Max's hands had tightened into fists.

Aurora grabbed her bra and top and threw them on. Devon pulled up his pants. He struggled with a shirt because of his injury, but he managed it, refusing her help.

"Devon," she whispered, "let me handle this."

He wouldn't meet her eyes.

"Are you both decent?"

"Yes, sir," Devon replied.

Her older brother turned around. She'd never seen his face this shade of red. Max glared at Devon, who returned the gaze. But Devon looked cowed.

"Am I going to get an explanation?" Max seethed.

"This is my fault. Entirely."

Aurora huffed. "I was definitely an active participant. I made the first move, so if anything, it's my fault. Don't you dare blame him, Max. It's none of your business what I do or who I spend time with."

Max hadn't taken his eyes off the other man. "It's my business when the guy you're naked with is *my* employee. Who I hired to *guard* you. Not...whatever he was just doing."

Okay, a fair point. But Aurora wasn't going to admit that. "He's not guarding me at all. He's off duty." Which completely ignored the fact that Devon had been her bodyguard earlier, when they'd first gotten intimate, but she was grasping at straws.

"Aurora, you need to leave," Max said. "Go back downstairs. I need to speak with my employee. *Alone.*"

"No. I am *not* leaving. You can be angry at me, but I won't let you take it out on him."

"Please," Devon whispered. "You're just making this worse. Wait for me downstairs, okay?"

Tears stung her eyes. But she did as he asked. Neither Max nor Devon even looked at her as she left the room.

Chapter Thirty-Two

Neither man spoke until the elevator dinged out in the main room, and Aurora was gone.

"Sir, I know it looks bad, but—"

Max fixed him with a murderous glare. "Please tell me it's the first time this happened. That you didn't touch her before today."

He was giving Devon an out. The chance to lie. But Devon couldn't take it. Any possible excuse had died on his tongue.

"I can't do that."

Max's eyes closed, a curse on his lips. "Did you sleep with her?"

Devon's stomach twisted painfully. He hated giving away any part of what he and Aurora had shared. Those moments belonged to the two of them, nobody else. Max didn't own his sister. Aurora would be the first to remind them of that.

Yet Max was Devon's boss. Not exactly a commanding officer, but a man who deserved his respect. Devon had a duty to respond.

"*Did you sleep with her?*"

"Yes."

Max slammed his palm against the wall. A vase shook on a nearby table. "If you weren't wounded already, I'd deck you right now."

Devon stood with his back straight, not breaking eye contact. Max had every right to be upset, and Devon had earned this dressing down. As far as his job went, he'd messed up. Been completely unprofessional. Not to mention breaking his express promise not to touch Aurora.

From the first minute that she'd kissed him, Devon had known deep down that this moment of confrontation was coming eventually. But that didn't make it any easier to see the disappointment on Max's face.

"I was absolutely clear when you took on this assignment. You were supposed to stay away from her. You gave me your *word*. My sister ran back home after a difficult break-up, so she was already in a bad place. And then she was traumatized by seeing Wolfson's murder. She was vulnerable. I needed somebody to take care of her at her lowest point, and you took advantage of that."

Devon blanched at the accusation that he'd ever hurt her. "I didn't intend for this to happen. But with all due respect, I don't believe that I took advantage of her. Aurora's not fragile. She's tough and assertive. She was clear about what she wanted."

"If I had any doubts about her consent, no one would ever find your body," Max growled. He paced like a caged tiger across the room. "I know my sister. I can accept her claim that she made the first move. Hell, maybe she did. But just because someone offers doesn't mean you have to accept. What happened to your fucking self-control, Whitestone?"

Finally, Devon averted his eyes, hanging his head. "You're right. I broke my word, and I apologize."

Devon wanted so much more than a few wild moments with Aurora. He cared about her. In fact, he was pretty close to falling for her. And he wasn't sorry about that, not for a second.

Yet he wasn't going to tell Max that. He wasn't going to make excuses or try to justify his behavior by professing his feelings for Aurora. That would just make him look like an even bigger asshole. Besides, Max would never believe him.

"What the hell am I supposed to do with you? Yesterday, I would've given you a fucking medal for what you did, and now..." He put his hands on his hips, shaking his head.

"I can pack my things and leave the office, if you'd prefer." He had to accept the consequences of violating Max's trust, whatever they might be.

If Devon did the honorable thing right now, then maybe Max would at least give his blessing when Devon asked to date her. Because of course, he still wanted more than just a few days with Aurora. A lot more.

But losing his job, though? His family's security? *Fuck.*

Max sighed. "Look, I'm not a robot. I know that emotions run high in these situations. You got Aurora out of some extremely dangerous binds. If not for you, I'd have lost her. That's why I was on my way up here to talk to you—to offer to switch you over to personal security full time."

"You...were?"

"Given your skills, it's where you belong. You're wasted behind a desk. I would've been a fool not to see that."

"Thank you, sir." He was so surprised that he didn't know what else to say.

Max walked back and forth across the room. The rage was draining from his face, and now he looked merely tense, if contemplative. Devon's boss was a very smart guy. In a matter of years, he'd built his security company into a small empire here in Southern California. Devon had seen his boss's ability to strategize before. And right now, he could see Max's mind working.

"Is that something you'd be interested in? Bodyguard duty

can be a lot riskier, as you've seen the past couple of days. Your family wanted you to stay out of danger."

"Honestly? I don't know." Ruby had urged him to pursue his own dreams instead of sacrificing so much for them. But what about his mom? She'd already lost a husband and a son.

"The pay increases with the risk, though. Your salary would be twice as much."

Twice as much. That was more than the pay range for most bodyguards, even those who were veterans with far more experience and training than Devon. He knew that Max had to have an ulterior motive for this offer.

But just think about this for a minute, he said to himself. *You'd be only a few months away from the down payment.* His family would have a place in West Oaks to put down roots, to grow. Ruby wouldn't have to go back to work, and his niece would have her mom around. His family would have the security he'd been fighting to give them for so long. A job like that wasn't easy to find, especially in a small town like West Oaks.

And Devon would actually enjoy the work. He'd just been thinking earlier that he wanted to be a bodyguard. He wanted to *help* people, like Kellen had. Here was Max, offering just that.

"I'd have to speak with my family. I'm not sure what they'd say, but I might be able to convince them. That is, if you're still willing to have me."

Max scrutinized him. "You slipped up, but...if we can manage to put this behind us, I'd like you to keep working for me. Which can only happen if you regain my trust."

"Of course, sir. What can I do?"

He tilted his head to the side, as if considering. Then Max's eyes turned cold and calculating. "Leave Aurora alone. Completely."

Devon blinked. "I'm sorry. What?"

"Stay out of her life. The sooner you're out of the picture, the sooner she can move on from all of this. I need your assurance that you won't see my sister again."

"Ever?" He couldn't be serious.

"Ever. Not socially. Not to date, not to hook-up. Nothing. Break it off clean. She needs a fresh start. And so do *you*. You said you wanted to earn back my trust. This is the way you do it."

Devon's immediate instinct was to refuse. He didn't want to stop seeing Aurora. But Max was letting him off easy, frankly. This was a second chance. He could fix this mess— make it go away.

All he had to do was give up Aurora.

Fuck. Am I seriously considering this?

He tried to picture the house, the secure future for his mom and Ruby, going to a job he loved every day… It did sound nice.

As in, too good to be true.

It was a fantasy to think they'd all be perfectly happy. His mom wouldn't be able to sleep knowing he was in danger. Ruby would still resent that he'd taken too much of the financial burden.

And how could he be happy in any job if it cost him a chance with Aurora? What kind of man would he be if he made that choice?

"If Aurora didn't want me in her life, that's one thing. But I can't do what you're asking. I care about her. A lot. I realize I haven't known her long, but—"

"You think you have feelings for her? That's testosterone talking. You should know better, given your training and education. But maybe you're not as ready to be a bodyguard as I thought. There are always attractive women in danger. There's always temptation."

"But Aurora's not just any woman."

Max scowled. "Exactly, she's my *sister*. I know what's best for her. That isn't you."

Devon clenched his jaw. "This isn't just a chemical reaction to the situation. I'd never claim to be perfect, but I have a lot to offer her." *My love, for one.* The realization took him by surprise. He'd never felt this way about anyone before. Maybe he wasn't ready to say those three words to her yet, but he wanted the chance to get there. In his gut, he knew Aurora was worth it.

"Good Lord. You're serious, aren't you?" Max's expression had shifted from annoyance to pity. "You think my sister's in a position to return any feelings you might have? After all she's been through? She just got out of a three-year relationship that ruined her confidence. She's been running for her *life* from some psychopath. And you think she's got her head on straight? You're fooling yourself."

Devon opened his mouth to argue, but the tightening in his chest stopped him.

Could Max be right?

Oh my god. Could he?

He thought of the uncertainty on Aurora's face just a few minutes ago, when she'd been in his lap. He had asked if she was okay, and she'd been about to tell him something. But then Max interrupted. What had she been about to say?

The events of the past several days spun through his mind. Aurora had seemed confident most of the time. Secure in her sexuality, enough that Devon had convinced himself she truly wanted him.

But she'd hinted at feeling insecure, hadn't she? There was the ex who'd made her feel bad about herself. And then there was the biggest factor, the worst part of all this—the violence she had witnessed. Devon knew firsthand that a horrific attack could blow someone's mind wide open, scrambling them up on the inside.

What have I done?

"Drawing this out will only confuse you and Aurora both." Max's voice was smooth, even soothing. Like he was more sorry than angry. "As soon as the danger's over, she'll wake up. Who's to say what she'll be feeling then? Don't throw away your career for some make-believe romance, Whitestone."

Shame burned him from the inside out. His shoulders slumped. "I see your point. I'll back off."

He'd give Aurora a few days to herself, at the very least. Until she had a chance to reflect on what she truly wanted.

And if she regretted everything that happened between them? If she wished it all away? If she actually felt he'd taken advantage?

If he let himself feel the true impact of that knowledge—if he'd caused her pain—it would break him.

Better to close himself off now.

"I'm very glad to hear that." Max's body had relaxed. "So, you'll accept the new position? We can put this behind us?"

"I'm sorry, but no."

Max took a moment to register the message. "No? You're saying *no*?"

"I can't accept. My mom will never feel secure if I'm working full time as a bodyguard." He spoke in a monotone, forcing the words out.

His desires, his dreams—that stuff didn't matter. It never had.

Accepting the assignment to guard Aurora had been a mistake in the first place. He should've remembered his primary duty—to his family. Instead, he'd put his family's security in jeopardy. He'd lost control, broken his word, and dishonored himself in front of his boss.

And worst of all, he might've taken advantage of Aurora's vulnerable state, just as Max had said. Devon had never been so disgusted with himself.

He looked down at the K tattoo on his arm. He prayed that his twin wasn't looking down on him right now.

"So you're saying you want to go back to desk duty?" Max asked.

Devon shook his head. "Given the circumstances, I don't think that's appropriate either. If I stay with Bennett Security, it'll seem like I chose my job over Aurora. I could never have done that." He would never have let her go because of his boss's demands. But Max was also her brother. Max knew her, and he loved her. How could Devon assume to know better than her flesh and blood?

"The only right thing to do is resign." *Which is what I should've done the moment that I kissed Aurora back.* Because after that first taste of her, he'd already been lost. He was going to have a hell of a time getting over her.

Max looked bewildered. Clearly, he hadn't expected this. Neither had Devon. In a matter of minutes, his feeble hopes had been stripped away. But he was seeing clearly again.

"I'm grateful to you for taking a chance on me, sir. And I'm truly sorry that your faith was misplaced."

With that, he gathered his few belongings and left.

Chapter Thirty-Three

"*I* need to know what's going on up there."

Aurora's eyes had been glued to the elevator for a while now. At one point, she saw the digital numbers go up to Max's apartment, and she'd held her breath. But then whoever it was went down to the lower level—the parking garage. She didn't know what that meant. The uncertainty was killing her.

Aurora started toward the elevator, but Lana held her back.

"They have to sort out their issues themselves. Max is his boss. You'll just have to wait."

"But waiting is the *worst*."

Aurora didn't even care so much about getting caught. But she was sick over the thought of Devon being in trouble. She had to defend him somehow. *I told him I would take care of him,* she thought. Maybe she couldn't protect him physically, not the way that a trained bodyguard could, but she'd still meant it.

Around them, Max's employees continued to work, though they'd been sending some curious glances in Aurora's direction.

"It's going to be okay," Lana said. "Max never stays angry for long."

"Are we talking about the same Max Bennett? Because my older brother is totally unreasonable."

"Then I'll talk to him."

"That won't help. You should have seen him, L. He was practically spitting. He's going to do something awful, I just know it."

Like the time he'd been in West Oaks on leave from the army, and Max caught a guy from her high school in Aurora's room with a hand in her pants. Her poor classmate had been so frightened he'd never spoken to Aurora again.

She knew Devon wouldn't get scared away like that. At least, she hoped he wouldn't. But Max could fire him. He could make Devon's life miserable.

And if he loses his job and can't take care of his family, it'll be my fault. How could I be so reckless?

That stupid, stupid lock. She should've checked it instead of just assuming. She should've been more careful now that they were in Max's domain. *I'm such an idiot.* And Devon was paying for it.

Finally, the elevator doors slid open. Max strode out, his face unreadable.

Aurora ran to meet him halfway. "What happened?"

"I'm busy right now."

"I'm not going anywhere until I know what you did to him."

"I didn't do a thing."

"Then where is Devon?"

Max's expression faltered, the mask of confidence slipping. "He's gone. He left."

"*What?*"

Aurora had yelled the word so loud that the entire room quieted, staring.

Sylvie started walking over. "Did you say Devon left? Is he all right?"

"He's fine." Max gritted his teeth. "Aurora, we shouldn't discuss this here. Let's go to my office."

"But he wouldn't just leave," Aurora protested. "What did you do?"

Max grabbed her wrist and pulled her toward the stairs. "Sylvie, everyone, back to work. You have plenty to do. Lana? Check that the courthouse has made the security changes I requested for tomorrow."

Lana arched an eyebrow at his order. The others watched them go.

Up in Max's office, he punched a switch, and the glass walls frosted over. "Okay, say what you need. But we only have ten minutes for this."

"You don't get to decide that. You don't rule my life, Max. You're not some dictator. And you're *not* my father."

He sat against the edge of his desk. "Maybe if our father cared half as much about you as I do, I wouldn't have had to step up. But I *did*. I always have. And I'm not going to sit by and watch you get hurt."

"Devon wouldn't hurt me."

"*Yes,* he would. Not on purpose, perhaps. He's a stand-up guy, I'll give him that. And a damned good bodyguard. But he messed with you, and that is not okay with me."

"You're not listening. Who I sleep with is *my* choice, not yours. And it was my choice. Completely. You had no right to interfere!"

Max stood up. "I'm not rehashing this same conversation again. It's a waste of my time." He started toward the exit.

"Wait a minute. Why did Devon leave? Did you fire him?"

He paused, hands on his hips, not facing her. "No, I did not. In fact, I offered him a promotion."

His answer stopped her in her tracks. "Then why did he go?"

"He resigned. He thought that was better."

So he'd left. Without stopping to say goodbye or explain. He hadn't said a single word to her.

This was Max's doing. It had to be.

"What did you say to him?"

Slowly, Max turned around. "Nothing that wasn't true. Aurora, I've seen this happen so many times. A bodyguard is protecting someone, and they fall into each other's arms. It's chemistry. His testosterone plus your adrenaline. That's exactly what I wanted to avoid."

"You made him promise not to touch me. Like I'm some weak little flower that needs her big brother to guard her chastity."

"No, I wanted to protect your *heart*. So you didn't do something you'd regret."

"I don't regret a single *minute* I spent with Devon. He doesn't either. I know it." Devon wanted to keep seeing her. It hadn't just been made up, or some physical reaction. She knew her own heart better than that.

Max crossed his arms, regarding her sadly. Like he didn't want to tell her the rest.

"Wait. Do you think he *does* regret it?"

Max shrugged. "At first, he didn't want to admit it. But then he really thought about the situation. He knew that I was right. He lost control of himself. I don't think he liked saying it. But that doesn't change the facts. He agreed with me that what happened was a mistake."

She stepped back, as if Max had delivered a physical blow. "He said there's nothing real between us?" Everything within her refused to accept it. She'd felt his sincerity in the way he held her and kissed her.

"He didn't say those words. But he agreed to stay away from you. Not to keep his job, but because he knew it was the honorable thing to do. Doesn't that answer your question?"

Aurora couldn't keep standing. Her knees weakened, and

she sank onto the couch. Tears sprang from the corners of her eyes. This couldn't be right.

"I want to talk to Devon. I want to hear this from him."

Max knelt beside her. "He chose to leave. Let him go."

Hot tears slid down her face. Devon was gone. He had chosen to go. He'd left *her*. She still didn't understand exactly what had happened. How so much had changed so suddenly when Max got involved. But if Devon cared about her, he'd have fought for her, right? But he didn't.

So, I'm on my own, she thought. *That's what I wanted from the beginning, wasn't it? I wanted to deal with my problems by myself.*

But the truth was, she'd never been on her own. As a kid, her brother found her a place to live, took care of her. Not long after she left California for school, Justin took Max's place. All her life, she'd been leaning on men. Devon was just the latest.

Max sat on the couch and put an arm around her. "I'm sorry, Aurora. I hate to see you hurting, and I hate that I had anything to do with it. Trust me, I don't want to be the bad guy with you."

"You must be sick of doing it."

"Being the bad guy? I know that it seems like—"

"No. Sick of *helping* me."

"Of course, I'm not."

"You *should* be. When I was growing up, I relied on you. I'm grateful that you stepped up when mom and dad couldn't. But ever since, it's like you still treat me like a kid. You didn't want me to leave California for college. When I came back, you stuck me in your penthouse apartment so you could keep tabs on my life. But I finally understand why."

"Aurora—"

She jumped up from the couch. "No, let me say this. I accepted a free place to live when you offered because I *couldn't* do it on my own. I took your help with finding clients

in West Oaks, too. I keep insisting that I'm strong and inde-
pendent, but every time I try, I fail. I *fail*."

Everything was becoming clear to her. She couldn't blame
Max for stifling her, not completely. She'd done it to herself.

"I'm going to pay you back for the rent. And for the cost
of having…" She couldn't say Devon's name. She swallowed
the sob that rose in her throat. "The cost of having a bodyguard protect me. Send me a bill, like I'm any other client."

Max was rolling his eyes. "I'm not going to do that. For
one, there's no way you could afford it."

"So make it a loan! Charge me interest, I don't care. I've
been taking your help when it suits me, and then getting pissed
when you expect to have a say in my life. I can't have it both
ways, can I?"

"You're not a client. I'd do anything for you because
you're my sister." He got up and held her by the shoulders. "I
love you. That's not conditional. I'm sorry if I ever made you
think otherwise, or made you feel like you aren't strong. You
clearly are. Look at what you've been handling these past few
days."

She could barely see for all the tears pooling in her eyes.
She rubbed them away, but they kept coming. "I don't want to
be angry at you anymore, Max. I can't… I can't take this
feeling…"

She didn't want to need her brother's help. She didn't
want to need Devon. *And I don't.* She pressed her hands into
her stomach. *I don't need Devon,* she repeated in her mind.

So why did she feel like she was being ripped open?

"I care about him. I think I could even love him someday.
That's crazy, right? I barely know him." In fact, she barely
knew what she was saying. She was babbling, spilling her guts
in front of her brother. "But I also know that he's the best man
I've ever met. It's no wonder he left. I'm this big mess who
can't take care of herself, and someone is trying to kill me, and
I'm so scared—"

Max wrapped her in a hug. "Hush, you're okay. You're okay."

The stress of everything that had happened the last days crashed down on her. The dam had finally broken. But Devon wasn't here to hold her up.

She did care for him—maybe even loved him already—as absurd as that seemed. She'd never fallen so hard or so fast for someone like this. The feeling was all-consuming and extraordinary and real. The pain of losing him was so intense that she might drown in it. But she had to make it back to the surface on her own.

No matter how much it hurt.

Chapter Thirty-Four

"*D*evon?" his mom cried. "Where are you?"

"In here."

He was slumped on the couch in the living room, feeling sorry for himself. He sat up just as his mother streaked into the room, dumping her purse and her bag as she went.

"Oh, my poor boy."

"Mom, go easy. Jeez." She was clutching at him, which aggravated his wounded arm. But her display of emotion annoyed him even more. Which was completely callous and unfair. He knew that. She had every right to be upset that her son had been shot, especially considering their family's history. But he wasn't feeling particularly understanding or generous at the moment.

She sat down beside him, pressing her hands to her face. "We were so scared, Devon. How could you take a risk like that? You said your job was supposed to be safe."

Ruby and Chase came into the room. Chase was carrying a sleeping Haley in his arms.

"He was protecting someone who needed help," Ruby

said. "I already explained that, Mom. She would have been killed if Devon wasn't there."

His mother nodded, but Ruby's words had only made her cry harder. "I'm just so thankful that you're here and you're all right. If anything had happened to you…"

They all knew the rest of that sentence. Devon practically knew his mother's fears by heart. He couldn't help softening. She was his mother, after all. He had made most of his decisions in the last year and a half based on not upsetting her.

"I'm sorry. I didn't expect the assignment to be so dangerous. But it's over now, anyway."

Aurora would be testifying in the morning. The danger had nearly passed, and if she needed a bodyguard going forward, someone else like Tanner would do it.

As soon as he'd left the Bennett Security office, he'd called Chase to let his friend know that it was safe for his family to come home.

Devon had to come straight here, to his Mom and Ruby's townhouse, so that he could see them. It was partly that he knew his mother would need to see that he was safe for herself. But he also didn't want to be alone in his sad, tiny studio apartment. Because then his mind would start spinning uncontrollably, thinking about Aurora and how much he already missed her, how much he wanted her. Even though he had no right. And how much of an asshole he had been to potentially hurt her.

"So, Aurora is safe?" Ruby asked.

"That's her name? Aurora?"

Devon flinched each time they said it. "Yes. Everything is fine now. For her, and for you guys. We were worried before that my identity could've been compromised. That's why you had to stay in a hotel. But now my coworkers are confident that nobody is coming after me. So, we can just try to get back to normal."

As if that were even possible. He'd lost his job. He'd lost

Aurora. So no, there was no going back to normal for him. But he didn't want to explain all of that to his family yet. He didn't want them to know how badly he had fucked up.

"I'll be right back," Chase said. "I'll just put Haley in her crib."

Ruby smiled at him appreciatively. "Thank you."

So that was new. Chase had been friendly with Ruby before, but now they seemed to share some deeper bond. What was that about?

Not that it was any of his business. Devon had no right to go all protective-big-brother on her, not after what he'd done.

Ruby came over to the couch and sat on Devon's other side. "Are you okay, bro? You've been through some serious shit."

Their mother tutted. "Language, Ruby."

"Mom, the guy just got shot. That is shitty. And he was in the army. Devon's used to hearing some salty language."

Mom shook her head, though she didn't argue.

Devon exchanged a glance with his sister. They were both well aware of their mother's idiosyncrasies. Megan White-stone was a woman who'd lost family to violence, who'd seen both of her sons serve the public and face danger. She knew just how terrible the world could be. Yet their mother insisted on observing every social nicety, as if proper behavior would somehow protect them from further heartache. As if they could shelter themselves inside a bubble, closing themselves off so tightly against every negative word or feeling so that no one could ever hurt them again.

Devon didn't blame her. He had done the same thing plenty of times, though for him it was all about shutting off his emotions. The Whitestones did what they had to do to get by.

Right now, Devon knew that if he let himself experience everything he was really feeling, he wouldn't be able to get up from this couch. He would do something ridiculous, like breaking down in front of his mom, and that would completely freak her out. He had to be strong for her. And for Ruby and for Haley. That was his real job. He just had to keep reminding himself of that.

"Earth to Devon. Are you going to answer my question, or are you just going to sit there looking wrecked?" Ruby smiled wryly at him, seeming to sense what he'd left unsaid—that he wasn't okay at all. "There must be something you need. Pain meds? Ice cream? A beer?"

He cleared his throat. "No, I'm fine. Maybe a shower."

He'd showered only a couple of hours earlier, but he wasn't going to let himself think about that. Because those memories would lead straight to Aurora, and he could already still smell her on his skin.

He stood up. Yep, a shower was exactly what he needed.

"Okay if I use yours, Mom?" He didn't want to wake Haley in Ruby's room.

"Of course." His mother got up, too. "And I'll make you some lunch. You must be starved."

They were keeping busy. Doing what they had to do to get by. Devon had the feeling that the next few days would be all about survival mode. He had no idea how he was going to get through them.

AFTER HIS SHOWER, Devon went out to the back patio while his mom cooked lunch.

He looked around at the yard. This townhouse was just a rental, not really theirs. But there was grass for Haley to run around in once she was bigger, and Ruby had planted a little vegetable garden along the side. The neighbors were quiet, and his mom and Ruby seemed to have plenty of space. The rent wasn't outrageous, either. It wouldn't be so bad for them to stay here a while longer. He had hoped to get them into a house of their own sooner, but now that he'd lost his job, that wasn't going to happen.

He'd have to find another job soon. Otherwise, his meager savings wouldn't cover the rent for more than a few months.

If he moved out of his own place and slept on their couch, then cut back on all his discretionary expenses, he could make this work. He could still provide for them the way he had promised.

But even as he tried to reassure himself, he felt the crushing guilt of having failed them. He had expected so much better. They all had.

He sat on a lawn chair. The patio door slid open, and Chase stepped out. "Mind if I join you? You seem like you're knee-deep in thought."

"Not really. Just trying to take it easy, I guess. Since that's what everyone seems to be telling me to do."

Chase's eyebrow raised, like he wasn't anywhere close to convinced. "Okay, what is it you haven't told us? Because I can tell there's more. You're beating yourself up over something. What happened?"

Devon closed his eyes. So it was that obvious. "I messed up. Bad."

"But you said Aurora was fine. She's safe."

"No, it's not her. I mean, it's not that she's in jeopardy. I wouldn't have come home if she wasn't in safe hands."

"Of course, you wouldn't. You'd never leave the job unfinished. So, what is it?"

"The problem is I don't *have* a job," he bit out. "I don't work at Bennett Security anymore."

"You what?" Chase plopped down on the chair beside him. "What the hell happened? Did you get fired?"

"I quit. But I didn't really have a choice. Aurora is Max Bennett's sister. And I slept with her."

Chase whistled. "Damn, Whitestone. I guess you're not the celibate monk we all thought you were."

"This isn't funny."

"Hey, I'm not laughing. But you're the last guy I would've expected to end up in a situation like this. Plenty of other men wouldn't have been able to resist the temptation, sure. But not you. Which tells me Aurora must be pretty damn special."

Devon sank further into the lawn chair, covering his eyes with his hand. "Yeah. She really is. She's amazing. And I ruined any chance I might have had with her."

"Why? Just because her brother doesn't approve?"

"Not only that. From the minute I met her, she's been adamant that she doesn't care what Max thinks. But there's a good reason Max told me to keep my hands off her. She was in a really vulnerable place. I should've known that she might not be in a position to…consent." Just saying those words killed him. A lump had lodged in his throat.

Chase frowned thoughtfully. "So, you think you misread her signals? Took things further than she wanted? That really doesn't sound like you. You're sure she wasn't into it?"

"In the moment? I was completely convinced that she was all in." The memories passed through his mind, unbidden. The desire in her eyes, her enthusiasm. Not to mention her explicit verbal permission. She had told him, again and again, how much she wanted him. More than once, she'd taken full control, making him come harder than he ever had in his life. Around her, Devon felt like he was gasoline, and she was an open flame. His skin started to burn, thinking of how eager she had been in his arms.

He loved that she was so comfortable with herself. She didn't apologize for being sexual, and she didn't hold back. He might not admit it to anyone but her, but he loved the way she bossed him around in bed.

And he was crazy about her outside the bedroom, too. Her brashness and smarts, her compassion and bravery and openness. She made him smile and laugh like no one else.

How was he ever going to get Aurora out of his system? If that were even possible.

"But that's the problem. How do I know that she won't come to her senses and hate me for what we did?" *I couldn't take that.*

"You really care about her. No wonder you've got yourself all tied up in knots." Chase crossed his legs, squinting up at the bright blue sky. "Have you asked her opinion on all this? Cause it sounds to me like you two really connected. I have no doubt you would've kept things strictly professional if you didn't feel something really intense for this woman. And if you weren't positive that she felt the same."

Devon rubbed his eyes. His nerves had been on a roller coaster lately, and he was afraid to hope. "I could give it a few days, then see if she'll talk to me. Maybe I'm wrong, and I'm overthinking this."

Please let me be wrong.

"You might not be thinking all that straight yourself. You're recovering from a gunshot wound."

Devon shrugged off the concern. His problem wasn't physical. "Maybe. But none of this changes the fact that I'm out of a job. Bills are coming no matter what happens with Aurora, and I need to be focused on what I'm going to do next."

"You lost your job? Devon, what are you talking about?"

He cringed, turning to see his mother in the doorway. Chase had left it cracked open. Dammit. His mom had over-heard. And Ruby was right behind her, peering past their mom's shoulder.

Just great.

Mom and Ruby came out onto the patio. They were waiting for an explanation. There was no reason to keep delaying. He might as well get it over with.

"I am no longer employed by Bennett Security. I decided to quit."

Ruby's mouth opened in shock. But his mother sighed, relief all over her face. "Well, I don't blame you. Your boss shouldn't have put you into that dangerous situation to begin with, after he promised that you wouldn't have to deal with anything like that. Devon, you did exactly the right thing."

He exhaled. His mom's approval only made him more upset because of all she didn't know. But he would just let her go ahead and believe what she wanted. Better that than tell her what he'd really been up to.

His sister, though, didn't seem nearly so pleased. "Why would you quit your job? For *us*? Are you serious right now? You said you liked being on bodyguard duty."

His mom's eyes narrowed in confusion.

"I guess I did, but Mom's right. It was too dangerous, and I need to be thinking of you guys. This is a lot more sudden than I would've wanted, but I'm going to get it sorted out. Don't worry about that."

Ruby paced across the grass, throwing her head back and roaring in pure exasperation. "When are you going to stop being a martyr and start worrying about *yourself*? It's getting really freaking annoying."

"Don't talk that way, Ruby," their mother said tightly. "You owe your brother a lot more than that."

"Of course, I do! We both do! Devon has been giving up everything for us, but when will it end? He's been miserable, don't you see that?"

His mom looked to him. "That isn't true, is it?"

Devon stood up, walking a few feet away. "I can't deal with talking about this right now. The job at Bennett Security is over. It's done. Okay? Let's just move on."

"Move on?" His sister laughed bitterly. "Like anybody in this family has ever moved on from *anything*. We pretend to be okay, but meanwhile, we're completely stuck in place. You expect us to watch you work yourself into the ground and pretend that we're grateful for it?"

Their mom tried to interrupt, but Ruby kept talking over her. "No, Mom. You know what? I'm not grateful to Devon for making himself miserable because it's supposedly what *I* need. What I need is a brother who is living the life that he wants. Haley needs an uncle who isn't afraid to pursue his dreams. Devon, what kind of example are you going to be setting?"

Devon was stunned into silence. Ruby had said some of these things before, but she hadn't revealed until now how angry she was. How disappointed she was in him.

Was he really setting a bad example? By giving up so much to care for his family, was he ending up hurting them, anyway?

There was just no way to win, nothing he could do that would satisfy everyone in his life, apparently. All this work had been for nothing, and he was just tired. So fucking tired of all of it.

Chase was biting his lip, looking down at the grass. Clearly, he wasn't enjoying being a part of this awkward family moment.

"Ruby, you should go inside and calm down," Mom said. "Come back out for lunch when you can be civil to your brother."

Ruby threw up her hands. "I'll come back when the two of you are finally ready to let go of losing Kellen and Dad. Because that is the real problem."

She stomped back inside.

"I'm sorry about that, Mom. I'll talk to her later. When we've both cooled down."

But his mom wasn't responding. Instead, she was staring off into the distance, eyes glassy.

Chase got up. "I'll check on Ruby. Or lunch. Or…something." He went inside, sliding the glass door fully closed.

Then his mom spoke. "Have you been unhappy? Tell me the truth." She was so quiet Devon could barely hear her.

The truth. Devon respected and valued the truth. But his sister was exactly right. He'd been lying to himself. Lying to his family.

"I've been unhappy. I'm proud that I can take care of you guys. I wanted that to be enough. But the desk job isn't what I would choose."

"Do you regret leaving the army?"

He really didn't know how to answer that question. "I wouldn't have left if you hadn't asked. But I don't necessarily think it was the right place for me, either. I would've missed out on seeing Haley grow. And meeting other people." Like Chase. And Aurora. "I'm really glad to be back here with you."

"Do you think Ruby is right? That I'm robbing you of the chance to pursue your dreams because I can't get over losing your dad and Kellen?" She was close to crying. Devon could see the tears hovering on her eyelashes.

He went over and pulled her into his arms. "None of us are over it. But maybe we've made mistakes. Maybe we could've done better. I could've been honest with you and told you what I was feeling. Instead of just pushing my emotions down and ignoring them."

She sobbed. "I've been so scared of losing you. But my fear has made you lose *yourself*. I hate to think that you would give up your own dreams because of me. What kind of mother am I?"

"Mom, please." He hugged her tighter.

"What do you really want for yourself, Devon?"

He wanted a lot of things. For the first time in a while, Devon was actually letting himself feel those desires. But wanting things didn't mean he could have them.

"I don't know, Mom. Really. I feel so mixed up right now."

"Well, please promise me that you won't give up on something you want because of me." She pulled back slightly, brushing the tears away from her eyes. Her breath skipped.

"I'm scared. I'm so scared every day that our family will get torn apart. But I guess that's already happened. The very worst...has happened to us."

"It did."

She swallowed hard, trying valiantly not to dissolve into tears again. Devon recognized the effort, knew how it felt.

"And we're still here, aren't we?" his mom asked.

"Yeah. We are."

He could see her standing taller. Forming some new resolve. He hadn't just gotten his strength and bravery from his dad. His mom was strong, too, in her own way. He had nearly forgotten that.

She put a hand on each of his cheeks, framing his face. "Things are going to be different. I know I have a long way to go to stop being afraid. Maybe I will never get there completely. But I can't allow you to make yourself unhappy. You have to be honest with me from now on. You deserve that. We both do. And I think..." Her voice broke. She swallowed again, and when she spoke again, she sounded adamant. "I know that your dad and Kellen would want that, too."

He nodded. And a little of the ache in his chest went away.

Chapter Thirty-Five

*A*urora lay in her bed staring at the wall. Her eyes felt swollen from crying. After her argument with Max, she had closed herself in the guestroom he had assigned to her, declining her brother's offer of dinner. Her stomach was too twisted up to even think about eating. But at least Max had otherwise left her alone.

There was a knock at the door. "Aurora? Can I come in?"

It was Lana. Aurora managed to make a sound of assent, and her friend came into the room.

"Oh, sweetie." Lana sat on the mattress. "Max told me what happened. I'm so sorry."

She was annoyed that Max had said anything. Aurora hardly even knew what had happened herself. But, of course, everyone in the office had to know by now that Devon was gone. They would naturally have been asking questions, and it wouldn't have taken long for the story to get around.

What were they saying? That Aurora had messed around with him and gotten him fired? Well, not exactly fired, but in enough trouble that Devon felt like he had no choice but to quit. Which was almost worse.

Devon had resisted her, over and over again. He'd told her

that his job was at stake. But she hadn't listened.

She'd been so selfish.

"Do you want to talk?"

"Not really."

Lana nodded. "I get it. When you're ready, I'm here. But in the meantime, we need to get things prepped for the morning. I'm going back to my place tonight, but I'll be back here first thing. We'll be leaving together around eight for the courthouse. Max said the security is all in place. So, you have nothing to worry about."

Aurora felt too numb to be worried about her safety tomorrow. "What exactly do I need to do?"

"Just tell them what you told me before. The truth. I'll question you first, and I'll ask pretty much all the same things I already have. No surprises there. Then, the defense attorneys will have their chance to cross-examine. They'll want to make it seem like you're not confident or credible. It's their job to undermine your testimony. We can go over some practice questions, so you're prepared for what they might try to do."

"I don't feel like it. Can we do that when you get here in the morning?"

"That's not ideal. But sure. I don't want you overly prepped, anyway. The most important thing is just to stand by your own memory and tell the truth about what happened. Beyond that, you'll be fine."

Lana explained a bit more about what to expect. How the judge had agreed to sit in, and a court reporter would record her testimony and the cross-examination.

Later, she would still have to repeat her testimony at the real trial, and any inconsistencies could be used by the defense to make her look untrustworthy. But the most important thing was that her testimony would be on record, so none of the defendants would have any reason to silence her any longer. Because if anything happened to her, the record of tomorrow's testimony could be read into evidence at the trial itself.

Aurora only half-listened, hardly caring about tomorrow. Before, she'd been nervous. Devon had offered to be there, and that idea had comforted her. She'd liked knowing that he wouldn't be far away, even as she had to face Dominic Crane and the other defendants in person—including Eric Madden, the ponytailed gunman who had killed Brandon Wolfson.

But now Devon was gone.

She just wanted the rest of this over with. So she could try to forget about everything that happened.

Lana finished her speech, but she didn't leave the room. Instead, she lay down beside Aurora.

"Remember when we used to share a room? You said I snored."

"Because you did. You were like a freight train." The memory coaxed a smile from Aurora's lips. Which was no doubt Lana's intention. But her mood wasn't going to be lifted so easily.

Lana rolled onto her side, facing Aurora. "But my snoring was nothing to your talking at night. You were always muttering about something. Usually, I had no idea what you were talking about. But once, when I was home visiting for the weekend—this was when I was in law school—you called out for your mom. One of the few times you asked for her in all those years I'd known you."

Okay, this conversation was definitely not lifting her spirits. She didn't know why Lana was bringing this stuff up. It was all ancient history, anyway.

Aurora's parents had come by sometimes; they hadn't completely abandoned her. But when it became clear they didn't plan to take her back, Lana's parents had started the process to become her legal guardians. Her parents readily agreed. In the end, Aurora had barely known her parents at all. She'd spent almost her entire childhood with Lana's family.

"Why would I ever call out for my mom? She was never

there for me. That's…pathetic."

"That is *not* true. And not what I meant." Lana sat up, crossing her legs. "When you were in high school, you always wanted to act like nothing fazed you. I was already an adult myself, but I saw how confident you were just as a teenager. The easy way you made friends and got boys to chase after you. To be honest? I looked up to you. Envied you, even. I was so awkward socially. But that night, when you were talking in your sleep, you gave a little of your secret away. You were just like everyone else. *We all* want someone to take care of us."

She rubbed Aurora's back. "Rory, you don't *need* anyone to look out for you. But you *deserve* it. I've always loved you like a sister, so I know that for a fact."

"I love you, too."

"Can I give you a little advice, from one sister to another?"

"I think I've had enough advice from siblings today. No offense."

"But it doesn't hurt to listen. Here's the deal. I think Max is probably right about one thing. Getting involved with Devon while he was your bodyguard was not the best idea."

Aurora grumbled, grabbing another pillow, and shoving it over her head.

"Hold on, I'm not finished. It wasn't the best idea, given the circumstances. But I *also* think that Max is being an idiot. Now that you and Devon like each other, Max has no right to try to keep you apart."

"But I fooled myself into thinking Devon and I really had something. At least, the start of something. If he cared, then he wouldn't have left."

"That's where you're wrong. I basically cross-examined Max about his conversation with Devon. I pulled out of him exactly what they both said. Devon told him he has feelings for you."

She looked out from under the pillow. "He did?"

"Trust me, I had to drag that out of Max. But you know

me, I always get the truth. As stupid as Max was being, he really thought he was doing right by you. But the fact is, he just doesn't know you as well as I do. I slept next to you, year after year, watching you grow from a little girl into a confident woman. I see that you and Devon have something that's worth pursuing. If it felt real to you, then you should trust yourself."

Aurora crawled up beside Lana, resting against the headboard. "You don't think I lean too much on men? Max, Justin…"

"Sweetie, you are a force to be reckoned with, whether you have a man in your life or not. That is the truth, and I would happily testify to it."

AFTER LANA LEFT, Aurora got out the laptop Sylvie had given her. She had to find some way to contact Devon. If he told her that everything between them was a mistake, fine. But she had to hear it from him.

Unfortunately, she didn't know how to reach him. Both of them had lost their phones when they'd fled Aurora's apartment building. If he still had that burner, she didn't know the number. She didn't even know his email or his home address.

Great way to start a relationship, she thought. *At least I know his last name.*

"Devon Whitestone" didn't seem like a common name, but he also lacked a social media presence. She found a listing for a phone number, but when she called, there was no answer. Just his voice on the voicemail message, which made her heart clench.

"I could ask Sylvie," she murmured aloud. "Or make Max tell me. Or maybe one of Lana's police detective friends can track him down?"

The more she thought about it, the more convinced she grew. She was going to find him and tell him how she felt.

Aurora Bennett was no pushover. She wasn't letting go of him without a fight.

Before she could organize a search party—or do anything else drastic—she saw a new email arrive in her inbox.

It was from Jennifer Scoville, Brandon Wolfson's former assistant, who'd helped Aurora plan the "Angels and Demons" party. Though that seemed like a lifetime ago.

Aurora had written yesterday to both Nadia Wolfson and Jennifer, asking if they recognized the driver of the black Escalade. Aurora felt sick, thinking of him. That man had shot Devon. Tried to kill her.

With her stomach roiling, she opened Jennifer's email.

Mrs. Wolfson doesn't know him, Jennifer had written. *I don't either. Sorry we can't help. Who is this guy? Is he someone we should keep an eye out for?*

Could Aurora have been mistaken about seeing the Escalade driver at the "Angels and Demons" party? At this point, she *hoped* she'd been wrong. She didn't want that man near Nadia or Jennifer.

Aurora checked her messaging app and saw that Jennifer was active. She called the woman, thinking that this would be an easier conversation to have verbally, instead of trying to convey everything in writing.

Besides, she'd missed seeing Jennifer. They had really clicked when they were planning the party together. And she hadn't had a chance yet to take Jennifer up on her offer of a spa day. She looked forward to being able to do something so normal with a new friend.

Jennifer answered, and her face appeared on the screen. "Aurora! It's so good to see you. I was just thinking about you."

"I got your email. Thanks for getting back to me. Never mind about the guy in the photo. I thought I saw him at The Lighthouse, but I could've been mistaken."

Jennifer's eyebrows drew together. "That's strange. But

why are you looking for him?"

"He's the person who attacked me yesterday. He wounded my bodyguard. We're not even sure exactly what he wants, who he's working for, but after tomorrow it won't matter so much. I'm scheduled to get my testimony on the record first thing tomorrow morning."

"Thank goodness. It's a relief to hear that."

They chatted a bit more about the ordeal of the past few days, and Jennifer expressed her shock over losing her employer.

"But on a happier note," Jennifer said, "Mrs. Wolfson has decided to hold her birthday party after all. I'm so glad she has friends supporting her."

"I was helping her with the arrangements. But I hadn't heard if she needed anything else."

"You don't need to worry about that. She really appreciates your efforts, but obviously you have way too much to deal with right now. We both want you to focus on yourself. Besides, she ended up deciding to hold the party tomorrow morning, making it a brunch instead. With just her very closest friends."

"That's a great idea." At least Nadia seemed to be doing all right. The woman had always been kind to Aurora. Eventually, the news would probably get out about Brandon's involvement with organized crime and human trafficking. Nadia Wolfson's friends would have to help her through that, too.

"I hope we can get together soon," Jennifer said. "Under better circumstances."

"Me, too."

Aurora said goodbye and yawned. It was nearly midnight. She tried Devon's number and once again got voicemail. Talking to him would have to wait until tomorrow. She wondered if, wherever he was right now, he was thinking of her.

Chapter Thirty-Six

*D*evon rubbed a hand across the stubble on his chin. It was past midnight, but he couldn't sleep.

He kept picturing Aurora. Remembering her taste. The way her skin had felt against his.

Stop, he told himself. *Enough*. As if his heart would listen.

Chase had gone back to his temporary lodgings for another night. Devon had offered his own apartment since Chase's house was in shambles right now after getting shot up. Chase had turned him down, saying that so long as Max Bennett was paying, he'd enjoy the fancy digs.

But Devon hadn't gone back to his own place, either. Instead, he'd stayed for dinner, fed Haley her bottle, and rocked her to sleep.

Now, his mom was in bed and Ruby was in her own room. Devon remained in the living room, staring at his laptop screen. He'd been trying to get his mind off Aurora by focusing on the men who'd attacked her. The Escalade driver, to be exact.

When he'd left the office earlier, he'd been sure Aurora was completely safe. But tomorrow, she'd be testifying. That meant going out into the open, at least briefly. If they'd missed something important, Devon wanted to know.

And despite the revelations from Dominic Crane and all of Max's and Sylvie's research, they hadn't found out the Escalade driver's identity.

That didn't sit right with him.

Devon decided to risk a call to Sylvie. He found her extension on the Bennett Security website and called using his mother's phone, since he didn't have one at the moment. *I'd better get a new one tomorrow*, he told himself, *because sharing my mom's cell is ridiculous*.

"This is Sylvie Trousseau."

"Hey, it's Devon."

"Dev!" There was a sound of rustling, like she was moving around. "Oh my gosh, it's good to hear your voice. Are you all right?"

He was getting tired of people asking that. But of course, Sylvie meant well.

"I've been better. Sorry to call so late, but I figured you'd still be at work."

"Excellent guess. It's Workaholics Anonymous over here, as usual, only nobody gets better. And it's not the same without you." There was a pause. "Everybody's talking about how you quit. I'm not going to ask what went down, because it's your business. But if you need an ear, I've got one. Two, in fact."

He smiled halfheartedly. "Thanks." He was relieved that he didn't have to go over his failings yet again.

Sylvie's voice lowered. "Aurora's really torn up. She was screaming at Max in front of the whole office. Whatever happened, it's clear she's on your side."

He didn't know what to make of that, so he just forged ahead. "I'm calling about Aurora's case. Any progress on ID'ing the Escalade driver?"

Sylvie huffed. "Nothing. It's like the guy doesn't exist. At least, not in California. I've been talking to all my contacts, both official law enforcement and not so official. Nobody knows this guy."

Devon walked across the living room into the kitchen. He was too full of nervous energy to sit down. "I keep thinking about what Aurora said. That she thought she saw him at Wolfson's club. But then, we couldn't confirm it."

"Right. That's bugging me, too. Crane insisted this guy wasn't part of his crew. Yet, if he *was* at the club, he must've had just as much knowledge as they did of our security cameras, because he avoided them so well. I've been over the footage from that party three times."

"But I'm wondering if maybe Aurora *didn't* actually see him at the party. What if she saw him at the club some other time, and the cameras had a better angle?"

Sylvie hummed thoughtfully. "That's not bad. It's entirely possible. Especially if he had some connection to Wolfson that we don't know about." There was the sound of fingers clacking against the keyboard. "Do you have a computer there?"

Devon glanced around. The laptop Sylvie had brought him yesterday remained at Bennett Security, since it was work property. His own was back at his apartment.

"I could use my sister's."

"Great. I'm going to email you a temporary link for access to our servers, so we can go over the footage together. Aurora was planning that party at The Lighthouse for several weeks, right? So, there's a lot to go over."

Devon rolled his neck, trying to release some of the tension there. "But do you think that would be okay with Max? I don't work there anymore. I shouldn't have access to anything."

Sylvie blew air between her lips. "I don't care what Max says. We need you on this team. Who else would be up at this hour working, except you and me?"

"Good point." Devon went over to his sister's room and knocked quietly. He asked to borrow her computer and then brought the device out to the kitchen table. "Okay, I'm ready. Opening my email now."

Sylvie's message was already waiting. He hadn't even realized that she knew his personal email, but then again, he shouldn't have been surprised. Everyone at Bennett Security went to Sylvie for help with finding people. She was better than anyone at combing through data and accessing info no one else could find. Maybe all her methods weren't completely above board, but she wasn't the type to give away her secrets.

He opened the message, and over the phone Sylvie gave him a one-time passcode to gain access to their servers. "You're sure this is okay? I have no idea what Ruby does on this computer. It could have viruses all over it."

"It's not ideal, but our connection is encrypted. And any access I'm giving you now will automatically cut off in twenty-four hours."

A few clicks, and he was on their database. "Should we divide and conquer? I'll start with the camera footage from a couple months back and you take the week after?"

"Man after my own mind."

They got off the phone and switched to a secure messenger. Devon combed through days of recordings. His heart leaped when he saw Aurora park in front of the club and get out. She'd been dressed in a suit and heels, which he'd never seen her in before. This looked like it might've been the first meeting with Wolfson's people.

He switched through the various camera feeds, tracking her through the club as she first met with a dark-haired woman, who Devon assumed was Wolfson's assistant. And then Wolfson himself and his wife. For several seconds, Devon couldn't tear his eyes away from Aurora's face. So open and animated, making the others laugh and nod. Of course, they had loved her. Who wouldn't?

He forced himself to refocus on his task—finding the guy who'd attacked her.

Devon's eyes were bleary, and he'd lost track of time when Ruby came out of her bedroom. "You're still up?" She was rocking Haley in her arms.

Devon sat back, stretching. "I had some stuff to finish." Though he hadn't had any sign of the Escalade driver in the videos from The Lighthouse. Maybe he was wrong, and this was all pointless. Maybe he was just wasting his and Sylvie's time.

"Everything all right?" he asked his sister.

Ruby glanced down at the baby in her arms, who was sucking contentedly on a bottle. "She still wakes up around this time every morning. Hungry little thing."

"Want me to hold her?"

"Would you? It's not going to bother your arm?"

"I'm slightly tougher than that, Rube. A baby isn't going to be the final straw that does me in."

Ruby turned over the bundle to him. He sat on the couch. Haley's round, brown eyes stared into his. She felt so impossibly tiny up against him.

Immediately, he thought of Aurora. She hadn't even met his family. They'd probably adore her. And they'd make him look good.

"You'd say nice things about me, wouldn't you?" he whispered to Haley. "Aurora would fall for it. Who could say no to that face?"

Ruby poured a glass of orange juice from the fridge. "What are you telling her?"

"Just uncle stuff."

"How to field strip an M-16 in ten seconds?"

He chuckled. "Something like that."

A kitchen chair scraped back as Ruby sat down. "Sorry I yelled at you earlier."

"No biggie. Must've been building up for a while."

"A long while." She looked down into her glass. "There's more. I accepted the job at the salon on Ocean Lane."

Guilt twisted its knife once again in his stomach. "Because I lost mine? I told you, I'll figure this out."

"That's not it. I accepted the job after the last time you and I spoke. I *want to work*, Dev. I want to pull my weight in this family, but even more than that, I miss being a stylist. I love making people feel good about themselves. And as much as I adore being Haley's mom, I can't deny this other part of myself."

Her fingers twisted together, and her eyes pleaded with him to understand. He couldn't remember the last time he'd seen his sister so nervous.

"I get it. We'll find the best day care for Haley, so that mom doesn't overtax herself. We'll make this work. Together."

She snorted a laugh. "This is going to sound awful, but maybe the near-death experience was good for you? Because I can't believe those words just came out of your mouth."

"What are you talking about?"

"You're the poster boy for self-sacrifice. Now suddenly, you're all chill about sharing the burden. It's…refreshing. Could it possibly have something to do with a certain woman you might have met?"

Devon groaned, and Haley's little brows knit together with a frown. "What did Chase tell you?"

That traitor. Spilling their private conversation to his sister? Really?

She tipped back the last of her orange juice. "He said you're crazy about her, but that you're not sure if it can work."

"You and Chase seem cozy these days. Anything you want to share?"

"Ha. So not going there. Quit trying to change the subject."

Devon sat quietly, hoping his sister would give up. But she

waited patiently for him to explain. "I was supposed to be
Aurora's bodyguard. You can guess why I had to quit. I never
planned on falling for her."

"Then *fuck your plans*, Dev."

He shifted his hand to cover Haley's ear. "Language?"

"It's just a word." Ruby smirked and plopped onto the
couch next to him. "But in this case, it's the right one. Plans
are all well and good. But we can never predict what'll
happen."

"Like losing Kellen. I know that. Uncertainty is always
there. But that's exactly when we have to stay the course and
remember what's most important."

Ruby shook her head. "No. Listen. When I got pregnant
by that loser, my first thought was about you. I was so scared
for my older brother to find out, because I thought you'd be
angry and judgmental. Of course, you weren't, thank goodness. But Kellen never got the chance to hear the news at all.
He'll never meet her. I hate that. Because he would've loved
her just as much as you do."

They both looked down at the precious girl in his arms.

"Haley wasn't planned," Ruby said. "But she's the most
wonderful thing that ever happened to me. That's life, Devon.
It's messy and scary and unpredictable. Sometimes, the worst
happens, and we can't prepare for it. It rips out our hearts
and lungs and we don't even know how we can keep going.
But the best things aren't planned, either. It's our job to recognize those opportunities for happiness and not let them pass
us by. Even if it means throwing all our plans out the
window."

The baby's eyes had fluttered closed. Ruby set the bottle
aside and shifted Haley back into her arms. Devon was sorry
to feel her warm weight disappear.

"I know it's scary to be out of a job. You don't know what
you'll do next. But do me a favor and slow down. Let me
worry about the bills for a while. Recognize the opportunity

the universe is giving you—to figure out what you truly want. If that's Aurora, then I really hope you'll go for it."

ONCE RUBY and Haley had returned to bed, Devon went back to work. But after scanning day after day of footage, and seeing Aurora several more times, he hadn't spotted anyone who looked like their mystery man. He clenched his fists in frustration.

"I've had no luck so far, either," Sylvie said when they got back on the phone.

His mind was straining for connections, but the pieces wouldn't fit. "I say we should take Aurora at her word. She did see the guy around The Lighthouse at some point. If so, what does that mean?"

"That he knew Brandon Wolfson. We've already considered that. But—"

"Wait a minute. What about the other people associated with the club? Like Wolfson's wife? Or his assistant? I've seen them all over the video footage. They were around the club all the time. What do we know about them?"

"I've got some basic background on them. The assistant is Jennifer Scoville. Single, a recent transplant from Las Vegas, where she was a personal assistant to some big-shot types before Wolfson hired her away. And Nadia Wolfson? A local to West Oaks. Just like Max, she's climbed the social ladder around here to the top."

"Vegas." Devon knew he was grasping at shadows at this point. But he was getting desperate for some kind of lead. "Do you have contacts in Nevada? If the Escalade driver is new to West Oaks, too, and he's been around The Lighthouse Club, could Jennifer be his connection?"

"Worth a try. But even Vegas is asleep by now." She stifled a yawn. "I gotta be honest. I'm fading."

Devon checked the clock. It was past four. The sun would be up soon. "Aurora's testifying this morning, right?"

"Yep. First thing."

Devon had no doubt that Max would have ample security in place. Yet unease still gnawed at him. "I don't like that we have this big question mark out there. No matter how much security is around her, she's still going out in the open tomorrow. Max can't control every single factor at a public building like the courthouse."

"I know what you mean. But this is out of our hands. Lana told me the defense attorneys refused to come to our office. They insisted on the courthouse because it's neutral territory."

All of that reasoning made perfect sense. Yet Devon couldn't shake that sick feeling in his gut—that there was a countdown clock somewhere, and he was running out of time. Maybe he was just upset over what had happened earlier, and it was really his guilt talking.

He appreciated what Ruby had suggested. Slowing down and considering what he wanted out of life. He planned to do just that. But only after he was convinced that Aurora was out of danger.

"I'm going to keep at it with the security footage. Just in case. Could you call Vegas as soon as possible to see if your contacts recognize our mystery guy?"

"I will. But try to get rest at some point?"

"At some point."

He might not work for Bennett anymore, and he might not be Aurora's bodyguard, but he cared about her. If she got hurt now, and he could've protected her, then it would be his fault.

Aurora wouldn't be safe until they'd found the man who was after her. Then, and only then—once she was truly out of harm's way—he would tell her exactly how he felt.

Chapter Thirty-Seven

*A*urora hardly spoke on the drive to the courthouse. Outside, it looked like just another beautiful morning in West Oaks. The sun shone on the ocean, and joggers and roller-bladers crowded the sidewalks. But she felt like it was still night, and she hadn't managed to wake up.

In the seat beside her, Lana reached for her hand. "Almost there."

Two of Max's bodyguards sat in the front seats. They were big, burly guys, and Aurora had missed their names. More bodyguards were traveling in the cars ahead of them and behind. Max was in one of those vehicles too, commanding the whole operation of getting her safely to testify.

But the one person she wanted to see wasn't here.

Lana had spent the morning going over everything yet again. But Aurora couldn't seem to hold on to her thoughts. "How long did you say this would take? I'm sorry. I know you already told me."

Lana squeezed her hand reassuringly. "It's okay. My questioning will last for about an hour. Then we'll have a break, and it'll be the defense lawyers' turn. I can't say how long they'll want with you. Probably several hours, and then I'll re-direct."

"Right." She wasn't looking forward to the back and forth. And if she didn't get her head together, she was going to get mixed up and say all the wrong things. No matter how she felt inside, she was doing something important. Even if Brandon Wolfson somehow deserved what had happened to him, his wife still needed justice, too.

Focus, Aurora told herself. *And this will all be over soon.*

Then she could crawl back into her bed and not get up for the foreseeable future. She almost laughed, remembering that she didn't even know where her bed was anymore. She had no interest in going back to her old penthouse apartment. Nor did she want to keep staying at Max's.

"Do you think I can stay with you tonight?" she asked. "Until I figure out what I'm going to do."

"Of course, you can. Anything you want. But Rory, things are going to get back to normal. I know that's hard to believe right now, but we'll get there."

If only she could believe that. But her life had already been on precarious ground before this, even if she hadn't seen it. Since the moment she'd returned to West Oaks, she'd been building her foundation on top of her brother's success. She had to start over and do things right this time. Find her own way. She just had no idea what that would look like.

And the thing she wanted to know most of all? If Devon would be part of that life. She hadn't had a chance to get in touch with him. She'd even looked around for Sylvie that morning, hoping that Devon's friend would know how to reach him. But Sylvie apparently had the day off because she was nowhere to be found.

Finally, they pulled into the courthouse and spoke to a security guard. The man let them through the barrier, and they drove into an underground garage.

Max got out of the SUV beside hers. "Everyone, get into

position. I want you all to be extra vigilant until we get upstairs."

One of the bodyguards opened her door and escorted her out. Additional guards flanked her on every side. She felt like a prisoner, rather than someone being protected. Somehow, she had felt much safer when Devon was the only one beside her.

Max and Lana walked ahead. Aurora and her guards followed, their footsteps echoing against the concrete of the parking garage.

They rode an elevator to the main floor, where police officers met them and escorted them through the metal detectors. Max and his team had to turn over their weapons. Aurora kept her eyes open, checking every face she passed. But she didn't see the Escalade driver who had attacked her and shot Devon. Nor did she see anyone that she recognized from the invasion of her apartment building.

But according to Lana, those men had worked for the Silverlake Syndicate, and Dominic had called off any further attempts on her. She wished she could feel reassured.

All this effort proved that everyone, especially her brother, knew she was still in danger.

Finally, they made it upstairs to the small courtroom where she would testify. It was far less ornate than courtrooms she had seen on TV. It seemed more like a conference room, with tables arranged in an odd configuration, and a few rows of benches for the audience.

Max's guards pulled her off into a corner. Lana came over and whispered, "Dominic Crane is just arriving."

At that same moment, the door to the court room opened. Dominic Crane walked in, escorted by officers. Aurora sucked in a breath. It was the first time she had seen him in person since right before Brandon Wolfson died. The man was even taller than she remembered, his form lithe and lean. His black hair was slicked back from his face, and he wore an expensive tailored suit. His features and pale skin had an ethereal beauty, like he should've been a model instead of a mobster.

Next, the other two defendants came inside, but they were in prisoner jumpsuits instead of designer threads. Aurora guessed that Crane's henchman hadn't made bail like he did, but she didn't care enough to ask Lana how it all worked. She preferred that these men weren't out on the street.

She studied each man in turn. There was the guy with a pointed nose and glasses, who looked every bit as mean as the last time she'd seen him. And then there was the man who'd pulled the trigger. Eric Madden. His gray hair was pulled back into that same ponytail, and his hard gaze roved over the room, meeting hers. A tremor ran through her body.

The day they'd killed Brandon Wolfson, these men hadn't known she was in the room. But she wasn't hiding anymore. And she refused to be afraid. These men, or someone trying to help them, had wanted to silence her. But today, they would hear her voice. They wouldn't be able to stop her.

"When can we start?" she asked Lana.

But Lana was staring at her phone, frowning. "Hold on, I just got a message from Eric Madden's lawyer. It looks like he's having some sort of delay."

She got up to confer with the other two defense lawyers. They were all whispering furiously, as if they had no idea what to make of this development.

A woman came in carrying a tray of drinks. She made for Aurora's side of the room, and Max stepped in front of her. "Can I help you with something?"

"Sorry, I'm with the clerk's office. I was assigned to help out today. I thought you all might be thirsty."

"Max, it's fine." Aurora waved the woman over. "I'd love a drink, thanks."

The woman handed her a paper cup of coffee. It tasted terrible, but the clerk kept hanging around, smiling, so Aurora sipped as much of it as she could. Besides, the extra caffeine wasn't a bad thing.

Lana came over to explain that they would have to wait a bit longer for Eric Madden's lawyer. He'd had some kind of emergency, and no one else from his law office could fill in.

"If we don't wait for him, we're going to have to cancel and reschedule. I don't want to do that."

Aurora agreed. So, there was nothing they could do but wait.

But after about half an hour, her stomach started to gurgle in a concerning way. She dismissed it at first as just nerves. But after several more minutes, the churning got worse, and she had to ask for the bathroom.

"Wait a minute," Max said. "Let me get my people in place in the hallways to secure the path."

"Max, anybody in this building had to get past the security and the metal detectors. I *cannot wait*. This is an emergency." If she didn't get to the bathroom soon, she'd vomit in front of everyone. She didn't want the defendants to see her in such a state.

Aurora barged past her brother, with her bodyguards scrambling to trail behind her.

The ladies' room was just down the hall. A bodyguard went in first to confirm that no one else was inside. By then, Aurora was getting desperate. At the bathroom door, Max said, "Go ahead. But if you take too long, I'm going to have to send someone in to check on you."

Without another word, she rushed inside, glaring at Max to leave her alone. She really didn't want any witnesses for whatever her stomach was doing. She barely made it to the toilet in time before she started to retch.

What was going on? She'd barely eaten anything since yesterday. She couldn't imagine that she had food poisoning. The coffee hadn't been great, but this seemed like an extreme reaction.

Thankfully, Max didn't make good on his threat to send anyone after her. She felt like her body was turning itself inside out. After a while, though, there didn't seem to be anything else left in her digestive system. But she was sweaty and feverish and felt completely gross. She would have to clean herself up as best she could to make herself presentable. Hopefully, washing her face and running her fingers through her hair would be enough. She would've paid a hundred bucks for a toothbrush.

But when she exited the stall, she found someone standing by the sinks. Aurora gasped, jumping back.

It was Jennifer Scoville, Brandon Wolfson's assistant.

Jennifer raised a finger to her lips, indicating that Aurora should stay quiet.

"You don't seem to be feeling so well." As if it were otherwise perfectly normal for her to be here.

"How did you get in here? Why are you at the courthouse at all? What is—"

Jennifer's hand moved from behind her back. She was holding a small black revolver.

She pointed it at Aurora.

"You are going to stay very quiet and do exactly as I say. Either that, or you aren't going to make it out of this building alive."

Chapter Thirty-Eight

"Devon?" Chase asked. "Man, did you sleep here?"

He opened his eyes and sat up. He was still at the kitchen table with Ruby's laptop open in front of him. He must've fallen asleep looking at the video footage.

Chase stood there in the kitchen, wearing his workout clothes.

Devon rubbed his face. "What are you doing back? I thought you went to the apartment Max is loaning you."

"I did. But I was up early for the gym and came to check on things. Also, your mom makes the best huevos rancheros. She and Ruby still asleep?"

"I guess so. Wait, why do you have a key to this house?"

"So I can help out when you're not around. Pretty sure you're the one who asked me to do that? Look out for your mom and Ruby while you were working?"

Devon's mouth twisted into a frown, even though Chase was right.

Chase opened a cabinet and threw Devon a protein bar. "Eat something. You look awful. And you have computer keys imprinted in your face."

Devon ran a hand over his cheek, feeling the indentations.

"What were you up so late doing?" Chase tore into his own protein bar.

Devon woke up the computer and logged back on to the Bennett Security server, relieved to see he still had access with Sylvie's passcode.

He explained to Chase that he was trying to explore a lead to the Escalade driver's identity. They suspected the man might have some connection to the Wolfsons and The Lighthouse Club. But they hadn't managed to find any proof of that yet.

"I've got a few more days of footage to go over. Want to help?"

Chase sat down at the kitchen table, swallowing the last of his snack. "Sure. My shift doesn't start until this afternoon. Might as well."

Once again, Devon started to scan through the surveillance footage. Chase complained that he was going too slow, so he sped up the replay. They were getting closer to the night of the "Angels and Demons" party.

He was running out of video. But there had to be something, some clue.

And then, there she was: Aurora stepping into the club in a long black dress on the night of the party. His breath caught, even though he knew she would've looked so much more beautiful in person. Thankfully, Chase didn't make any smart comments.

They slowed down the replay as they combed through those final hours just before the party began. They had to go camera by camera, so it wasn't possible in an efficient way to see all the footage chronologically. They had to piece it together as each camera angle revealed a bit more of the story.

Chase sat forward. "Go back. I think I saw something."

Devon moved the time back slightly. They were watching a camera that had been aimed at an alley on the side of the club. It faced an exit door. Not the one that Crane and his men had used, which had very conveniently not had a working camera on it at the time. This exit door was over by the kitchens. Several times, workers came in and out.

"All I see is people hauling trash to the dumpster. What is it?"

"Start moving forward," Chase said. "Slowly. I thought I saw someone that didn't belong." The seconds ticked by, and then Chase pointed. "There. Pause it."

Devon studied the screen. Chase was right. There was a blond woman stepping out of the exit door. She was wearing an evening gown, not the typical clothing for the employees they'd seen using this door otherwise.

"I think that's Mrs. Wolfson." Devon moved the video forward several seconds more.

And then another face came into view. This was a man, barrel-chested and burly. He stepped out of the shadows of the alley and spoke briefly to Mrs. Wolfson, keeping his face tilted away from the camera. But for one brief moment, he turned, facing the lens.

Devon took a still image and zoomed in. Bennett's high-quality cameras didn't disappoint. They could see the man's face clearly. He had gray hair, a ponytail. An observant gaze.

"Do you recognize him?" Chase asked.

"No."

It wasn't the Escalade driver. Devon wasn't sure who this guy was, or even if this meeting with Mrs. Wolfson meant anything at all. He hit his thigh with a fist, cursing. All this effort had led them nowhere once again.

"Wait," Chase said. "He seems familiar. I feel like I *should* recognize him. But it's just not coming to me."

"I'll send the photo to Sylvie. Maybe she can place him." Her photographic memory was a major asset. If this guy was connected to the case at all, Sylvie would know.

After finishing his review of the recordings, though, Devon

hadn't found anything else useful. And he hadn't heard back from Sylvie, either about the photo or about her contacts in Vegas. Maybe she was getting some much-deserved sleep after their late night.

"So, we're basically back to square one." Devon rested his forehead in his hand.

Chase sat back down at the kitchen table, chewing on a second protein bar. Mom and Ruby still weren't up.

"But what about the leak of Aurora's identity as the witness?" Chase asked. "How did Crane's men, or this Escalade guy, find out about her? You don't still think it was anyone in my department, right?"

"No, we pretty much ruled that out. Even the cops who were stationed outside Aurora's building didn't know they were guarding her. That's another mystery. Nobody knew, except a few people in the DA's office and a handful of Bennett Security employees. And then a few more people, including you, after the first attack on Aurora's building."

That was something else that didn't add up. So much about this case just didn't make any fucking sense.

"And the filing clerks that work for the court," Chase pointed out. "They would've known too. Because Lana filed the sealed complaints."

"Hold on. The what?"

"The complaints? The official documents that charged Crane and the others with murder? The DA's office filed them under seal, right? Meaning their contents remained secret until the court unsealed them later, after the police made the arrests. So those people you mentioned knew, but so did the filing clerk that entered the documents into the record. And whoever else at the court records department who had access."

Devon jumped up, energy rushing through his veins. His exhaustion was gone. He looked for his mom's cell phone. Where had he put it?

Chase kept talking, not seeming to realize the urgency Devon was feeling. "But those workers deal with sensitive records all the time. It's pretty far-fetched to think they would have leaked that information."

"I don't care what's likely or not. It's possible. And Aurora is at the courthouse right now."

He found the phone on the kitchen chair. It must've slipped while he was asleep. Devon called Sylvie, praying that she would answer.

"Hello?" She sounded sleepy, but he'd apologize later for waking her.

"Sylvie, is Aurora at the courthouse now?"

"I think so. Based on what Lana mentioned yesterday. Why?"

"I was just talking to my friend Chase, and he mentioned that the records people at the courthouse would've had access to those secret court documents that Lana filed with Aurora's identity. Is that something you looked into? When you were trying to figure out how her identity got leaked?"

"Oh my god. How could we have missed that?"

There was a sound of things moving, and Devon guessed that Sylvie was walking around her place.

"I just sent a message to Max. I told him to be on the lookout for anything strange at the courthouse."

Devon exhaled. "Good, thank you."

"I think he's got at least six of the guys going with Aurora today. If anyone tries something, they'll be ready. But this information could help. Thank you, Dev."

"Hold on, wait. I'm guessing you haven't seen my email? I found something in the footage from The Lighthouse Club. From the night of Wolfson's murder. It looks like his wife, Nadia Wolfson, is talking to some guy in an alley, like they didn't want anyone to see them. Chase and I couldn't tell who the guy was. But maybe you can."

"Yeah, I'll look." There was a pause while Sylvie pulled up

the message. Then she drew in a sharp breath. "I know exactly who this guy is. This is Eric Madden. Aurora witnessed him pull the trigger and kill Brandon Wolfson. What was he doing talking to Wolfson's wife?"

"That's exactly what I want to know." Devon didn't like this, not at all. They had assumed Mrs. Wolfson wasn't involved in her husband's shady business dealings—because she claimed to have no knowledge. She certainly hadn't said anything about knowing the guy who killed her husband.

The same man that Aurora was testifying against *right now*.

"Is it possible you could locate Mrs. Wolfson?" Devon asked. "If she's involved with these people, then we have no idea what she might be planning. Or what side she's really on."

Sylvie's fingers clicked on her keyboard. "I'm sending you Mrs. Wolfson's address. She lives up in the hills above West Oaks, in one of those fancy mansions overlooking the ocean."

Devon knew the area, though he'd only been up there to consult on some expensive custom security systems. "Do they have a Bennett Security setup?"

"Even if they do, I can't start looking at their cameras. That would be a gross violation of company policy. So that's an absolute no go. Not happening…." Sylvie had said all this in a robotic tone. "Oh no, look at that. I have an appointment soon. Better run. I'll talk to you later."

The line cut off. But Devon understood what Sylvie had really meant. She hadn't been refusing his request. Exactly the opposite—but if she was going to access the cameras at the Wolfsons' property, then it had to be off the books. The subject was way too sensitive to discuss over an open cell phone line.

They could view the footage from The Lighthouse Club all they wanted because Max was consulting on the case, and the police had taken possession of everything that could be evidence related to the murder.

But they had no such permission to be sneaking a look inside Mrs. Wolfson's private home to spy on her.

Sure enough, Sylvie wrote to Devon using an encrypted message. *Good news and bad news. Wolfson's estate used a Bennett Security system. Bad news is that it went offline after the murder. Apparently, our tech contacted the widow to see if she needed assistance, and she said she wanted to discontinue the service.*

Devon wrote back to ask if she had any of the previous footage from the home stored in the company databases.

I'll see what I can do.

But almost right away, Sylvie wrote again. *Max is calling. Stand by.*

Devon cursed, anxious to find out what was going on.

"Any updates?" Chase asked. "I can tell something's going on over there from your face, but I have no idea what."

Quickly, Devon tried to fill in his friend—that they suspected Mrs. Wolfson might have more involvement in the conspiracy than they'd realized before. "But if Sylvie can get access to their camera recordings from before the murder, it might show who the Wolfsons were associating with. Maybe Wolfson and his wife knew all of these people a lot better than we thought."

Maybe they'd even find the Escalade driver among them.

The phone rang again, and Devon grabbed it. Sylvie sounded breathless when she spoke.

"Devon, they've taken her. Aurora is gone."

Chapter Thirty-Nine

*A*urora could hardly breathe. "Where are we going?"

They were crawling through an air ventilation system. It had connected to the courthouse bathroom—that was how Jennifer had snuck inside. But Aurora still couldn't understand what Jennifer had to do with any of this.

"Just keep moving," the other woman said from behind. "Don't make me ask you again."

Aurora was trying not to panic, but every second, Jennifer was forcing her farther away from any help.

Had Max figured out she was missing yet? Would he realize they'd gone into the air ducts? She felt like ages had passed, but it had probably been just a few minutes.

"You did something to the coffee, didn't you? Did that woman know? The one who gave me the drink?"

"We had to get you into the bathroom somehow. She gets paid to do what we tell her, not to ask questions about why."

"But…"

Jennifer's hand grabbed Aurora's calf and pinched. "Shut up and move faster, you little brat. So fucking entitled, aren't you?"

She blanched at the woman's cruel tone. Jennifer had been

so kind before—obviously, all for show. *But why?* Aurora's mind demanded. *Why is this happening?* For now, she kept her mouth shut. She was afraid of what Jennifer might do if she didn't.

Aurora kept crawling forward inside the narrow shaft. Dust tickled her nose. Her eyes watered as she stared forward in the dark, trying to see what lay ahead. But only small amounts of light filtered in through the metal walls of her prison.

Eventually, she ran into a barrier. "The shaft ends here. What now?"

"Just push. The panel should be loose."

Aurora pushed on the thin wall, and it collapsed away, clattering against concrete. Jennifer shoved her from behind, and she stepped out into the parking garage.

Aurora inhaled, ready to scream for help. But then she felt the sharp pressure of the gun barrel in her back.

"Don't even think about it. This way."

They rounded a corner, and Aurora saw a white delivery van.

In front of the van stood the man who had attacked her and Devon. The nondescript, blue-eyed man who'd been following her for days.

She forgot about Jennifer. Forgot about the gun. She turned and tried to run, desperate to get away from him. But the man closed the distance between them in a few short steps and grabbed hold of her. He shoved his hand over her mouth, lifting her into the air as she kicked.

He shoved her into the back of the van and onto the floor. Jennifer slid inside and held the gun to Aurora's forehead. "You still have a chance of making it out of this. *If* you cooperate. But if you make this difficult, I won't hesitate. Do you understand?"

Aurora nodded. "Who is he? That man?" He hadn't said a word. Aurora realized that she had never heard him speak.

"My fiancé," Jennifer said. "Beck Neuman. Though I

think you've already met him a time or two?'"

Jennifer's fiancé? What the hell?

What else did they want from her? If he and Jennifer wanted her dead, why hadn't they already done it?

Her mind worked, trying to come up with some way out of this. She had something that these people needed—otherwise, they wouldn't keep her alive.

But would they truly let her go after they got it? She didn't believe that. Beck had been perfectly willing to shoot her just days ago. All she could do was lie here and wait to learn more, hoping that she could come up with some way to escape.

Or that someone figured out where they were taking her. Because she certainly didn't know.

Beck got into the front seat and the engine revved. He eased out of the parking garage, pausing only briefly at the exit.

The truck drove slowly at first, winding through the downtown streets. Aurora listened carefully, counting the seconds as they passed. Then the vehicle picked up speed, clearly now on the freeway.

With every mile that passed beneath her, her panic grew. But the counting helped keep her calm. When she'd gotten up to ten minutes, they exited the freeway and were back on city streets. She couldn't see through any windows but guessed from the car's movements.

Then the truck began to climb. That meant they were in the hills north of West Oaks, in the fancy neighborhood full of massive houses that dotted the seaside cliffs. The most envied real estate location in the region, a place Aurora had never personally visited in all her years of growing up here.

But why would Jennifer be taking her to this area? She couldn't imagine that Jennifer could afford a house here on an assistant salary. Max probably had friends here, but—

Then it dawned on her, just as the van pulled to a stop.

The doors opened. A salt-scented breeze ruffled her hair. She could hear waves crashing against rocks.

Jennifer pulled her upright, still aiming the gun. Beck reached into the back and yanked Aurora outside.

$\mathcal{T}$he light turned red, and Devon slammed on the brakes. He screamed a curse.

"Ow," Sylvie complained from the phone, "can you turn down your volume a little? I'm trying to concentrate."

"You think I'm not?"

"Green light," Chase said from the passenger seat.

Devon stomped on the accelerator, and the car lurched forward. "How much farther to the turn?"

"Half a mile," Sylvie responded. "You're almost there."

After they'd learned from Max that Aurora was missing from the courthouse, Devon had jumped straight into his car. He hadn't even known a destination, just that he couldn't stay put while those bastards had Aurora.

She was out there somewhere, and he had to find her.

It was Sylvie who'd realized where they had to go. "Max said that Eric Madden's lawyer is missing, too. Clearly, it was a ploy to delay Aurora's testimony so they could snatch her first. This was planned. And we know, because of you, that Eric Madden is tied to Nadia Wolfson."

It wasn't proof that they would find Aurora at the Wolfson estate. But Sylvie had also heard back from her friends in

Vegas—they'd identified the Escalade driver as Beck Neuman, a suspected hit man for organized criminals in Nevada.

Neuman would want to take Aurora to a secure, isolated location. Wolfson's cliffside estate fit the bill.

It wasn't much, but it was the best lead they had.

Max and his team had also identified the delivery van that must've carried Aurora away from the courthouse, and the police had issued a BOLO. So, Aurora's kidnappers couldn't have taken her very far. They would've wanted to get off the streets. Max had people spreading out all over town at this very moment, checking other possible locations where Aurora could be hidden.

But Devon had been the closest to the hills. He was going to beat everyone else there. At least Chase was with him, in case this got messy.

"Do we know yet if that delivery truck came into Nadia Wolfson's neighborhood?" Devon asked.

"They probably came through a different route. Only one side of the neighborhood has a manned guardhouse, and we already know this Beck Neuman guy isn't sloppy. He wouldn't have gone that way. I have my team checking security cameras around town for me, but I have my hands a bit full between you and Max."

Sylvie's voice was tense, and Devon couldn't blame her. They were all working as fast as they possibly could.

But if we don't find her in time... He wouldn't let himself finish that sentence. They were going to find her. *He* was going to find her. There was no other option.

Chase spoke into his own phone briefly, then lowered it. "Backup from West Oaks P.D. is a few minutes behind us. But until we can confirm that Aurora is at the Wolfson estate, they won't order in the SWAT team. Someone in Lana's office is working on a search warrant, but we only have threads to go on at this point. It probably won't be enough."

Devon slammed his palm against the steering wheel in

frustration. Neuman could only be minutes ahead of them, considering how quickly Max had realized she was gone from the courthouse. And yet, the man was running circles around all of them.

I'm going to kill him for this. And if he lays a finger on Aurora, I'm going to make it slow and painful.

He drove even faster, barely making it through the next yellow light before it switched to red. Chase grabbed onto the dashboard. "Careful, man. If we don't get there, then we can't help her."

"The turn is coming up," Sylvie shouted through the phone, watching their progress on her computer.

"I see it."

Devon's tires squealed as he turned and started climbing the road into the hills. Sylvie had already spoken to the guard at the gatehouse, and the man waved in acknowledgment as they passed.

Devon sailed around the curves as they climbed higher and higher into the hills. He squinted when they turned toward the ocean, the sun glaring off its surface.

By the time they pulled up to Wolfson's property, Devon's lungs were aching. He'd been holding his breath.

"The gate to Wolfson's driveway is already open," Chase said. "Looks like there's a crowd here."

Devon pulled into the parking area. There were at least a dozen fancy cars here, Teslas and Range Rovers and Audis. Devon's modest sedan stuck out in these lush surroundings just as much as Devon himself did.

He and Chase jogged to the front door. It was already open, with a stern looking man barring the way.

"Are you here for the party?" The man eyed Devon and Chase's informal attire. They both wore jeans and T-shirts. Chase didn't even have his uniform on.

"We're here to speak to Nadia Wolfson," Devon said.

"I'll inquire if Mrs. Wolfson is available." His tone

conveyed that she probably wouldn't be. The man retreated inside, closing the door in their faces.

Devon looked up at the house. It had a red brick facade and elegant white pillars. It looked more like a plantation home straight out of the south than a California beachside escape.

It took all his self-control not to burst through the door and demand answers. His fingers drummed rapidly against his thigh.

"What are they doing in there?"

"It's only been about a minute," Chase murmured. "We have to play it cool. We have no other choice until that warrant comes through and backup arrives."

Devon knew that everything his friend said was the truth. But that didn't make it any easier to wait.

The door swung open, and Devon took a halting step forward. Nadia Wolfson stood there, dressed in simple white, a look of concern on her face.

"Can I help you? This isn't the best time, whatever it is you're selling. I'm in the middle of an event."

The sound of voices and tinkling dishware came from further in the house.

"We're looking for Aurora Bennett. She's been kidnapped. Eric Madden and his associates are trying to keep her from testifying—associates that include *you*."

Shock rippled across her features. "Why would I want to do that? My husband was the one Eric Madden killed. I want nothing more than to see him and Dominic Crane behind bars. But Aurora is missing? That's awful. What happened?"

Devon kept throwing questions at her, but the woman didn't betray anything. If she was lying, then she was quite the actress.

But if she was really involved in this conspiracy, as they now believed, then she'd have to be.

"You're welcome to come inside," Nadia said. "You'll just

find a bunch of women who're here to commiserate with me. It's a dreary way to celebrate a birthday, but at least I'm not alone."

Devon and Chase went inside. But after several minutes of walking through every part of the Wolfsons' plush residence, they hadn't found anything that hinted at Aurora being here.

Devon spotted Jennifer Scoville in passing. Like the other party guests, she watched him curiously, sipping a glass of champagne.

"Any updates on your end?" he asked Chase quietly in the hall.

His friend shook his head. Devon checked his mom's phone, which he'd brought with him. Sylvie hadn't sent any further updates.

"Thank you for your cooperation," Chase said to Nadia. "We'll come back later if there's more."

"With a warrant, I trust? Because I think I've been more than generous with my time. And my home."

Chase nodded. Devon couldn't even get a word out. His throat was too tight. They'd wasted at least half an hour, and they had absolutely nothing to show for it. He and Sylvie had been wrong. Maybe Mrs. Wolfson was still involved, but Aurora wasn't here.

They went back out to the car, got in, and slammed their doors. He sent off a quick text to Sylvie telling her that they'd reached another dead end.

"Our backup got diverted to a car accident," Chase said. "Not that we needed it, apparently. With a warrant, we could get access to Nadia Wolfson's computers and documents to prove she was involved. But without more evidence first to implicate her, I doubt the warrant's coming."

And Aurora was still out there somewhere. They had no idea where she might be. Devon paused behind the wheel, unsure of what to do next. He was at a loss in every possible way.

If not for his colossal screwup, he might've been with Aurora at the courthouse today. He didn't know if he would've been able to prevent her kidnapping, but at least he would've had the chance.

He'd failed her. Now she was paying for it.

"We can't keep sitting here," Chase said. "Let's head back downtown, check in with Sylvie, and see what else we can do."

Devon started the car and turned around, heading slowly back downhill.

The phone rang. It was Sylvie. He picked up. "Say you have something. Anything. Please."

"I might. The house next door to Nadia's sold in just the last few weeks. And guess who the buyer was? Jennifer Scoville. Brandon Wolfson's former assistant."

Devon swung the car around while Sylvie was still talking. He drove past the Wolfson residence and onto the next driveway, which was farther uphill. A sprawling white stucco house appeared, its windows dark. Unlike Nadia's place, this house seemed deserted.

They jumped out of the car and ran to the front door. Chase knocked frantically, but Devon was tired of wasting time. He went around the side of the house, where he'd be concealed from the street. He averted his face, covered his arm with his shirt, and bashed a hole in a window.

But there was nobody inside when they searched. No sign of Aurora at all.

Where was she?

---

Chapter Forty-One

*A*urora sat in a stiff wooden chair, her hands bound behind her. Beck Neuman stood casually across from her, holding the revolver. He hadn't taken his eyes off her once.

"Not very talkative, are you?" she asked.

"Throat surgery." His voice was scratchy and low. "Cancerous tumor. I nearly died."

"How upsetting for you."

He nodded, as if she were sincere. "I realized I wanted more out of life. To have a family. I asked Jennifer to marry me. My fee for this operation will get us started."

"Heartwarming," Aurora deadpanned.

The guy was a psychopath.

And she still didn't understand what he wanted with her. They'd parked in front of a white stucco house, and Jennifer had disappeared. Beck had carried Aurora down a set of stairs along the cliff to this guesthouse.

At first, she'd been terrified. But the longer they sat in silence, the more her anger took over. She didn't know this man. He had nothing to do with her. Yet he was willing to kill her, all in the name of settling down and starting a family? Aurora couldn't imagine being that twisted.

Yet Jennifer was far worse. She'd looked into Aurora's face time and again, pretending to be her friend. Aurora was pissed at herself for letting that happen. She'd probably beat herself up about it later. But right now, she let all that rage fuel her.

She was going to get out of this, and she was going to make them pay.

Starting with Beck Neuman—because he had shot and wounded Devon. Even if she could somehow forgive everything else this man put her through, she was not going to forgive that.

Neuman eyed her, like he could somehow see the thoughts passing through her brain. "No one's going to find you here. Might as well accept that now."

She looked through the huge windows at the view. The guesthouse was small and modest compared to the grand white house uphill, but the ocean panorama was breathtaking.

"We'll see," Aurora said.

Then she heard footsteps approaching along the path.

Nadia Wolfson appeared in the windows. She slid open the glass door and walked inside.

"*Nadia?*" The nausea in Aurora's stomach increased. She had suspected that Mrs. Wolfson could be involved, but hadn't wanted to believe it.

"I'm sorry about this." The woman did truly look regretful. "I'd hoped it wouldn't be necessary."

"Why am I here?" Aurora's wrists strained as she pulled at her bindings. "I want an explanation."

"I suppose I owe you that much." Nadia took a seat in a comfortable upholstered chair, her long legs crossing. "It's not personal, Aurora. At least, it didn't start that way. I never wanted you to get caught up in this. You were supposed to plan the party where Brandon would die, take your generous pay, and go home none the wiser. But you had to complicate things."

"You planned your husband's murder. Didn't you?"

"Jennifer helped." Nadia stood up, sweeping her hair over her shoulder. "Oh, don't look so shocked. Brandon was really as despicable as they say. It was his choice to start laundering money for Dominic Crane and the Silverlake Syndicate. But that's how I met Eric. He hated working for a weak leader like Crane, and I hated my husband. We both saw a way to free ourselves. Take control of our situations. You seem like a strong woman. That has to be something you understand, right? Wanting to forge your own path?"

Aurora didn't give her the satisfaction of agreeing. But Nadia went on anyway.

"It was my idea for Brandon to divert funds from Crane for us to start our own competing enterprise. Eric helped from within the Syndicate. Meanwhile, we made sure that Crane found out about Brandon's betrayal just when we wanted him to. I set up the 'Angels and Demons' party as the perfect opportunity for Crane to deal out vengeance. Eric was right there, to make sure that Brandon didn't survive the night, even if Crane was too soft. Which he was. There was never supposed to be anyone there to witness Eric pulling the trigger. I'm sorry you had to see that."

"But you were planning to blame the murder on Crane? How was that supposed to work, without any witnesses or evidence? Because Crane was never going to be the one to fire the gun."

A man like Crane never got his hands dirty. Aurora could tell that much about the man, whatever else she thought of him.

Nadia shrugged dismissively. "I never intended to send Crane to prison. The plan was always to undermine Crane's position within the Syndicate. We helped Brandon cheat him and make him look like a fool. Eric was going to take advantage of Crane's weakness within the organization and make his move to seize control. That part of things is still going forward, at least. Crane isn't going to be the leader of the Syndicate for long. But I can't allow Eric to wind up in prison. He's my ticket to a powerful role within the Syndicate. They should have a West Oaks native like me in charge of their operations here. It's good business sense, which they might've seen if I wasn't a woman."

"So, you had to make sure I didn't testify against Eric. You hired *him* to get rid of me." Aurora tilted her chin toward Beck Neuman, who still watched her impassively.

"Crane's allies went after you first. The Syndicate has informants all over—including inside the court records department. They passed on your identity as the witness, and I already knew where you lived. I gave them access to the Bennett Security system at The Lighthouse Club so they could figure out your brother's weaknesses. Of course, I was hedging my bets, sending Beck after you as well. Sadly, the Syndicate goons botched the job, and prolonged all this mess. Then Crane put out the word to leave you alone. Yet one more sign of his weakness and his selfishness—because he was guaranteeing you'd testify against *Eric*. As if Eric was expendable, just a pawn. So, Beck carried on himself."

The man nodded. "But I wouldn't have gotten anywhere without your and Jennifer's help."

Aurora glared at the woman. "What did you do?"

Nadia had the nerve to look sheepish. "None of us had any idea where you'd gone after you fled your brother's apartment building. But then, you and I had that video call. I could see the old water tower through the window of the house where you were staying. I've lived in West Oaks since I was a child, even longer than you. I'd know that water tower in a heartbeat. It didn't take much effort to pinpoint exactly which house you were holed up in. You never should've spoken to anyone while you were there, Aurora. It was foolish of you to be so trusting. The real world is too harsh for a girl like you."

Aurora tugged at her wrist ties again, shaking with fury. "You sent Neuman to kill me. You've wanted me dead this whole time. Why am I still sitting here? Why are you keeping me alive at all?"

Lines appeared in her otherwise flawless skin. "Because you sent Jennifer and me Beck's picture yesterday. Obviously, you and your brother were getting way too close. I couldn't let you discover my part in this. You're here to tell me everything that Max and Lana Marchetti know. Have they learned Beck's real identity?"

"Yes," Aurora spat out. "Sending the photo yesterday was a test. My brother knows you're involved, and any minute he's going to show up. His people have probably already surrounded this place."

Nadia slowly shook her head, regarding her like a disappointed mother. "I don't think Aurora has a future on the Vegas poker circuit, do you, Beck? She really needs to work on her bluffing."

Damn. It had been worth a try. "Then I'll make a deal— let me go and I'll testify that Crane pulled the trigger. I'll say that Eric was never inside Wolfson's office at all."

"All right. I'm convinced." Nadia headed toward the glass door. She paused with her fingers around the handle. "Convinced that you don't know a thing that I need to worry about. Beck, you can toss her off the cliff, and the current will get rid of her. I should get back to my guests. I told them I was upset and needed some time alone, and they'll be worried. My party was already disrupted enough by your friends looking for you."

My friends? Who had been looking for her?

"Wait! Nadia, please." Aurora's chair nearly tipped over as she struggled. But Nadia was gone, leaving the glass door open. Cool, salty air blew through the room.

Beck advanced on her. He still had his gun, but he wasn't using it. Probably so there wouldn't be a bullet in her body that could serve later as evidence. She'd simply wash up along the coast somewhere, and no one would have any idea she'd been here.

Aurora kicked at him. Her heel connected with his knee, and he grunted in pain. "Don't make this harder on yourself."

He pulled her up from the chair, leaving her hands still bound. Neuman forced her outside, half dragging and half carrying her. Aurora kept kicking, but it wasn't any use.

"Help me!"

Neuman pushed her toward the edge of the cliff. The low metal railing pressed into Aurora's hip. Her weight tipped forward. She saw the white foam. Heard the crash of the waves on the rocks below. Hair whipped across her face in the wind.

"*No*," she screamed.

"Neuman, take another step and you're dead."

She knew that voice. "Devon?"

He was here for her. He'd really come.

Too fast, Beck spun himself behind her. She felt his gun barrel at her temple.

Devon stood on the cliffside path, holding a weapon in both hands. His shoulders were back, his face a mask of concentration. He wore civilian clothing, but he was every inch the soldier.

"It's over. Give up and step away from her. *Now*."

Chapter Forty-Two

*D*evon faced down the man who'd shot him. The man who'd tried to kill him and Aurora both.

Beck Neuman.

The man who now held a gun to Aurora's head.

"You've got nowhere to go, Neuman. It's over."

They'd seen Nadia when she climbed the stairs up the cliffside. Chase had grabbed the woman, and Nadia had made up a whole story about how Beck Neuman was holding Aurora hostage. As if she herself were just another victim.

They'd deal with Nadia Wolfson later. Chase would make sure the woman didn't go anywhere. Max's team and half the police in West Oaks were currently speeding toward this location. Backup might be minutes away, but Aurora was in danger *now*.

Devon took a step closer. The man jabbed the gun at Aurora's temple, making her scream. A red scratch appeared on her skin. Devon swallowed down his rage.

"Drop your gun," Neuman said in a harsh, scratchy voice. "Or she dies."

"If she dies, then you do."

Devon was trying to remain calm and professional. But the

other man's eyes bored into him like he could spot every source of weakness.

"I saw you with her before. I saw the way you looked at her. You won't risk her life. All you have to do is put down the gun."

"Devon, don't," Aurora cried. "He'll kill you."

Devon's shoulder ached with the same knowledge. He searched for a hole in Neuman's defenses. But the other man was well-trained, too. He was keeping Aurora in front of him as a shield, their bodies pressed against the cliffside railing. There was no way Devon could shoot Neuman without risking her. And even if he managed to hit Neuman, the man might still plummet over the side of the cliff, taking Aurora with him.

"Decide," Neuman rasped. "I'm going to count down from three."

Devon had run out of options. Dammit, he had no choice. "If I do, will you let her go?"

"Same moment your gun drops. Not before. Three...two..."

He couldn't save both Aurora and himself.

Neuman's lips drew together to count down to one. Devon's hands loosened on his weapon.

At the same moment, Neuman's gun lost contact with Aurora's temple, shifting to point at Devon.

Aurora screamed and threw herself into Neuman. The killer lost his balance, and they both tipped toward the cliff.

Neuman was teetering at the railing, about to go over. He clamped onto Aurora's arm, still trying to aim his gun with the other hand. Aurora grasped behind her for the railing, horror on her face.

Devon fired two quick taps at Neuman's chest. The man's body convulsed, arms flying wide and letting go of Aurora's arm as Devon sprinted forward.

He grabbed hold of her waist just as Neuman flipped over the railing.

The man didn't cry out as he fell. They only heard the surf thundering against the rocks.

Devon untied Aurora's hands, then lifted her into his arms. She was crying and holding him tight around the neck.

"You came for me."

"Of course, I did. I'm sorry it took me so long."

He carried her back toward the safety of the guesthouse. Sirens wailed nearby. "You nearly gave me a heart attack when you knocked him off balance. You almost fell." Devon hadn't felt anything but a low simmer of anger during the confrontation, but now his pulse was speeding so fast he thought he'd pass out. "I doubt Max will be happy about that."

"Who cares about Max?" Aurora touched his face. "I couldn't let Neuman hurt you again."

"Thank you." He smiled, wiping her tears. "I guess that means you're not mad?"

"You idiot. I never was."

"Maybe I should've talked to you before I quit my job and left yesterday?"

She laid her head against his shoulder. "Just don't do it again."

"Don't worry," he murmured. "I'm not going anywhere without you."

"Promise?"

He hadn't been so great about keeping promises lately. But this one, he was determined not to break.

"Yeah. I do."

MAX WAS one of the first to arrive, right behind the initial group of squad cars.

"Aurora!" He ran toward his sister.

She let go of Devon. They'd climbed up the cliffside stairs and now stood in front of the white stucco house.

Max swept her into a hug. "Are you hurt?"

"I'm okay. Thanks to Devon."

The moment Max set her down, she reached for Devon again, hooking her arm around his waist.

"Whitestone," Max said stiffly. Devon braced himself. But his boss held out a hand. "Thank you for saving her."

"Yes, sir. Nadia Wolfson was responsible for a lot of this. But the police are taking Jennifer Scoville into custody as well. She's at the house next door." Aurora had already told the officers that Jennifer kidnapped her from the courthouse.

"And Beck Neuman?" Max asked. Sylvie must've told him the guy's name.

"Dead."

Understanding passed between the two men. Max nodded. "I can't describe how grateful I am that Aurora's safe and sound."

"Grateful enough to give him his job back?" she asked. "Because you're so full of shit, and you admit it now?"

Max eyed his sister. "Possibly. I can acknowledge when I'm wrong.

"What about saying you're sorry?"

"Devon and I will discuss it later."

Devon figured that was as good a response as they'd get, so he cut off the subject. "Lana's here. She'll probably want to talk to Aurora."

The police made their arrests, ambulances came to check for injuries, and the coroner's van arrived to deal with Neuman's body, though Devon guessed it might take some time to find it in the water.

After hours of interviews at a police station, they found themselves back at the Bennett Security office. Aurora was across the room talking with Lana and Max. She would still have to give her official testimony against Crane and Madden and the others at some point. But not today.

Occasionally, her eyes darted over to Devon's, like she was making sure he was still close.

"Your exile didn't last long." Sylvie had snuck up on him. "All you had to do was single-handedly save the boss's sister."

"It wasn't single handed. Couldn't have done it without you."

Sylvie shrugged, smiling like she couldn't disagree. She held open a box of pizza, but Devon shook his head. He'd already eaten some, though he hadn't tasted it. He was too exhausted.

"And I don't have my job back yet. Max deferred that discussion till later." Though Devon's former boss had, in fact, apologized for underestimating Devon and Aurora both.

"Isn't the real question whether you want it?"

She was a smart one, this Sylvie Trousseau. "All I know is that I want to be with Aurora."

Sylvie nudged him with her elbow. "Good thing Aurora seems to want that, too."

He nodded. It was a really, really good thing. The best.

Finally, Aurora finished with Lana and Max. She smiled at Devon, heading over.

"Hey," Sylvie whispered to him, "if you and Aurora want to sneak away, I won't tell."

It was tempting. Devon had driven his car back here, so they had a getaway vehicle. Devon had also checked in with his mom and Ruby, promising that he'd return his mother's cell phone as good as new.

But he didn't plan to go back to his family's place tonight. Aurora could meet them another time.

Tonight, they still had a lot to discuss. They'd need to do that alone.

"What about Bennett's surveillance cameras in the parking garage? They'll see us leave."

"I could *never* tamper with those. How dare you even suggest it?" Sylvie winked. "I'll talk to you later. You get some rest... Or not."

"I'll owe you."

"You'll pay me back, eventually." Sylvie walked away backward. "I have no doubt about that."

Aurora reached him and slid her hand into his.

"You want to get out of here?" he asked.

"As long as nobody's chasing after us? Then yes. I *definitely* want to get out of here."

Chapter Forty-Three

*D*evon unlocked the door and let her inside. "So, this is my real apartment. Not exactly a penthouse."

He switched on the light, and Aurora glanced around. They were in an average apartment building several miles away from the ocean. Not too far from the area where Aurora had grown up.

Some people might think that the houses and structures around here were a little old, a little worn. But the trees were tall, and children played games out on the sidewalks.

The inside of his studio apartment definitely looked nothing like Rick Harrison's penthouse. Yet it was perfect for Devon. There were photos of his family all over the walls and shelves. Snapshots of Ruby, Devon in a tan beret and camo, Devon holding a baby that Aurora guessed was his niece.

She saw a photo of Devon along with a mirror image of himself. The two brothers had their arms around one another, one of them holding a football, both wearing easy smiles. Just a casual, candid moment.

"You and Kellen?"

"Yeah. When I was on leave the last time that I saw him. I wish he could've met you."

"I wish that, too."

She took Devon's hand as she walked through the rest of the space. The kitchen was mainly a sink, hot plate, and dorm fridge. The bathroom was down the hall. But everything was neat and tucked away. He hadn't even left any dirty dishes in the sink, which was Aurora's worst habit.

"I know it's not much, but…"

She pulled him toward a small couch facing the bed. "I love it. You've made it really nice. It feels like you—cozy."

He sat beside her, their fingers entwined. "There's a lot more I'd like to share with you. I'd really like you to meet my family. If that's something you want."

She nodded. "Absolutely. I can't wait. But first, I need to know—why did you really leave yesterday? I know what Max said to you. Lana got that out of him. But I haven't been able to figure out why you took off without saying anything to *me*."

"I may have freaked out a little. Just because this is happening so fast, and I was afraid that I was putting too much pressure on you. I wanted to give you some space. In case you needed to think about what you really want from me."

Space? She didn't want space at all.

She crawled closer to him. "It *is* happening fast. That's true. I was afraid you were having second thoughts."

"About you? I want you in my life, Aurora. In whatever way you're comfortable with. I'm sure of that."

Warmth spread through her insides. She leaned in to kiss him. His lips were sweet, tender. She wanted to feel the rest of him. Needed his skin against hers.

But then she pulled back before they could get carried away. There was more that she had to tell him.

"I need to change some things about myself. I mean, the way I've been approaching my life. I don't want to rely on Max so much anymore. Not because I'm still angry with him, but because I want to have a good relationship with him that's free of so many complications. He did overstep, but I'm the one who led him to believe I couldn't stand on my own. I want to find my own clients, build my business on my terms. And I want my own place, too, based on what *I* can afford. Hopefully…close to yours."

Devon smiled. "That sounds really nice. I've enjoyed being your neighbor before."

"I promise I won't be so noisy this time." She bit her lower lip, tired of joking. She wanted him to know how she really felt about him.

"Devon, I'm falling for you. I don't want space. Do you?"

She'd whispered these words. He pulled her into his lap, his breathing growing heavy. His focus had gone soft with longing.

"No space. I definitely don't want any space between us."

Their mouths connected. Almost immediately, she deepened the kiss. She needed him closer. They broke contact only so that she could pull off her top, and their mouths collided again. Devon's fingers pushed her bra straps aside, yanking the fabric down to expose her breasts. He lifted her higher so he could suck one nipple into his mouth. A rush of desire pooled in her belly.

He let the nipple go so that he could suck the other one. His eyes flicked up at her. God, this man was sexy.

"Make love to me," she said. "Please."

"You don't feel like being bossy?"

"No. I want you to have me any way you like." She whispered into his ear. "I trust you."

He got up from the couch in one swift motion, bringing her with him. He crossed the room to the bed. There, Devon set her gently on the covers.

"Lay back." He grinned when she obeyed. He removed the rest of her clothes, one piece at a time, covering every inch of bare skin with kisses. His fingers slid her panties away. But instead of tasting or touching her center, he stood up and took a step back.

"You are so beautiful. Especially when you're being quiet."

She kicked a leg at him. "Oh, shush. Don't make me sorry I put you in charge."

Laughing, he fisted his T-shirt and pulled it off. His expression shifted back to lust as he unbuttoned his jeans and pushed them past his hips, then did the same with his boxer briefs. He squeezed his hand around the base of his erection. The tip glistened.

"You want me?" he asked huskily.

"Yes. Please."

"Then touch yourself. Show me that you're ready for me."

Yikes. Her entire body felt like it was combusting with need. Devon in charge was absolutely doing it for her. She spread her legs and brought her hand to her core as he watched, just as she'd done in Chase's bathroom days ago. Only this time, Devon wasn't holding back, except to tease her. He was driving her crazy.

"Fuck. Look at you. You're soaking wet."

"Wet for you."

He fetched a condom from a drawer. Rolled it on. He walked toward her and stopped at the edge of the bed. "Turn around. Hands and knees."

"Yes, Lieutenant."

He smacked her lightly on the hip when she was in position. She couldn't help giggling.

Then his cock slid home, stretching her, and her giggle turned to a moan. He wrapped his arms around her upper body, lifting and bracing her so that her back was against his chest. He cradled her against him as he began to thrust. Aurora gasped at the sensation.

"You like that?" He kissed the back of her neck.

She couldn't make a coherent sound, so she nodded. Devon had complete control over the way they moved. Yet she also felt completely supported. She'd given herself over to him in every way—for this round, at least—and it was perfection.

As his movements grew more urgent, he reached around her to massage her clit. Her orgasm came on her fast and intense. He pumped into her with his own shuddering release, then scattered her back with kisses as he lowered her to the bed.

"What do you think?" he asked once they'd caught their breath, and he'd discarded the condom. "Did I do okay? Will you let me be in charge again?"

"Hmm, maybe. If you ask nice, and I'm in the mood for it."

"Still a firecracker, I see."

Aurora yawned. He pulled the covers over them and cuddled her close. Her eyes drifted closed.

"Sleep. You're safe with me."

I know, she meant to say, but she was already dreaming.

Epilogue

One Month Later

*A*urora slipped on oven mitts and pulled a roast from the oven. "Looks amazing. Is everyone hungry?"

"The mashed potatoes are ready." Ruby was stirring a pot on the stove. "Just need to warm the rolls. Dev, can you grab them?"

Devon was busy bouncing Haley, but he used his free hand to pull his mom's dinner rolls from the fridge. He and his niece both were enjoying watching Aurora and Ruby tag-team in the kitchen. All his favorite women, right here under one roof.

"How'd I ever get so lucky?" he whispered to the baby, who gurgled that she had no clue.

His mom hustled out of her bedroom, heading for the door. "I just heard someone drive up. It must be them."

Aurora had been joining him for Sunday night dinners with his family. They all loved her, just as he'd expected. Unfortunately, Ruby always seemed to have a new embarrassing story to share about him, and Aurora was only too eager to hear.

Sometimes he caught Aurora and his sister whispering and laughing together, and he wondered what they were conspiring about. And watching Aurora read bedtime stories to Haley brought a joy to his heart that he never could've anticipated.

Aurora had folded into his life just as easily as she folded into his arms—at least when she felt like being held. Just as often, Aurora turned the tables on him, and he was loving every second of it.

His mom opened the front door just as Max and Lana arrived on the stoop. There were exclamations and greetings and hugs. Lana cooed over Haley.

Max clapped Devon on the shoulder, handing him a bottle of red wine. "Have you had a chance to go over that new client file I sent? They want us to start protection on Monday."

"Hey, no talking business tonight." Aurora took the wine and started opening it. "Unless you all want to hear every detail about the wedding I'm planning for my latest clients. They're doing a cosplay theme—elves and wizards and everything."

All the women shouted their encouragement, while Max and Devon both promised there would be no further shoptalk.

"Boo," Ruby shouted. "We want elvish wedding details. Bring on the Pinterest boards."

You'll get wedding details, Devon responded silently. *Just you wait.* Minus the elves, anyway.

Eventually, Ruby would get to come ring shopping with him. As soon as Devon was sure Max wouldn't object that it was too fast. And, most importantly, that Aurora would say yes. There was no rush. Only Haley knew his secret, and she wasn't telling anytime soon.

Devon was back to working at Bennett Security, and he'd

accepted the promotion to bodyguard. His mom still struggled with the risk, but she'd made it clear that she could handle it as long as he was happy. And she'd remarked more than once lately that she'd never seen him so content.

As for Aurora, she'd already secured a couple of clients, including the epic fantasy-themed wedding in question. She wasn't working for the West Oaks wealthy yet, but Devon had no doubt she would get there. And she was building her success entirely on her own foundation, which meant a lot to her. Devon felt her pride every time she told him about her latest win.

The roast went on the table, along with the mashed potatoes, a dish of roasted carrots, and his mom's homemade yeasted rolls. He held Haley in one arm so that his sister could eat. His gunshot wound hardly bothered him at all anymore, though it had left a scar that Aurora insisted was ridiculously sexy.

"Want me to take a turn holding her?" Aurora asked.

"It's all good. Once Haley's asleep, I'll just throw a napkin over her head, so I don't spill gravy on her."

"Such a sweet uncle." Aurora leaned in to kiss him, and Max pretended to grumble from the other side of the table. But everyone else hooted.

"I know we aren't supposed to talk about work," Lana said after a while. "But I have an update on the case against Nadia Wolfson and Jennifer Scoville. If you'd all like to hear it."

"We certainly would." Devon's mother set her fork roughly on her plate. "I want those two bitches to burn."

"Mom, language!" Devon and Ruby both said at the same time. Aurora only laughed.

Lana explained that Jennifer had just accepted a deal. She would plead to a lesser degree of kidnapping and menacing, instead of the original conspiracy charges.

In exchange, Jennifer had told the authorities everything about Nadia's plans. Jennifer would also be required to help pay restitution for all the property damage and havoc their conspiracy had caused. Their mole inside the courthouse had flipped on Nadia, too.

But the district attorney hadn't offered Nadia any deals. Her trial would be starting in several months. It was sure to get a lot of media attention.

Aurora had already completed her early testimony against Madden, Dominic Crane, and their pointy-nosed associate. From everything that Lana and the police had learned from their informants, the Syndicate wasn't going after her any further. Aurora would have to repeat her testimony later on at the trials—apparently the DA wanted to try the various defendants separately, though Devon wasn't sure of all the details. Aurora would have to testify at Nadia Wolfson's trial as well.

But Max had arranged for a bodyguard detail to keep an eye on her until they were sure all danger had passed. Not Devon himself, but a shifting lineup of people he worked with and trusted.

"From what I've heard, Dominic Crane has been ousted as the head of the Silverlake Syndicate," Lana said. "I don't know yet who's taking charge. A bunch of different factions are now vying for control, and his lawyer isn't in any hurry to get Crane to trial. But maybe Crane will want to testify against his former friends. Bringing down an organization like that would make the West Oaks DA's Office look pretty good, assuming the Feds don't decide to swoop in and steal all the credit."

Devon hoped that Lana got her wish, but he didn't like the thought that Dominic Crane would get off easy. Maybe he hadn't directly wished Aurora harm. But Crane was a criminal, and he was at least partly to blame for Aurora being in danger in the first place.

"You don't think he'd be afraid to testify?" Aurora asked.

Lana scoffed and sipped her drink. "A guy like him? No way. He just needs to feel like he's getting a sweet enough deal in exchange for his cooperation. Crane might look handsome, but he's still a snake."

"Enough about them." Max lifted his wine glass. "I propose a toast—to Devon. For saving my sister's life and making her so happy. I'll always be grateful, so long as he never breaks her heart, because then all bets are off."

"And to Aurora," Ruby chimed in. "For saving my brother's life."

They'd all heard the details of those moments outside the cliffside guesthouse. Devon held Aurora's hand under the table, meeting her gaze with a smile. *I love you*, he mouthed.

"Love you, too," she whispered.

"Hear, hear," the others said, and clinked glasses.

THAT NIGHT, Devon was glancing over the email from Max when Aurora came over to him. She was hiding something behind her back.

"I found a friend I thought I'd lost. You'll never guess."

They were spending the night at Aurora's apartment, which Devon didn't like as much as his own. She still hadn't finished unpacking. Boxes littered her already cramped space. But Devon had resolved not to unpack for her or complain.

Her messiness did occasionally cause arguments—but clashes with Aurora always led to fiery chemistry in bed, and he had no problem with that.

She produced the object from behind her back. It was the huge green vibrator she'd used as a hammer back at the penthouse.

"It's the Incredible Hulk!" She bounced down onto the couch. "Do you remember?"

"How could I possibly forget?"

She wiggled the thing at him. "Should we invite him to play tonight?"

He liked the sound of that, but he was going to tease her about it first. "A threesome? Not sure I'm okay with that. Should I be jealous?"

"Never." She tossed the vibrator aside and kissed him. "There's nobody for me but you, Devon Whitestone."

"Not even Rick Harrison and his hedge fund?"

"Not even him. I'd take Devon the bodyguard any day."

"You mean Devon, *your* bodyguard."

"Damn right."

"And you're mine."

"I'm your…what?"

"Just mine," he murmured between kisses. "All mine."

∾

Don't miss the next Bennett Security book, HEAD FIRST, Lana and Max's story.

Lana is about to begin the most important trial of her career. But Max Bennett, her sexy star witness, keeps catching her eye. Even worse? They share a history. When a faceless stalker threatens Lana, the owner of Bennett Security will go to any lengths to protect her. The real challenge? Trying not to fall for her.

Also by Hannah Shield

Acknowledgments

Many thanks to my editor and my criminal law consultants. Any mistakes—and creative license—when it comes to legal proceedings in this book are entirely my own.

I'm so grateful to my beta readers and advance reviewers! Your support means the world to me.

About the Author

Hannah Shield once worked as an attorney. Now, she loves thrilling readers on the page—in every possible way.

She writes steamy romantic suspense with feisty heroines, brooding heroes, and heart-pounding action. Bennett Security is her debut series. Visit her website at www. hannahshield.com.

Made in the USA
Middletown, DE
03 November 2023

41878807R00182